Mike Chinn lives in Birmingham with his wife Caroline and their tribe of guinea pigs. He's written fiction that runs from Westerns to Sword & Sorcery and Space Opera, via Horror and his British Fantasy Award short-listed Damian Paladin pulp adventure stories (along with its ever expanding universe) to the occasional Sherlock Holmes pastiche, as well as editing four books for The Alchemy Press (*Swords Against the Millennium,* and *Pulp Heroes* volumes one to three). The Batrix & Scilli books grew out of his love of Fantasy fiction and Alistair MacLean style thrillers, and a desire to somehow combine the two.

CITADEL OF THE MOON

MIKE CHINN

CITADEL OF THE MOON

FIRST EDITION

ISBN

978-1-7390938-3-9

Printed and bound by IngramSpark

SALADOTH PRODUCTIONS

Hall Green, Birmingham
United Kingdom

PROLOGUE

THE FIGURE ON THE bed shifted position nervously. Chains rattled. The filthy cot he lay on, though crude, was soft and comfortable, although he'd spent so long in irons that his wrists and ankles were marked by both ancient scars and fresh lesions. The stained, coarse brown woollen robe wrapping his spare frame was, by now, as familiar as his unwashed skin. All of these were now so commonplace that it's doubtful his mind even registered them. It was the gathering of shadows as night fell – suggesting soft, huddled shapes in the corners of his cell – that always caused him to tremble. Nightfall: the time he most loathed, feared, yet lusted after; the reason he was manacled to the cold wall above his bed while his legs were gyved to its steel frame. The subtle refinement to his torment.

The dark grew ever more profound. The dirty window set high up in the cell's longest wall let in precious little light during the day. By nightfall, only a Full Moon shining directly through the thick glass made any impact on the gloom.

His diamond-blue eyes flickered wildly under a ragged, almost colourless fringe. His filthy hair and beard were tangled and stained by traces of the food he was occasionally brought – starvation by neglect was not an option for him, and he would never have the willpower to simply stop eating. His nervousness clattered the chains again, and he froze. Had he heard the soft arrival of his cell's other, occasional occupant?

He held himself rigid, apparently not even breathing. He remained frozen until the unexpired breath would be tormenting his lungs. Perhaps even more so than his fear. It bellowed out and he took another gulp of cleaner air.

"Very good, Brother." The voice was low yet vibrant, coming from the darkness. "I almost believed you were going to drive yourself into a swoon this time. My lovely, eager boy."

He clutched at his chains, head darting wildly as his eyes strove to pierce the gloom.

"Let me be!"

He had tried to shout the words, but all he seemed able to force through his throat was a feeble croak. Words were wasted anyway, no matter how strongly they might be delivered. She could never let him alone. Not while the Sun was below the horizon.

She stepped into what little light his grudging window allowed through, feeling her form solidify and take shape as his gaze fell upon her, defining her. Each night was the same, yet with subtle, almost indiscernible differences. The face of a child, no more than ten years old, and framed by long waves of black hair. A cloak – dark as her hair and obviously meant for an adult – dragged on the soiled floor behind her, swamping her tiny body.

She pouted like a favourite grandchild denied a treat. "You don't look happy to see me, my love." Her voice, although coming from childish lips, was neither young nor innocent. It oozed with experience and heavy irony. It was the voice of someone who'd enjoyed a thousand lifetimes of pleasing men and women – in every conceivable way – while saving the greater pleasures for herself. "Don't you want to play anymore?"

"Witch!" he croaked. "Leave me! Leave me!"

"Witch?" She stepped a little closer, coming to within an arm's length of his filthy cot. "You insult us both, Brother." She flicked aside the edge of a cloak which was no more substantial than cobweb, briefly exposing her naked, unnaturally voluptuous body. "Time to play," she murmured.

He began to shriek, tearing his throat raw. Every night he did this – hope fighting against bitter experience. There was no one to come to him, no one to help him. And all the while she simply stood watching him, just beyond reach, her too-young lips taut with a sardonic grin.

Eventually, his ranting quietened as he exhausted himself. His protests were following the familiar nightly pattern; perhaps he no longer had the strength to break it. Or maybe he thought that very familiarity would help him resist.

"How long?" he whispered, almost inaudible. "Oh ye Powers Above and Below. How long?"

She waited until his ragged breathing evened out, the smile never leaving her lips. She filled it with as much invitation and promise as mockery, knowing she was all but irresistible.

Finally, she moved in closer, each step made with an exaggerated sway of her hips. He watched her every move – his eyes apparently unable to tear themselves away. She noticed his body responding in spite of his protests and her smile widened. There were no secrets between them.

"I am a patient girl, my sweet," she whispered. "But even my patience isn't limitless. Give in to me, give in to yourself. You cannot deny that it's not what you want. Look at my body, imagine how it would feel. How smooth, how round. Think of the delights you will find deep inside my flesh—"

"Be silent!" His voice was a harsh rattle.

"Don't be cross, my love; it's not in your nature." Her smile turned demure, her eyes – suddenly visible in the thin light – flared yellow. She ran her gaze along his wasted form, her hands over his coarse robe.

She felt him tensing, his hands tugging at the manacles. His legs jerked painfully against their restraints. Blood started to trickle down his wrists, opening fresh wounds.

She climbed sinuously onto his wasted body, teasing him with her hands. She ran them along his sleeves, his arms, his wrists, stopping just before the manacles. Instead, she dabbed a finger in the fresh blood, put it to her lips, and lazily sucked the finger clean, making sure he could see.

She was straddling him now. She could simply take what she wanted in a moment, chained as he was; he couldn't stop her. But that wasn't the game. She was bound never to steal, he must give.

With a flick of her arms, the over-sized, diaphanous cloak billowed aside. She swayed her ripe body before him, so close even his manacled hands could reach. If only he would.

"Here," she crooned, "am I not desirable? Am I not luscious? The shortest, simplest of words, my sweetness, and all this can be yours. You know that. There is no sin in it. No wrong..."

"Let me be!" he wheezed between clenched teeth. His eyes remained open, though, fixed on her. His hands half-rose, his fingers twitched; perhaps – in his mind – already caressing her curves.

She laughed: low and sensual. There were no secrets between them. "Yes, look at my body; feast on it! Picture the delights we could enjoy together: entwined, thrusting... And that most exquisite release, again, and again. Every night ... every month ... every year..."

His gaze moved upward, onto a nose she knew was small, slightly upturned. Even in this barest of illumination he could probably make out the scatter of freckles across its bridge. He stared, undoubtedly fixing his gaze on them, concentrating. Anything but look on her inviting body, or into her tawny, hypnotic eyes.

"My lips ache for your touch, Brother," she cooed. She pulled herself upright, her nose and freckles moving out of his eyeline. Now his vision would be filled with hips and soft thighs. "Kiss me, my love..."

For an instant, his neck strained forward. His tongue flickered across his chapped lips. Then he fell back again, his face a mask of self-loathing.

She allowed herself a momentary smile of satisfaction. One night he would weaken, it was inevitable. That he had resisted so far was a wonder; but he was, after all, merely human.

He raved wordlessly at her, spittle flying across her perfect skin. Tears flowed down his cracked cheeks; she answered with mocking laughter that echoed throughout the cell – but no further.

The game was, once again, under way.

CHAPTER ONE

THE SKY GREW LIGHTER. The firmament had managed to survive the night without boiling monsters, no wizard had rained down magical destruction from it. The house facing us from across the road had remained stubbornly silent. Another joyless watch was over.

I slipped my watch out of a waistcoat pocket and glanced at it. Dawn was just under two hours away. Good. Some other fool could waste their time staring at an empty mansion. I wanted sleep, food, and *chavet*, although not necessarily in that order. The delightful agonies of withdrawal had begun some time earlier, and my bottle was empty.

Snapping the watch closed, I dropped it back into its pocket. I wanted to stretch, yawn, make those disgusting early morning noises most of us seem to feel so necessary, but I couldn't break cover. Just in case. I had to remain concealed in the wild stand of trees across the road from the mansion until my relief came. I prayed he wouldn't be late this morning. Just for once.

I'd passed the point where I believed we'd been misinformed about *Gosigné* Mawinnek's attractive, Scan Feta retreat days ago. Now, I was convinced the whole mission was an attempt by Under-Director Risnek to drive me mad. That yes-man's yes-man had never liked me.

The feeling was mutual.

There was a rustle of movement to my left.

"Scilli!" hissed a voice. I relaxed, dropping my hand from the butt of the Alva repeating pistol tucked away in my topcoat.

Sadly, it wasn't my relief, but Krajicek Fochs. Fochs was another Bureau employee caught up in a seemingly endless operation; I recognised his less than cautious voice. He was also another one of the Under-Director's non-favourites. Mainly because, like me, Fochs had the nerve to have been forcibly enrolled at a wizard's seminary as a baby, and the misfortune to not be a fully indoctrinated Chrysomancer when the war was over and we were all friends again. Except for the Chrysomancers, obviously. Risnek never could tell the difference between the lost and saved. It was one of his more endearing qualities.

"Fochs," I acknowledged his foggy silhouette, as it thickened out of the pre-dawn air. "I hope you've come to tell me it's all been a big joke, Risnek's laughed himself into a seizure, and the High-Director's signed off my premature retirement with full pay."

Fochs' expression – permanently frozen into a fishy stare behind his thick eyeglasses – faltered. Looking like a stunned turtle, he smoothed what remained of his thinning, pomaded hair. "That's not exactly—"

I stopped him before he could rumble on further in his pedantic way. "Then we've got to hurry up and wait, yes?"

"No."

I sighed the sigh of a man doomed to eternal disappointment and leaned against the half-dead tree at my back. "We're not going in?" I said, injecting as much pleading into my voice as I could. It was wasted on someone with Fochs' sensitivities.

"Up until four days ago, we were certain Deynah was still a member of the group." He was determined to forge on, regardless of how much I already knew. As project controller, I was supposed to know better than he, but Fochs had never been the kind of man to be side-tracked, not once he'd decided to impart whatever gem of information he'd been saving up.

"But you don't any longer—" I tried to interject. I would have been better employed attempting to detour an iceberg.

"Then we lost all trace of his signature. There was no indication that he'd been killed, just the loss of the abaston trace linked to his aura."

"Maybe he lost the crystal."

"You know perfectly well the cross-link has a range of several miles. No one has left or entered the house since we lost the trace."

"That you know of."

"We've been monitoring all this time, Scilli. No Chrysomantic magic has been used."

"And what if they don't use Chrysomancy?"

He stopped long enough to take a breath, blinking at me with his magnified eyes. "The Bureau is fully aware of the suspicions both you and the late Sanej entertained about other forms of magic. But so far, you've signally failed to produce any proof."

"Scan Leroth: bureau operatives killed in a bizarre explosion – cause unknown. Instances of peculiar abductions and deaths in the Kant – cause unknown. The assault on the Capitol last month: three senators simply disappearing while under Sharpshooter escort, another two previously healthy senators dropping dead with unaccountable fevers – causes unknown. How much more proof do you need?"

"They are not proof, Scilli, merely unanswered questions."

"You remind me of a heteromorph I used to know…" Fochs wasn't improving my mood any, and me mentioning Scan Leroth had awakened unpleasant resonances. The similarities with this stakeout were uncomfortable. I didn't want it ending the same way.

Over six months had passed since Sanej – who'd been my partner back then – and I had wasted similarly futile nights watching a deserted merchants' house in the eastern seaport. Eventually, Sanej had ordered a raid, and we'd lost over half our force in an explosion of no recognisable cause. All that was recovered, before the entire building collapsed, was an exhausted fragment of abaston crystal, recently carved with the profile of a long-dead king.

Then Sanej had been murdered during an undercover operation – leaving me with as many questions as theories. But, as Fochs was so quick to point out, there was no proof.

I looked back at the house. Its pale sides were beginning to glow like dying coral in the growing pre-dawn light. It was three storeys high, with twenty half-moon windows along the front wall, and a shallow, tiled roof. Its grounds were neatly laid-out with lawns and parterres, and a grove of Cotechatlu palms beside the main, wrought iron gate. Quite the picture. And like most pictures, most of it lay cryptically beneath the pretty facade.

"We can't wait any longer," Fochs insisted, his tone fussy. I nodded.

"Get everyone into position," I sounded even more tired than I felt.

"We go in on my signal."

He busied himself away, goggling face smug with the belief he'd forced me into an unpleasant position. That was half true – what I was imagining was a whole lot worse than unpleasant – but a self-important ninny like Fochs would never be able to force me. My devious conscience was all I needed – some individually perverted sense of what was right and wrong. Deynah might still be alive in that villa, a prisoner, with just enough left worth saving. As long as a treacherous voice, cunningly hidden in my mind, kept insisting on that possibility, I'd have to find out.

The Bureau knew me very well and used its advantage to the hilt.

I slipped out my watch again. The minutes spun past as daylight grew stronger, the villa's front wall changing from coral to pale lemon to sharp white. If Fochs didn't get everyone in position soon, there'd be no point in attempting the quiet, unobtrusive swoop I'd planned. No mad charges like Scan Leroth. Every conceivable outcome anticipated. Every one of us had been fully briefed, and seventy percent casualties had been declared well within the criteria of success.

Which demonstrated only too clearly the sort of mind that plans these ventures.

Fochs appeared again, batting aside a growth of ferns twice his height. Behind his thick lenses, his eyes looked glazed and luminous. I hoped it was simply a distortion caused by the glass and not the exhilarating rush of battle-fever. I've heard some soldiers get it in the moments before a fight. It often ends badly, for them and everyone around them.

"All ready, Scilli," he gasped. He sounded on the point of collapse. What was he going to be like once we were actually inside?

"You lead the assault on the west side," I ordered. Then he'd still be in the shadows, I reasoned, the safest position and nothing to do with keeping him as far away from me as possible. "Your watch?"

He tugged a heavy, double-cased beast out of his waistcoat and flipped it open. Both our timepieces were synchronised to within fractions of a second. The Bureau never stinted when it came to equipment.

"We start in thirty seconds from..." I waited for the seconds dial to reach the top "...now."

Fochs vanished. I wasn't wrong: he was drunk on the idea of taking such a major part in the operation. If he actually lived through it, I promised myself to take him to Grif Ditya's for the best dinner he'd ever had.

The second hand swept round with uncomfortable speed. It seemed as though Fochs would never have time to get to his men.

Thirty seconds passed. I shouted a command and burst from cover. Silently, twenty men – all armed with pistols – followed. Uniformly clothed in unremarkable charcoal suits, we were a band of freelance mourners, searching for business.

We dashed across the narrow road, keeping low. Not that anyone in the villa could fail to see us. The gates weren't locked, and we were through in a moment. We were at our most exposed during the dash to the villa's walls, but there were no shouts from the building, no shots, no magical defences. It was unnerving.

All twenty-one of us slammed up against the west wall of the villa. I signalled north and south, and my group split into tens, as per their training, fanning out along the building. Ground-floor windows were the targets. Already open, preferably, although we all knew enough ways to force a locked window without alerting the household.

Rapidly, in total silence, we made it inside. There were three open windows. All twenty-one of us slipped through as a choreographed whole that made me proud. But the continued silence and lack of response rattled my nerves.

The villa was in darkness, except for the east-facing walls, which were lit by the rapidly approaching dawn. It was decorated in classical style, with plastered walls, dark-varnished floors, open staircases and a great deal of heavily embroidered furniture. The ceilings were ribbed with fake beams, and everywhere the rooms were filled with oil-lamps in the latest style, brass and steel, polished to mirror-finishes, and not one lit. There was an underlying scent of beeswax and lamp-oil.

My group swept the ground floor without being told. Nowhere was left unchecked. Cushions were uprooted, cupboards and drawers opened, closets scoured. The only sounds were of rubbered boot-heels on polished floors. There was nothing. Nothing to hint the villa wasn't the retreat of a normal, everyday businessman with the time and money to indulge his tastes. Not even the signs of a mistress – and it was a matter of record that *Gosigné* Mawinnek had several.

I hoped Fochs was having better luck.

The Sun was a degree above the horizon when our search came to a futile end. Nothing in any of the above-ground storeys, so I reasoned there must be a basement. Maybe several. Many fashionable villas across Ramini were built on the sites of old ruins; at one time it had almost been obligatory. I was betting that Mawinnek had a maze of ancient, stone-built cellars under his highly polished floorboards.

I was in one of the salons, thinking hard, staring at the floor as though I could force my vision through. I heard the rapid footsteps, and I knew it was Fochs before I looked up. His fishy stare was disturbed; all the excitement had gone out of the chase. Mawinnek wasn't playing fair.

"Anything?" I asked, by way of something to say. I already knew the answer. He wouldn't be here looking so piqued otherwise. But at least he was still breathing. That was a plus.

"Not a thing." He was trying to match his expression to the sulky tone, but on his face, it didn't fit. I shoved my hands into my trousers' front pockets and tapped the floor with a toe. It sounded solid enough.

To give Fochs credit, he caught on fast. "Cellars?"

"It's all we've got left."

The pout vanished, his goggling stare catching fire once more. "Then I'll find them!"

He was racing back to join his men before I could stop him. I hoped the older, more experienced heads amongst his team would stop him before he did anything rash. I shrugged and faced my own, disconsolate bunch. They'd been hoping for some action, too. *Gosigné* Mawinnek had disappointed them.

"Clean up and secure the place," I said. "We'll hand this whole sorry mess over to the relief. Whenever they deign to turn up."

"Scilli!" came Fochs' sudden, excited yell, "I've—"

It wasn't much of an explosion, just a vivid, actinic flash that drowned the entire house in light. My ears popped in the displaced air. When I'd picked myself up from the floor, there wasn't a sound.

In a hallway, almost at the centre of the villa, a rectangle stood proud of the floor. Residual energy sparked around its corners, a stark purple against the rosy dawn light. The air smelled sweet, slightly metallic. Fochs was huddled nearby, folded in on himself like a newborn baby. He was dead.

A member of Fochs' own squad gently turned the body over. Fochs sprawled across the floorboards, his hands charred lumps, clothing white with ash. Even his eyeglasses were buckled, the lenses warped and partly melted.

"What happened?" I asked, more for clarification's sake than anything else.

"He spotted a groove, running at odds with the boards," said the one who'd turned Fochs' body over. "Before I could stop him, he tried to prise it open." He pointed at a molten splash against the wood. Up to that moment, I hadn't spotted it. So much for my vaunted powers of observation.

"Knife?" I asked. The other nodded. I found myself sighing again; it was a good day for sighs.

"I think we can assume the spell's done its worst," I said, knowing nothing of the sort. I just figured it was time we had some decent luck.

I stepped over Fochs and crouched to look at the raised piece of floor. It was a trapdoor, of course, disguised just enough to fool anyone not actively searching for it. That probably explained the spell. Mawinnek would know the door couldn't stay hidden forever. So, he overlay it with a simple defensive spell, one that would kill anyone impatient enough to try and open it. A trapdoor indeed.

Except there were more than one of us. Somehow, I didn't think that possibility would have passed Mawinnek by.

"Which means there's something down there, waiting for us," I finished the thought aloud.

Nobody looked happy at my words. The number of volunteers to investigate didn't exactly crush me. They were all waiting for me to lead. One of the joys of being appointed controller.

Taking a firmer grip on my pistol – though I don't know what use

I thought it was going to be – I nudged at the trap with the toe of my boot. Reluctantly, it flipped over into a fully open position. The hinges couldn't have been oiled in years: they screamed in outrage. Someone lit a match and tossed it into the hole. Several steps glared against the blackness before the match hit bottom and flickered out. Not far down, then. If an unseen someone chose to grab my ankles as I stepped through the gap, at least I'd survive the fall.

Taking a match out of my own lucifer case, I stepped onto the top step. The bottom was hidden by the dark, so I wouldn't go all dizzy and lose what little respect I might still have amongst these men. I doubt any of them knew about my little problem with heights – it's not the sort of thing you toss into conversations at staff dinners – and I wanted it to stay that way. I get enough grief being known as a failed wizard, without letting on I get nose bleeds in tall-heeled boots.

I took two steps down. The darkness didn't get any more revealing. I struck the match. The sphere of illumination was just enough to show me the floor, several feet below, but nothing else.

I descended quickly, eager to reach the bottom, not wanting to be framed in the dawn-lit trapdoor. If anyone down there was going to take pot-shots with a pistol or crossbow, the match was the only target I was willing to give them. And I wasn't fool enough to leave it close to any part of me I couldn't live without.

The match began burning my fingers. I dropped it and lit another. Holding the light up, I scanned my musty surroundings. The cellar appeared to start at the wall immediately behind the stairs. From the echoes my scuffling boots raised, I guessed it was pretty large, with few, if any, projecting walls. I held the match out level as far as my arm would stretch. I wanted to see any obstacles, not find them with my face. I needn't have bothered.

I'd taken just a dozen steps into the void, shuffling warily, when a faint glow pulsed some distance ahead of me. I took another step, and it pulsed a little brighter, one more and it grew brighter still. Whatever it was, my presence had activated it.

"What's that?" someone called from above. They must have seen the glow. But I wished he'd kept his curiosity a little quieter.

"I don't know. I'm taking a look. Get everyone out of the villa, just in case."

Fearless, thoughtful Scilli. Always putting the lives of his men before his own.

With each step, the light grew brighter. It was like racing towards a heatless furnace while barely moving your feet. The walls of the cellar were growing clearer: dank, nitre-encrusted curves of ancient brick. The air was fragrant with the scents of mould and damp. As I'd guessed, the foundations of Mawinnek's villa were old ruins. Another time I'd be impressed by the symbolism, now I was more caught up in what I could see a hundred yards ahead of me, clearly blazing in a blue-white flame.

It was Llyscu Deynah, or had been, once. I hoped that whatever made Deynah the man he was – his soul, if there are such things – was long gone.

He was trapped in what looked like a skeletal, metal chair. His face was rigid, eyes glaring, hair standing erect from his skull, writhing like it had acquired all the life the man that had been Deynah had lost. His hands were half-clenched against the chair's thin arms. All about him, sinuous as any python, were blazing coils of thick, white light, undulating and writhing against his flesh and clothing. Wherever they crossed, there was another, brighter flash, and another coil was born. As I watched a thin, new-born coil wriggled towards his face and slowly tunnelled up a nostril. His expression never wavered. I took that as a good sign – for him, anyway.

A luminous tear oozed from his right eye. It was several moments before I realised it was another tendril – or maybe the same one – squeezing past the eyeball.

Raising my pistol, I fired, straight for the centre of Deynah's brain. If the bullet ever reached his flesh, I never saw it. Instead, a vivid purple spark flashed across the front of the blaze. The coils began to whip furiously. Deynah's body twitched as new tendrils grew with frenzied speed.

I fired again. Another flash; even more coils. Belatedly, it occurred to me that I'd just done the very thing Mawinnek wanted. The trapdoor had been a warning. Deynah was the real trap.

I turned and ran. I'd done enough as a hero, now it was time to be practical. Getting further away from Deynah wasn't making the light any dimmer, quite the opposite. As I reached the stairs, two brilliant tendrils coiled themselves around the bottom of the handrail. I cleared the steps two at a time, kicking the trapdoor shut behind me. It bulged as something below pressed up against it.

Hoping everyone was clear of the house, I ran for the front door, not stopping until I was past the gates. Everyone seemed to be watching, appreciating my athletic performance. I yelled: "Take cover!"

Maybe it was the panic on my face: suddenly, I was the only one around. I raced across the road and dived into the shrubbery. An instant later, a colossus behind me coughed.

I watched in awe as the villa came apart. It wasn't a vast explosion; paradoxically, there was almost a sense of order to it. Walls shivered apart, throwing disintegrating windows across the grounds in precise arcs. The roof hurled tiles in a wide circle. Although I heard the smash of debris falling all around me, the exploding villa was unnaturally quiet. Merely the softest of pops as it disassembled itself.

A spout of blue-white brilliance coiled upwards, detonating in a silent, sky-filling flash. For a moment, everything on the ground had twin shadows.

I pulled myself out of the cover of a gnarled wasp-oak. On the opposite side of the trunk, at the same level as my cowering head, a hand-sized shard of tile was embedded three inches into the striped bark.

Chavet withdrawal chose that moment to remind me of its presence. It had just been sitting back and enjoying the excitement, finding out if I'd make it through this time. No sense wasting all the suffering on a dead man; an endless toothache-like pain spreading all the way up from my feet to my crown. A crown I'd be missing right now if I'd been on the opposite side of the wasp-oak.

I heard rustling around me: the sound of several men getting carefully to their feet. I pulled myself upright, dusted crushed leaves off my coat and tried not to look as if I wanted to throw up.

"Anyone hurt?"

There was a chorus of negatives. If anyone had done more than break a fingernail, they were being brave about it.

I spared the razed villa a sour look. Another Scan Leroth. That only two lives had been lost this time – and one of them before the assault – didn't cheer me. Under-Director Risnek would want my head served up with an apple in my mouth – along with bacon rolls, fried potatoes, and herb bread.

A wave of pain flowed over me. I clutched my gut, swore eloquently and at length, but carefully under my breath.

"Same old Scilli," came a voice from immediately behind me. I lurched about, raising my pistol. There was a single figure: small, rotund, with neatly clipped and oiled hair. His barrel-like figure was neatly clad in the blue and gold uniform of a lieutenant-commander of the Internal Bureau. He stuck out a podgy, though immaculately manicured hand. "A pleasure to see you again."

For a moment, I was stumped. I didn't know this person. My reputation wasn't that big, surely? Then I recognised the blue-lensed eyeglasses the man was wearing. Those, and the Bureau uniform, told me everything. He wasn't a man at all.

I stuck out my own hand. "Batrix. You're looking ... well."

The heteromorph squeezed my fingers briefly before dropping his arm. The smile was businesslike. "Thank you. I feel well. I wish I could say the same of you."

I shrugged. Batrix knew me well enough to make a diagnosis from my visible symptoms. I wasn't about to explain.

He reached inside his tunic and pulled out a small bottle, clear glass, the liquid inside glowing a faint, cold blue. "I think you deserve a congratulatory drink."

I tried not to snatch at the bottle, but it was hard to be civilised at such a time. Yanking off the cork I took a deep pull on the hated contents. Immediately the gnawing ache subsided. It looked like I might live to hate another day.

"Thanks." I slipped the already half-empty bottle inside a coat pocket and gave Batrix what I hoped was a grateful smile. His own mouth twitched at the corners. I tried not to burst into tears at the unrestrained emotions crowding that moment.

Instead, I wondered how many reverses the heteromorph's peculiar, magically created physiology had made since our last assignment together, how many changes of gender with each Full Moon. He was much shorter than I remembered, with a lot more girth. I wondered if he would always be the same weight, regardless, the flesh simply reorganising itself to suit his height.

And now my head was clearer, a realisation struck me. "You brought that order – the one to go in!"

Batrix had the grace to look a little uncomfortable, but I didn't know his present form well enough to read him properly. "Indeed, Scilli. Along with a further order from Under-Director Risnek. You are to return to Wael Edra immediately."

Wael Edra: the Ramini Republic's new capital and home of the Bureau's headquarters. Quite a jaunt to Scan Feta. To send someone like Batrix such a distance – even if he were only a heteromorph – meant Risnek had something serious on his self-absorbed little mind. Something more than roasting me over a slow fire.

"Immediately, eh?"

Batrix nodded, a smile tweaking at his mouth. He remembered me too well.

"As I recall, the next coach to Wael Edra doesn't leave until tomorrow, Batrix."

He produced a watch, the twin of my own. "At exactly this time tomorrow."

"Then there's no hurry. How about dinner at Grif Ditya's tonight?"

The heteromorph frowned. "I believe that is the most exclusive, and thus most expensive restaurant in Scan Feta, Scilli. Might I enquire as to the occasion?"

"Let's just say, I owe it to someone. What d'you say?"

Batrix continued to stare at me through the blue lenses. Finally, he nodded. "As I said, same old Scilli."

CHAPTER TWO

RISNEK'S OFFICE WAS BURIED deep in a drab, inconsequential government building on the west side of Wael-Edra. The brand-new paving slabs that spread out on either side of the over-ornate columnated front doors – pillaged from some Chrysomancer Lodge was the rumour – were already being dug up. No one seemed to know why.

There was a lobby on Risnek's floor; it was right outside his door, used as a waiting room, before being admitted to his eminence. The light from the gas-lamps lining the dark panelled walls highlighted the dust in the air. I couldn't tell if it was part of the lobby's ancient charm, or an extra delight thrown up by the work outside.

I was sitting and waiting, not patiently. The moment Batrix and I had stepped off the stagecoach from Scan Feta, a messenger had handed me an urgent message: *Get to Risnek's office. Now.* No time to wash off the dust of travel, get a drink, eat, even rub out those intimate bruises caused by Ramini's unmaintained dirt roads. So I'd come. And sat. And waited.

It was another of the Under-Director's little games. This time it was the *I'm in charge so you'll damned well do what I say, when I say it* one. I've played before.

On the far side of the lobby, nearest Risnek's door, was a flat desk. Bent over it was a tall, lean, dark-haired lovely whose name, according to the polished mahogany plaque on the desk, was *Ingosigna* Drienn Afromett. She was dressed in a steel-grey dress with a high collar and fashionably puffed sleeves. The pleats in the lace at her wrists and throat had been pressed sharp enough to draw blood. Her only concession to jewellery was a simple gold watch pinned to her breast. Her chestnut hair was scraped severely back from a face that looked far too pale. I wondered if she ever went out much. The large dark eyes under angular eyebrows didn't look as though they were in the habit of warming up too often.

"Will Risnek be much longer, *Ingosigna* Afromett?" I asked, probably for the hundredth time.

"The Under-Director is in conference," she replied, no-nonsense, also for the hundredth time. "I'll send you in when I have the opportunity."

I almost thanked her, stopping myself just in time. She wasn't listening to me. I could have asked her the time in peasant Balgysan for all the difference it would have made. I continued sitting and waiting. More time passed. Nobody went into Risnek's office or came out. The delightful Drienn Afromett shuffled one pile of papers into another.

Half an hour or so later, the door opened, and two men backed out, laughing. A third man was holding the door for them, encouraging the laughter. I didn't need to look to see it was Risnek. But it was the other two who interested me the most: Beshbigl and

Spyru, two of the High-Director's own personal secretaries. Since when had they become such bosom pals with the Under-Director?

They all shook hands heartily, then Beshbigl and Spyru crossed the lobby and went out through the only other door. Risnek dropped the grin off his face and looked as though he'd never smiled in his life. He stared expressionlessly at me.

"Scilli. Come in." His door closed over the last word, cutting it short. I got to my feet, smiled sweetly at *Ingosigna* Afromett, and went in.

Risnek's office was long and dim and quiet. The windows all along one wall were covered in drapes the colour of the wood panelling. Even in winter, the office was too warm; in summer, facing south as it did, the heat was often unbearable. Today didn't feel as though it was going to be exceptional. There was a thick carpet that matched the drapes. On one wall was a large, paler square; ten years ago, a not particularly flattering portrait of Sendivogius, the Archimandrite, had hung there. Times change. Risnek would most likely have replaced the painting with a full-length portrait of himself years ago, if it hadn't been for the High-Director's oft-repeated contempt for the kind of man who liked hanging over-sized personal likenesses behind their desks.

There were two desks in the office. One, a plain functional affair surrounded by chairs; the other, a grotesque and expensive chunk of mahogany that blended well with the dark, unadorned wall panels. Risnek shuffled himself into place behind the mahogany thing and sat in a tall leather chair. He motioned me to sit at the other desk, well away from him, and, very obviously, in a slightly lower seat.

In the dim room, Risnek was a little more than a well-fed ghost. His suit was pale grey, edged in grey silk. His hair had gone an almost colourless yellow, common in men who had been blond in their youth, and it was dragged across his scalp in a pointless attempt to disguise his growing baldness. The few lines his face had surrendered to were deep, and his features were beginning to sag. His slightly fleshy lips were more often pouting in a sulk than smiling.

He reached for a huge cigar from a green stone box. He trimmed and lit it, taking his time. My time didn't count.

Finally, growing tired of the game, he leaned back, and through a haze of blue smoke said, "The assault on *Gosigné* Mawinnek's villa was less than successful."

"Don't blame me," I said. "I never wanted to go in from the start."

Risnek showed no sign of even hearing my comment. He drew on his fat cigar, his cheeks sucked in, and he blew out another cloud.

I changed tack. "The whole operation was obviously blown. Deynah didn't stand a chance from the outset. Mawinnek already knew who and what he was..."

Risnek deigned to glance my way. "You are implying that someone within the Bureau is leaking information?" He didn't look convinced.

"Do you have another explanation? We go into the villa, there's no one home, the place is booby-trapped – with Deynah left as a parting gift. Mawinnek clearly knew we were coming."

"As ever, you are over-dramatizing the situation, Scilli. Deynah may have been unmasked. He made an error that revealed him to Mawinnek. Modern interrogation techniques are quite thorough—"

"An experienced hand like Deynah wouldn't give himself away just like that, especially to someone like Mawinnek, who just happens to own the biggest private army in the Republic—"

"*Gosigné* Mawinnek is a respected banker, one of the richest men in Ramini. To date, we have singularly failed to prove anything remotely sinister with regard to the private security force he runs—"

I didn't falter. I'd been bracing myself from the moment I'd sat down in the lobby outside. "On top of which, field operatives are specially protected against all known interrogation methods." I managed to finish my speech without jumping over his desk and choking him silent.

Risnek's lips thinned. "Don't presume to lecture me on operational policy, Scilli. I think I may consider myself all too aware of normal procedure. More so than you, I imagine..."

I wasn't going to argue that point with him. He could think what he liked, it didn't hurt me any.

"The most important task of the Internal Bureau is the security of the Republic," Risnek was saying. As I'd expected, it sounded like I was going to get one of his lectures. "For that single reason alone, I accept that we must use all of the resources available to us. No matter how exotic."

"If you mean magic, Under-Director, say so. I'm a big boy now, I can take the shock."

He put down his cigar. "I make no secret of finding the use of Spooks distasteful, Scilli. I never have, no matter how tame or well-trained. But a weapon is a weapon. However, I still consider the utilisation of untrained wizards both pointless and needlessly expensive." He raised his cigar again and took a puff. The room was starting to smell like one of those exclusive, rich-boy-only clubs, the thresholds of which I'm not supposed to cross. His pale mouth twitched into a reasonable facsimile of a smile. "After all, what contribution do people like you make, Scilli?"

It was a question I'd heard many times before, and not just from Risnek. After a while, it doesn't bother you so much. "Because we know how Spooks think, Risnek. Even without the full knowledge and skills of an indoctrinated Chrysomancer, we can still recognise the signs; smell them. Because of what they did to us, we hate them even more than you do. But best of all..." I pulled the ever-present *chavet* bottle out of my coat and slammed it on the desk "...because you can control us just as easily as they did!"

That seemed to cheer Risnek. His smile broadened until he looked almost human. The wizards had made me, and thousands of others like me, an addict to *chavet* so they could exert control all the easier throughout the formative, rebellious years. But the wizards are defeated, *chavet* is illegal, and only certain departments within the government can still procure the stuff. The Under-Director knew that given a choice between the Department and a supply of the hated drink or no *chavet*, eventual insanity and probably an agonising death, in the end I, and all my contemporaries, would jump through whatever hoops the government put in front of us for the hated liquid.

On bad days, it was hard for me to remember who I hated most: the spell-singers or the Bureau.

"Why the attack on the villa?" I asked, just to change the subject.

"Information had come our way that Mawinnek was about to flee. The Bureau had invested too much money in the operation to watch it end so precipitously."

"Left it a little late, didn't you?"

"As you say. An unfortunate end to what was, up until then, a perfect operation."

"Good of you to say so."

"Credit where it's due, Scilli. Shame about Deynah and Fochs, though."

"They were both seminary boys, Risnek. I'm sure you can find it in your heart to forget them."

All of his cultivated friendliness evaporated. "This continual surliness in the face of authority will never help you to escape from your present position."

"I like being face down in the mud with your heel on my neck."

"No wonder your last department was so keen to be rid of you." He sighed like a martyr. "You think you're clever, Scilli; you think you're trouble. Well, I'm both more clever and more trouble than you'll ever be. Remember that. It might save you pain."

I said nothing. Risnek's opinion of his own intellect was well known, if not universally shared. His true genius lay in exploiting others' weaknesses. It had taken him far, while winning him few friends. But Risnek was not the kind of man who cared much about anyone else; his self-regard took up most of the day.

"However, enjoyable as this passing of the time is, it isn't the reason I summoned you."

I can't say I was surprised. "You wouldn't have sent Batrix so far south to find me if you'd just wanted to insult my upbringing, Under-Director. Not when you could have saved it all up for my eventual return."

"I have another job for you—"

"Related?"

He drew in a deep breath. "I really can't say. Perhaps. Perhaps not. It will require you working with that heteromorph again; the High-Director seems to feel you built up a good rapport during your last encounter." He paused to raise his cigar again. "It was in female form, I believe, at the time?"

"For most of it, yes."

"Pretty?"

He was almost seventy years old. Somehow, he seemed to think that his advancing years and receding hair made him irresistible to women. The truth was, he used his position in the Bureau ruthlessly. No young secretary – like Drienn Afromett outside – was likely to say no, not when it meant losing their job and receiving such a poor reference they'd likely never get another elsewhere.

"I didn't notice."

"Then that *chavet* must do more to you than I thought."

There would be no point in telling him that *chavet* doesn't do anything, except make you fatally addicted to it. Other than that, it might just as well be coloured water, except water will slake a thirst. I've never known *chavet* do that.

"If you ever feel the need to sample a drop, Risnek, call me first."

"Go to hell, Scilli."

"I have. It's not all it's cracked up to be."

A ribboned wad of papers flew across the void between us and slapped onto my plain desk. I had to hand it to him, Risnek was accurate.

"Your memoirs?"

"Your next operation. Read through it while you're having your face done."

I raised the papers, riffling through them and picking up the odd word. "A pilgrimage?" I said, unable to contain my surprise. "Surely not religious?"

Risnek made a disgusted sound deep in his throat. "Thankfully, no one has seen fit to repeal the Suppression of Religions Act yet. No, this is a purely secular affair – a family who claim they can trace their descendancy back to native Anesicci. Why they should want to, is beyond me." He drew on the cigar and blew out another noxious cloud. I wondered if he was trying to drown the imagined smell of pre-colonial natives. "They want to visit their lost homelands, some lake called Grémasicci Boya, just north of Qaijente."

I dropped the papers back on my desk. "And what's the Bureau connection? Are they Spook sympathisers? God-worshippers? Deflowerers of under-aged virgins?"

"You can be quite crude at times, Scilli. No. Simply put, they have asked the government for assistance on their journey. You will provide it."

"You mean we're there to keep an eye on their deviant, anti-social behaviour?"

He smiled like a bilious hog. "There has been some disquiet recently amongst certain 'factions' in the larger towns. It seems it's presently fashionable to regard the aboriginal inhabitants of Ramini as idolaters. Worse, in fact, than the Chrysomancers who first subdued them."

"The people can't take their revenge on the Spooks – since they've either become respectable politicians or conveniently vanished – so they're picking on some impotent, more visible group. We don't change, do we?"

"Your cynicism does you credit, Scilli. Close the door on your way out, will you?" One of the politest dismissals I'd ever had from Risnek. I scooped up the papers, slipped my *chavet* bottle back in a pocket, and walked out.

Outside, I blinked in the comparative brightness. *Ingosigna* Afromett was still at her desk, redistributing bits of paper. She paused, giving me a look that signalled that she'd been listening at the keyhole. Other than that, it was quite enigmatic. I wondered if she'd been able to hold the old lecher at bay, after all.

I gave her my best smile. "I don't think he means anything by it," I said. "We're not betrothed, or anything."

Her pale face almost flushed to a healthy colour, from the crisp edge of her lace collar to the tight roots of her hair. A simple human reaction, whatever the reason behind it.

I walked out a happy man.

CHAPTER THREE

BATRIX WAS ALREADY OUTSIDE Doctor Bezdichnij's waiting room. The heteromorph exuded the healthy glow of a man just returned from his barber, which was ironic, since nothing resembled a barber-shop more than Bezdichnij's surgery. All the same, I wasn't entirely happy to see him. Despite Batrix's somewhat bizarre – and now illegal – origins, his distrust and loathing for all forms of magic were well known. At least, by me they were. Besides, I've never liked being watched when under the ministrations of the good doctor.

"You survived Under-Director Risnek, then?" Batrix asked with the faintest of smiles. Supported by his oddly prissy body and overshadowed by his blue eyeglasses, the smile looked out of place.

"I have before, no doubt I will again." I placed one hand on the doorknob. "Are you coming to watch, or is there something else?"

Batrix cocked his head to one side. "It is a never-ending source of amusement, Scilli, the way your brash manner clashes with an obvious, underlying insecurity. Does one imply the other, I wonder?"

"You've lost me," I said, knocking on the door with my other hand. Not waiting for a summons, I walked in. Batrix followed, closing the door silently behind us.

The waiting room was deserted. The wooden panels covering the walls were grimier by several centuries than those in Risnek's office. Only five, rather worn high-backed chairs were in residence, all pushed neatly against the panelling. A faded carpet covered most of the floor, doing its best to distract the minds of anyone waiting from the scuffed boards underneath. It wasn't doing such a good job.

"Bezdichnij!" I called out. An echo bounced off the stark walls a couple of times before losing its nerve and quitting. Somewhere, a chair scraped on wood, a thick voice muttered. A section of the wall panels slid open, and Doctor Vis Bezdichnij shuffled through.

He was tall, and thin to the point of agony. An eagle's beak nose detracted attention from his hairless, polished cranium. His unusual height had bent his spine over the years and dragged his shoulders down. Now, he looked like some ageing, flightless bird, permanently on the defensive. He was dressed in a dirty suit that had been out of fashion for fifty years; its lapels were streaked with ominous brown stains.

He raised his head like it was carved from heavy marble. "Scilli." he said, in a voice so gentle and stuffed with caring you wanted to throw yourself at his feet and hug them. Not the voice of a man who, if the rumours were true, personally supervised the vivisection of over five thousand men and women during the war.

"Good day, doctor. I'm here to be made beautiful."

"Even my magic has limits, Scilli." He glanced towards Batrix and nodded his head ponderously. "Lieutenant-Commander. I've had no orders regarding yourself, although a heteromorph would be an intriguing challenge."

"I am here simply out of my own interest, doctor," said Batrix. "I find each lunar transformation quite enough."

"Understandable." He turned slowly, indicating the open panel. "This way, if you would, *Gosigné* Scilli."

I stepped though the opening. On the other side, the barber-shop revealed itself: a small room, this time clinically white. A single, pedestal chair stood in the centre of the room, reflected in the wall-mirror it faced. There was a simple glazed bowl and glass shelves, anonymous bottles of prettily tinted fluids lined up along them. Against another wall, beyond the vision of anyone seated in the chair, was a glass-fronted cabinet. Even a cursory examination of the objects placed carefully along its shelves would have instantly shattered the homely image.

"You know the procedure, Scilli," came Bezdichnij's seductive voice. I walked up to the chair and lowered myself into it. I took one last look at the man sitting in the mirror opposite: black frockcoat and trousers, plain waistcoat, plain tie and a collar that clearly needed replacing. The image of a none-too prosperous man, outfitted by charity and cast-offs. The face above the clothing was equally unmemorable: ordinary colouring, slightly over-long dark hair, large moustache. I'd been doing this too long to wonder how much of that was the real me.

Bezdichnij approached from behind. He ran his hands through my hair as though it was something he'd discovered under the carpet. He pinched my cheek. "Good work, eh?" he sighed.

"If you say so. Shall we get on?"

His image stooped over my head in the mirror. He looked surprised. "Got somewhere to go, Scilli?"

"Anywhere."

"I'd almost believe you were nervous," he laughed softly. "You know, it doesn't hurt."

He had a strange idea of what was meant by not hurting. "Let's just say, I don't trust people who enjoy their work as much as you."

He laughed again and disappeared out of the mirror. I didn't try to follow his image. He'd gone to the cabinet, that's all I needed to know.

"You have gone quite pale, Scilli," said Batrix on my left.

I turned to look at him. "I suppose you look forward to all your transformations?"

He pursed his lips. "Look forward? They happen, Scilli, I cannot alter that. Pleasant or unpleasant, such things are a function of what I am."

I waved a finger at my face. "Well, this is part of what I am, too. It's a part of the job. And not one they mention in the advertisement."

Bezdichnij reappeared behind me. In his hands was a selection of polished steel instruments. They all looked about as harmless as razor blades. He was also clutching a fragment of abaston crystal: his own, attuned stone. The source of his power, as with all Chrysomancers.

Even over the six feet separating us, I could feel Batrix stiffen.

"Don't fret, Commander," said Bezdichnij as he placed the shiny instruments around the wash basin. "I know my tools look a little menacing, but they are perfectly harmless. Despite the appearance of my little workshop..." he waved a thin arm at the walls "...I am not some red-handed surgeon-barber."

"That is not your reputation from the war," said Batrix. His tone wasn't friendly. I glanced across, quickly so no one would notice. His round face had somehow gone as rigid and unyielding as stone. The coloured glasses made him look almost threatening. It was a disturbing image.

For a moment I wondered if Batrix wasn't along to make sure I wasn't harmed by the doctor. The heteromorph had some very inflexible views about wizards.

I watched Bezdichnij in the mirror as he slowly faced Batrix. "The war ended ten years ago, Commander. What I did then, I have had many opportunities to regret. I have worked blamelessly for the new government ever since."

"Or put another way, Batrix," I added, "the Bureau controls his supply of *chavet* as much as it does mine. If Bezdichnij misbehaves, no *chavet*. No *chavet*, madness and death, eventually. I don't think he's likely to try anything."

"Thank you for putting my case so sympathetically." He didn't sound grateful.

For a while, the silence was thicker than molasses. Then Batrix cleared his throat daintily. "If I have insulted you in any way, Doctor Bezdichnij, please accept my apologies. Scilli will tell you, I am not a person to extend trust easily."

"He still doesn't trust me," I said. "Last time we met, he tried shooting me."

Bezdichnij turned his shiny head back to look at me in the mirror. The huge nose loomed over my head. "Then he has good taste, Scilli. Next time, Commander, make a better job of it. Now, hold still."

He pushed my head back against the chair's head-rest. Picking up his sinister collection of instruments, he began clicking them together with the negligent ease of practise. Despite suffering dozens of times, I couldn't resist trying to watch in the mirror. But my head was too far back, and forcing my eyes to look down just made them ache.

With a flourish, faster than he'd moved so far, Bezdichnij lay the assembly around my head. Where it touched, it was icy. Much colder than steel has a right to feel. Adjusting it deftly, he placed parts along both sides of my nose, against my cheek-bones, my temples and forehead. A few turns of tiny screws, and it was locked in place. And so was I. From this moment, until he was finished, all I could do was trust in the doctor's skill, and how much a slave to *chavet* he was.

There was a click immediately above me, and through my restraints I felt the snap of something being clamped in place. In the mirror, I could just about see the reflection of Bezdichnij's abaston stone where it now crowned the steel assembly.

A moment later, it pulsed with golden light, blinding me. I clenched my eyes, but the dazzling light still cut through.

"Now, this might sting a little," I heard Bezdichnij murmur reassuringly. If I could, I would have laughed. My eyes already felt as though he was pushing hot needles through them.

The odd, indescribable crawling sensation started almost immediately. It felt as though my face was trying to get up and walk away by itself. Pins and needles jabbed away at my scalp. Deeper down, I swear I could feel the bones of my skull straining and heaving at their sutures. It didn't hurt one bit.

At some time, eventually, everyone undergoing this process suffers hallucinations. Bezdichnij and his fellows explain it away as a reaction to the changes taking place, nothing more than dreams – typical of the kind brought about by anxiety. Others claim that it's actually some kind of personality change, accompanying the new face being grown. And even though it's never been proved that the faces that Bezdichnij form over the restructured skulls are even based on real people, some of the more imaginative claim that the images are somehow produced by the distressed souls of the ones whose faces have been stolen. Obviously, the latter opinion is vigorously discouraged.

All I know is that I'd never suffered from anything, until that day. One moment, I'm in the chair, eyes aching like hell, face squirming as though it was growing worms, the next, I'm in the middle of chaos. All around me, smoke-ragged figures in armour that glowed like the Sun fought with primitive swords and axes. It was like something from Ramini's ancient history, years, maybe centuries, before the colonisation from the Old Lands. I could hear the screams and howls of battle, the injured and dying, even smell the stench of blood and shit. The air was black, ripped through with crimson.

A huge, blinding light drifted across the scene. At random, it would snatch a figure from the melee with what could have been long, thin tendrils. It was hard to see against the brilliance. I was the only one who seemed to notice or care.

The formless shouting began to take on a shape. Gradually, the embattled figures slowed and lowered their weapons. They were all beginning to turn and face me. The shouting was a word – a name. The air was growing brighter, and the name, clearer. It was being chanted by a million throats. I knew it. It was...

The drifting light blazed stronger. The smoky figures boiled away under its impact. I could no longer keep my eyes open...

The name... it was...

"Scilli!"

It was my name...

"Scilli!"

Someone was shaking me, as well as yelling, none too softly, in my ear. I blinked open my eyes. The blinding light was gone. I remembered where I was. Batrix was nudging my shoulder, Bezdichnij calling my name. The metal apparatus was gone, and I found I could move. I pulled myself out the slouch I'd fallen into.

"You've finished," I muttered. My mouth was bone dry, and I noticed how raw my throat felt.

"I finished half an hour ago," Bezdichnij said quietly. He backed away, his body slowly drooping into its habitual stoop.

"We were unable to wake you," Batrix added.

"I've had a lot of late nights." I rubbed at my sore eyes, feeling the dried tears all around them.

"You had one of those hallucinatory episodes, didn't you?" Bezdichnij was dis-assembling his metal pieces, placing them carefully back in the cabinet. "What happened?"

I tried to remember, to make sense of what I'd experienced, but it was already starting to fade, like all good dreams. "There was plenty of shouting, and a bright light. Probably the light from your abaston crystal. And they were all calling my name."

"A curiously rational interpretation of the imagery," commented Batrix. He was smiling as though it hurt.

"I thought you preferred the rational," I said, getting out of the chair. Oddly, I ached all over, except for my face.

"I do," admitted Batrix. "You are the one with the taste for the exotic."

I snorted. "Anyway, let's see what you've done to me, doctor." I leaned towards the mirror.

I've never been partial to red hair, especially the bright, almost orange kind. It always seems to go with a deathly pale complexion, and freckles. Bezdichnij had given me everything – all except the freckles. Carrot-headed, white-faced, pale blue eyes. The only strong feature staring back at me was a thick, darker-tinted beard that mercifully covered half of the face.

"Don't you have anything in blond?" I asked, rubbing fingers over my fresh, pale cheeks.

"You're always ungrateful, Scilli. I do what I'm told, no more, no less."

"What d'you think, Batrix?" I turned to the heteromorph in appeal. One look at his expression told me there was no sympathy there. I sighed and looked back in the mirror. "Ah, well. Maybe it'll grow on me."

I was out of Bezdichnij's workshop and almost out of the waiting room when it struck me. A lot of the strange dream had faded, and I could no longer remember what the voices were chanting. It was a name, sure enough, but I was suddenly very certain that, after all, it wasn't mine.

CHAPTER FOUR

BATRIX HAD BEATEN ME to the stage terminal. It didn't surprise me. The heteromorph had a punctiliousness that would shame a Pomino Thryme clock. He didn't look unduly shocked that I was late, with barely two minutes to go before our party left.

The whole terminal was strident with passengers – both potential and discharged – vendors of hot snacks, drink and tobacco peddlers, newssheet hawkers, and an unguessable number of cutpurses and pickpockets. Almost a dozen stagecoaches were parked indifferently along the street – leading off a corner of Wael Edra's main square – dazzling in their various liveries, different for each route.

But the Anesicci weren't relying on a routine stagecoach. Even if there were any overnight stages on the route to Qaijente, it was doubtful any of the coaching companies would want to let a private party use their franchised stop-overs. Not for a price the Anesicci could match, anyway.

The huge, six-wheeled coach they'd hired was in brilliant black and yellow, drawn by four massive aurochs. Built for endurance rather than speed, it had four windows on each side. Entry was through a door in the rear. It reminded me of one of the carriages designed by the late Professor Alva for his Scan Leroth to Scana Carsofi railroad train. For a moment, I thought I felt nostalgic, but it was more likely dread at the thought of spending a couple of weeks sitting in one of the notorious coach seats.

There were two more waggons in the train: canvas-topped, four-wheeled supply carts, pulled by just a pair of aurochs each. The whole thing didn't look like much and was probably worse. I wanted to assume the Anesicci knew what they were doing, but I didn't feel all that generous.

I handed my single chunk of luggage to the driver's boy. He disappeared in the general direction of the supply waggons, and I wondered if I was ever going to see it again.

Batrix had already climbed aboard, so I grabbed a handle on the coach's rear door and swung myself through the narrow entrance. Inside, it had been made to look as much like someone's parlour as possible: drapes, chairs and recliners covered with antimacassars, a polished table against the front end, and a particularly ugly rug that clashed in every way possible with the floral wall-coverings. We hadn't started moving, and already I felt besieged.

"Morning," I said to Batrix, before smiling and nodding to the three other passengers who were already on board. One was a woman sitting rigidly on an ottoman, thin and shrivelled, her harsh, unsmiling face outlined by a battered red bonnet. A silver and turquoise amulet hung down her black dress on a long chain; it looked like a grotesque, misshapen humanoid. Next to her sat a man as huge as she was small. I wondered how he'd squeezed himself through the doorway. His bloated, puffy face was as humourless as the woman's and as red as her bonnet. The third was another man, of medium build, medium colouring, medium age, reclining easily in an armchair. He was so ordinary it made me suspicious. If I'd wanted to ride the countryside while attracting no attention, I'd probably make sure to look just like he did. He was the only one who returned my smile. It didn't mollify me one bit.

"Looks like we're in for a happy trip," I remarked to Batrix, just loud enough for them all to hear. The comment slid off the two hard faces, Mr Ordinary simply smiled again. It looked as if my ride to Qaijente was going to be one long party.

Batrix settled himself into a chair at the back of the coach, right next to the left-hand window closest to the door. "Make yourself comfortable, Scilli," he said, smoothing out creases in his trouser legs only he could see. "Once the rest of our party has arrived, we will be off."

"Glad to see I'm not the only one who isn't punctual," I said, finding myself a chair as close to the centre as I could and dropping carelessly into it. Mr Ordinary leaned out of his own seat, aiming a hand in my direction.

"I'm Romino," he said. "Gen Romino."

I took his hand and pumped it once. "Wilonek Scilli. And this is Lieutenant-Commander Batrix."

Romino shook Batrix's hand with enthusiasm. "You'll be the government men," he said, as though he found the idea overwhelmingly exciting. "The agents."

"Agents?" remarked Batrix. An eyebrow rose above one of his lenses.

"You know: keeping us safe."

"Safe from what?" I asked. Before Romino could answer, the huge man shifted in his own seat. For some reason, I thought of a whale beaching itself.

"You must excuse Romino," he said in a curiously high voice. Maybe it had to stretch itself to get out from inside his obese torso, or maybe it was something to do with the scarring around his throat. He'd fought in the war, at Drsitu Forek, but his file was predictably niggardly with details. "He has a rather excitable nature and has a tendency to treat life like some cheap novelette."

Romino turned to him, still smiling. I wondered how long it would be before I lost patience with someone so damned cheerful. "Life is a novelette, Echosic," he said. "But not so cheap, I hope."

"And you are...?" I prompted the big man, now that he'd taken the time to speak. He paused a moment before laying a massive paw over one of the woman's thin hands.

"*Gosigné* and *Gosigna* Echosic. We are the spiritual leaders of this pilgrimage."

Spiritual? There was a word that didn't get to see daylight too often these days. Even without the various bits of legislation that had sprung up after the wizards' defeat, such terms were often too emotive for most people.

"Don't let Rhys hear you saying that," said Romino.

"Rhys?" I prompted.

"Rhys Ecozar," supplied *Gosigna* Echosic. I didn't need to be looking at her expression to hear how low in her estimation he was. "He is the final member of our pilgrimage." She reached inside a reticule lying on her lap and withdrew a small watch. Snapping it open, she glanced at it, her dour face growing more sullen by the instant. "And true to form, he's late."

"A man after my own heart," I said aloud, all the while thinking that Ecozar wasn't the last member. Risnek hadn't given me that file just to clear space on his desk. I'd spent a good proportion of the previous night going through the details, learning the names. I'd allowed everyone to introduce themselves mainly because the engraved likenesses included with each biography were so basic, they could have been anyone. But there was another woman: an *Ingosigna* Sotha Ponac. Where was she? And why had *Gosigna* Echosic so obviously excluded her?

A moment later, I had my answer. The tardy members of the group swept into the coach, arms around each other, laughing gaily. Even the mountainous disapproval of the Echosics couldn't put a dent in their high spirits.

"Sorry we're late," said Ecozar. He was a strikingly handsome man, with short black hair, trim moustache and sideburns. His suit was a deep red – almost the colour of blood – while his waistcoat was mint green. He probably thought he was being daringly unconventional; I just wished Doctor Bezdichnij had made me colourblind. "A touch of last-minute shopping."

Ingosigna Sotha Ponac held up a bundle of small packages, all tied neatly in clashing ribbon. She was as striking as Ecozar: tall and slender, wearing a bustled dress and pea-jacket in silver and black, her auburn hair pinned up under a wide-brimmed hat. Green eyes sparkled mischievously. I'd probably seen more beautiful women before, but right at that moment, I couldn't recall where.

"Not often you get a chance to go shopping in Wael Edra," she said. Her husky voice matched the rest of her perfectly.

Batrix, Romino and I came to our feet. There are times when observing the social niceties is a pleasure.

"We're in no rush, madam," I said.

She glanced at me. For a moment, the sparkle dimmed, and a tiny frown creased her brow, then she was all light and air again. "Thank you, *gosigné*. You have me at a disadvantage..."

Gosigné Echosic cut in before I could answer. "I might remind you that we are on a pilgrimage to our ancestral home!" His high voice couldn't convey the authority he so desperately needed, but it was loud enough. I noticed that he hadn't bothered getting to his feet.

"Indeed," chimed in his wife. "This is a journey to remember what it is to be Anesicci, not to indulge in frivolity!"

Ingosigna Ponac coloured slightly and dropped her gaze. "I apologise, *Gosigna* Echosic," she said softly. "You are perfectly correct."

It didn't take long to figure that Sotha Ponac had about as much Anesicci ancestry as Batrix or me, with her colouring, which might go a long way to explaining *Gosigna* Echosic's coolness towards her, but it didn't explain what she was doing here. She wasn't married to Ecozar, nor was she – at least, according to Risnek's files – his lover. This was a strange trip for a single woman with no obvious connections to the Estates.

Echosic levered himself out of his chair. It was even more like some vast oceanic mammal dragging itself out onto dry land. "Now our numbers are complete, I will instruct the waggon master to set off without further delay." The effort of getting to his feet had left him breathless, pale and sweating. It would have been better if he'd asked someone else to go. I was about to volunteer, when a new voice from the rear of the coach cut in.

"Not yet, my dear fellow, not yet. Give me time to stow me own gear, eh?"

The voice was so familiar. It brought back memories I'd thought long dead and washed away on an ocean of *chavet*.

I turned, hoping I was wrong, knowing I wasn't. Standing in the doorway was a flamboyant figure in a long, red-lined cloak. His near-black hair was streaked with white at both temples, and he sported a moustache even finer than Ecozar's. The deep blue of his suit was perfectly matched by his striking eyes. He was leaning easily on an ash cane.

It was him, sure enough. "Steganesh," was all I trusted myself to say.

He stared hard at me for several moments. I could feel his eyes drilling through to my spine. "And you are...?"

He wouldn't have recognised me, of course, thanks to Doctor Bezdichnij's tender ministrations. "Wilonek Scilli. We were at Madrasaté Seminary together."

He raised one eyebrow in surprise. "Fancy. My dear fellow, what have they been doing to you? You look positively ill!" He didn't sound so thrilled.

"You know this man?" Echosic wheezed from behind me.

"We've met," I agreed cautiously. Until I knew exactly what Steganesh was doing here, I wasn't going to commit myself any more than I had to. He was conspicuously absent from Risnek's files.

"Indeed?" Batrix wasn't giving anything away by his tone, but I recognised the signs. He was intrigued, and not a little bit suspicious. I was pretty sure he had every reason to be.

"Very well, I've known Steganesh for over ten years; known him quite well. We've both saved each other's lives. He was one of my closest friends, and I don't trust him any further than I could throw him with one arm. So, Petran, what are you doing here?"

He began peeling off a pair of pale orange kid gloves. "Well, I needed a lift to the north of the Anesicci Estates, and I heard you were headed that way. I thought I might ... hitch a ride?"

"Did you, now?" Ecozar stepped up to him, a challenge in his eyes. I wondered if he knew how much peril he was in at that moment. Maybe he wanted to impress *Ingosigna* Ponac? "And are you aware that this is an Anesicci pilgrimage?"

"Perhaps I'm Anesicci."

"With all due respect, sir," Echosic piped, "I doubt that."

"And neither are Wil, or the uniformed fellow over there who is giving me the most dreadful glare, or ... this delightful lady." Steganesh bowed to *Ingosigna* Ponac, raising a gloved hand to his lips. She smiled, the fire in her eyes blazing higher.

Steganesh straightened, but he didn't release her hand. "If you make an exception for them, can you not also make one for me?"

"No!" *Gosigna* Echosic's retort was sharper than a musket-shot. And had a similar effect. Steganesh dropped *Ingosigna* Ponac's hand and stepped back a little.

He turned to Batrix, his face sliding into serious planes. "Perhaps we might hear from the government? That is an Internal Bureau uniform, I believe. A ride to Anesicci is all I ask. I will gladly provide my own provisions. Even a fee, if such becomes necessary."

"You have so far failed to answer Scilli's question, *Gosigné* Steganesh," Batrix said, calm but firm. "Do so, and I will consider your request."

"I must protest!" Ecozar turned on the heteromorph. "You know that there are certain portions of society motivated by nothing other than hatred of the Anesicci! They'd like nothing better than to destroy our past, our heritage! How can you be sure this man isn't allied with such people?"

"Maybe because Petran has never been able to side with anything or anyone in the past," I said. "His one abiding interest is himself."

He half-smiled at me, showing perfect teeth. "How true."

Ecozar shook his head. "Unless his own self-interest and that of the anti-Anesicci lobby are the same. Or they've bought him."

Steganesh looked hurt. He dug inside his coat and pulled out a long, pale brown cigarette. "My dear fellow, there's no one alive who could afford me." He waved the cigarette in the air, and it lit by itself.

"Not even the Archimandrite?" I asked.

He smiled again. "Sendivogius and I haven't been on speaking terms for some time. I rather suspect he'd like to see me dead."

"So you say." Ecozar was certainly pushing his luck. I would have to take him to one side and explain a few realities to him later.

"I am still waiting for your answer, *Gosigné* Steganesh." Batrix had the patience of a rock-face at times. I wondered how he did it.

"Oh, very well!" Steganesh pulled off his cloak with a flourish and draped it over his free arm. He took a pull on the cigarette and blew out a cloud of aromatic smoke. "I know all about this little trip to the lake, and how certain members of the Senate are opposed to it. Whether you wish to believe it or not, I do have some Anesicci blood – a maternal great-grandmother, or some-such. I thought I might be of some help."

"How?" demanded Echosic.

"He's a wizard," I said before Steganesh could give his own reply. It probably wasn't going to be truthful, and I didn't want too many lies getting in the way so soon. "A third *shakrat* Chrysomancer. And I think it might be true about his Anesicci blood."

Echosic collapsed back into his seat. I felt the whole coach tremble.

Ecozar stepped further away. *Ingosigna* Ponac barely moved, only her head, which she cocked slightly to one side, shifted.

"May I remind you that we're running late!" snapped *Gosigna* Echosic. "If the gentleman wishes to share the trip with us, let him."

I had a feeling that a decision had just been taken. Whether it was the best one, I couldn't say.

"Yes, yes..." Echosic's voice sounded higher and hoarser than before. This time, he didn't volunteer to get things moving. "Gen, would you inform the waggon master that we're setting off promptly."

Romino leapt to his feet, face eager. As he pushed past us and disappeared out of the rear door, it occurred to me that he'd remained silent for the last two or three minutes. He was the only one without an opinion and the urge to share it.

"I'll keep out of your way as much as possible," Steganesh was saying.

"See that you do," said *Gosigna* Echosic. Despite her instantaneous consenting to Steganesh's request the moment she'd learned he was a wizard, I could detect no fear of him – in either her face or tone. Maybe she was just a good actress.

The coach gave a lurch. We all swayed, momentarily off-balance. Ecozar put a steadying arm around Sotha Ponac's shoulders. She allowed it to rest there, for just long enough, before shrugging him aside. All the while, she didn't once look at his face.

Then Romino leapt back through the door, grinning cheerfully. "We're off!" he called, somewhat redundantly.

"So it would seem, Gen." Echosic spoke with the weary tolerance of a parent towards a loved but trying child. "Now sit down." He turned towards the rest of us. "All of you, please take a seat. There are plenty, I'm sure."

"Too many, it looks like," *Gosigna* Echosic muttered as we shuffled around the wallowing coach, looking for chairs. Ecozar and *Ingosigna* Ponac found themselves a sofa against the mobile parlour's right wall. Steganesh sat himself down at the table. As Romino returned to his original chair, I joined Batrix at the rear of the coach, picking a ludicrously ornate yet amazingly uncomfortable armchair.

"One day, the eclectic range of your friends will cease to amaze me," Batrix murmured, speaking just loud enough for me to hear.

"Petran's not exactly a friend," I replied.

"But not an enemy either?"

"No." It was hard to describe how Steganesh and I stood with regard to each other. We'd known each other for years, were as sociable as two people could be under such circumstances, and I could no longer bring myself to trust him.

"Perhaps you would like to tell me something about him?" Despite his polite phrasing, Batrix wasn't exactly making a request. I sighed and drew out my *chavet* bottle. I took a discreet swig. I had no idea how my travelling companions viewed addiction.

"Petran Steganesh was one of the last wizards to attain full indoctrination before the war put the brakes on the Spooks' activities. As I said, he made third *shakrat*, which tells you he's good. He's very good. But he's also something of a wild card."

"He certainly behaves somewhat differently to other wizards," Batrix commented. I kept forgetting, just because he acted all urbane and proper, dressed in his pretty uniform, that Batrix had spent an undisclosed number of years as a Chrysomancer's slave, the normal role of a Shifter before they were emancipated at the war's end. It was hard to believe, especially after considering the unguessable numbers who had died doing the same thing.

"There's something in his make-up." I was watching Steganesh as he sat at the table. He wasn't moving, or at least, he wasn't moving anything I could see. "Something even the nuns and tutors at his seminary couldn't destroy. Rebelliousness, arrogance, massive self-reliance... I don't know what. But it left him largely untouched by their domination. Except for the *chavet* addiction, which was forced on every poor soul schooled at their damned seminaries, he's no more a tool of the Spooks than I am."

"That should be celebratory, but your voice is very bitter, Scilli. What happened?"

I continued to stare at Steganesh. "He asked me to trust him. And I did." He must have felt the pressure of my gaze since at that moment he turned and smiled, his best, most charming smile, the one that has mice dancing joyously onto the traps. "Then he tried to kill me."

CHAPTER FIVE

BATRIX SAT BACK IN his chair. "Kill?" He took another look at Steganesh. I wondered how his thoughts were drifting. "Yet before, you said he'd saved your life."

I almost laughed. I've been told I have a rather strange sense of humour. "Yes. I think he had a sudden change of mind. He's very capricious."

"An entertaining travelling companion."

The coach lurched suddenly. I pushed a drape aside and peered out of the nearest window. We'd cleared the centre of Wael Edra and were now heading through the dusty suburbs. Dwellings were large and infrequent, mostly villas similar to Mawinnek's Scan Feta retreat. But the road was still a rutted, dusty axle-breaker. After ten years, President Thinos still hadn't got around to improving civic amenities, even in the capital. There might have been votes in it, but not as much prestige. To survive another term of office, Thinos needed prestige; he couldn't live on his war record forever. Come the next elections, there'd be first-time voters for whom the war was a distant, childhood nightmare.

Prestige was expanding a network of rail-roads across the Republic, based on Alva's prototype. It was in the encouragement of all-new industries, science and engineering – the advancement and enrichment of Ramini and its people without resorting to the magic so popular with our previous, barely missed tyrants.

"Do you know as much about this job as I do?" I asked, out of a need to say something.

"Not knowing how much you were briefed by Under-Director Risnek, I find that impossible to answer," Batrix replied. He sounded almost smug.

"This is no time to be getting pedantic. All Risnek told me – and all I got from the files he passed on – was that this is simply an Anesicci pilgrimage back to some part of the Estates they consider sacred. Due to the mounting anti-native pressures in Senate, we've been assigned to keep an eye on things. Maintain the peace."

Batrix nodded. "That is more or less the crux of it."

"So why us?" I leaned towards him, the heteromorph leaned back, keeping the same distance between us. "Why two Bureau members, rather than a waggon-load of soldiers with big sticks and even bigger muskets? They would be more effective in a fight, should it come to that."

Batrix was quiet for some moments. Was he weighing up my comments and preparing a suitable answer? Or was he concocting something to satisfy my curiosity, while not answering anything? Ever since we'd left the Bureau building together, I couldn't shake the feeling that Batrix knew a lot more than he was telling. If that was the case, it prompted the obvious question: why? If there was some reason for keeping me in the dark – other than protecting my easily hurt feelings – I hoped it was a damned good one.

"Perhaps the government do not wish to be seen actively siding with an Anesicci faction," he said at last. "Providing troops would be tantamount to President Thinos declaring his opposition to the anti-native lobby, and in the strongest terms. I do not think he can afford to risk a split in the Philosophic Party at this time. It would also leave him open to demands from other pre-Colonial fundamentalist groups."

I wasn't convinced. "That still doesn't explain us. I don't know about you, but I don't think the Bureau took me under its sheltering wing just to ride shotgun on religious treks."

"No," agreed Batrix. His tone was odd. "You belong to what is often referred to euphemistically as the 'dirty tricks department'."

I found myself trying not to smile. Government was all about dirty tricks, and worse. The subtle bit was getting someone else to do the nasty parts for them. "You still don't like the idea, do you."

"It seems to me to be a dishonourable way of conducting business."

I couldn't disagree there. "So Risnek sends, instead of a bunch of armed men, who would be too visible, a uniformed member of the Bureau and a grubby little spy. I'm sure that'll help *Gosigné* and *Gosigna* Echosic sleep more easily in their bed tonight. If I were a member of a minority, with almost a quarter of the government out to legislate me into extinction, I'm sure the thought that people like us were actually here to keep a very close eye on me would never enter my head!"

"I am in a minority, Scilli." He said it so softly, without rancour. "The only heteromorph in the Bureau, in the entire government. As far as I know one of the last of my kind – if not the very last – unless the Spooks are illegally growing others elsewhere."

He was right, of course. And ironically, so was I – a trainee wizard who'd been rescued from the Madrasaté Seminary before I'd been fully indoctrinated. Still a free mind, but with no magical skills – no attuned abaston stone, even if I had – and an addiction to a substance that is proscribed and growing increasingly hard to source, a drink no one outside the Chrysomancers' tight little circle knew how to brew.

I don't think the Anesicci needed me siding with them: they had enough problems.

"So what is your opinion?" Batrix prompted me.

I flopped against the hard back of my chair, noisily blowing out air. *Gosigna* Echosic frowned in my direction, checking I wasn't about to damage the furniture. She glanced away again.

"I'm not allowed opinions, Batrix, I'm too young for them. They might make me ill."

"Very amusing—"

The coach lurched again. This time, very audibly, I could hear the driver swearing from his perch, high up at the front. Judging by the tightening of *Gosigna* Echosic's mouth, so could she, and she wasn't amused. Personally, I thought it demonstrated he had an inventive turn of mind.

"Thinos really must do something about these roads," Steganesh called lazily.

"I'm sure President Thinos has more important things than the state of our roads taxing him at present," *Gosigna* Echosic snapped. From the way she'd stressed President, anyone would think he was a close and revered colleague.

"Name one," Rhys Ecozar butted in.

"The President was good enough to personally endorse this trip," Chato Echosic piped up. "Despite your bias, Rhys, he has shown himself a man of good faith—"

"He's a man who needs votes, Chato. Until he gets back in, an Anesicci vote is as good as another other's—"

"That's uncalled for, Rhys—"

"—and if he isn't re-elected, all his goodwill is just so much desert sand."

"Calm down, Rhys." *Ingosigna* Ponac laid a gloved hand on his shoulder. After a token resistance, he lay back in his seat again.

"Yes, Ecozar, do what your *hotechl* tells you!" *Gosigna* Echosic's voice was soft – barely audible above the road noise – but the venom more than made up for it. Sotha Ponac flushed, her beautiful features briefly hardening into brutal lines. This time it was Ecozar's turn to mollify her. From the way she snatched her arm away from his hand, I don't think he was trying hard enough.

"For such a straight-back, the lady has a pretty foul mouth, wouldn't you say?" I murmured to Batrix.

"You understood the term?"

"Well, I know it makes 'a whore who's giving it away' sound pretty tame."

For a moment, I actually thought Batrix was going to blush, but he disappointed me. "You have an erratic, yet strangely detailed education, Scilli," he said.

"Me? I'm just a seminary boy, Commander. I wouldn't know anything about that kind of thing."

The coach lurched for the third time. I smacked the back of my head against the side, giving me an excuse for some imaginative cussing of my own. I heard a thin screech, followed by a dull thud. Once my eyes had found something like focus again, I saw *Gosigna* Echosic was being helped off the floor by Gen Romino. Her husband was just sitting, doing nothing to help, looking apoplectic.

The driver was bellowing. This time he didn't just sound furious; there was an edge to his voice. Nerves, maybe even fear.

Highwaymen? This close to Wael Edra? Unlikely. But I patted my Alva repeater in its pocket, just in case.

I pulled the drape back again, slowly. Suburbs had given way to countryside. Fields of some yellow-flowering plant stretched away to the smooth horizon. The land was still gently undulating, nothing like as flat as it would get further south. Aside from the fields and a few birds, I could see nothing unusual. It was unlikely that just the sight of a few crows would get the driver into a lather.

The coach was still moving, and guessing from the increasing number of jolts my tender bones were being subjected to, somehow, we were speeding up. Aurochs are big, steady animals, at a good pace they can easily outwalk a man, but anyone who can get more than a good-natured plod out of them is some kind of genius. They aren't made for it, neither physically nor temperamentally.

"What is the fool doing?" I heard Ecozar complain.

There was another outbreak of wild shouting, then a sound I'd hoped I wouldn't hear on this journey: gunfire. Muskets, by the sound of it, or carbines.

The coach lurched drunkenly, swerved – rattling us all in our seats – and came to a swaying halt. Outside, it had gone uncomfortably quiet. I could actually hear the creak of the settling springs.

There was another shot, followed by a heavy thud that vibrated dully along the roof. The driver was hit. There was a second, incoherent shout – a boy's voice this time – abruptly stilled by more gunfire.

"What is going on?" Sotha Ponac hissed. She sounded confused and edgy – hell, so was I – but not frightened.

"Bandits!" Echosic wheezed.

"More like government men who think we're far enough away from Wael Edra to kill us!" Ecozar muttered.

"If so, they are remarkably naïve," Batrix said.

"Or careless," I added. I still couldn't see a thing from the window. I was going to have to get out. I pulled out my repeater and started towards the door. I heard the sound of Batrix's footsteps falling in immediately behind me.

"You'll be needing my help too, Wil." Steganesh stood up from the table and began to weave his way through the slightly disarrayed furniture. In his hand was an egg-sized chip of opalescent stone, shot through with fine golden veins – his abaston crystal. It was a damned sight bigger piece than the one he'd had last time we met.

"I hardly think that will be necessary," Batrix said, drawing himself up stiffly. I couldn't say which he was refusing: Steganesh or his crystal. Both, most likely.

"How do you know?" Steganesh towered over the heteromorph, beaming his best smile. It looked more like the grin of a shark.

"If they were Spooks, they wouldn't be using firearms," I said. "Professional pride."

"Strange times," said Steganesh. "Perhaps their crystals are exhausted."

"While your own is new and vibrant, I expect." Batrix's tone was definitely chilly, I recognised it so well. Quite a change not to be on the receiving end.

"Actually, about half-charged, I'd say." Steganesh rolled the crystal about his fingers like one of those illegal stage magicians juggling a coin one-handed. It seemed appropriate. "Still, more than enough to fly this pony-trap to the Moon and back."

I was getting impatient. "We don't have time for this. Steganesh, come if you must. Batrix, keep a close watch on him."

"I have every intention of doing so."

I eased the rear door open. Someone had had the foresight to grease the hinges, and it swung back without a sound. There was no one at the back; no huge bandits with skin and teeth problems, heavy cutlasses and bigger guns. The two trailing waggons were at a stand-still, the nearest some thirty feet away. I couldn't see its driver.

I stepped to the ground as slowly and noiselessly as I knew how. At a crouch, I eased myself around the back of the coach, peering one-eyed around the corner. If someone up at the front was using us for target-shooting, I wasn't going to stick my entire head into view and shout "boo!"

"See anything?" I didn't need the stifling scent of too much lilac water to tell me that was Steganesh.

"A group of riders," I whispered back. "I can make out seven, but there might be more on the other side of the coach..."

"I'll look." Steganesh backed away before I could argue.

Batrix shuffled closer. "Do you have any idea who they might be?"

"Not from here." The Sun was still low, and it was shining from behind the riders. All I could make out were vague silhouettes. "They're not doing much, apart from blocking our way."

"There are none the other side." My nose told me Steganesh was back.

"Seven, then."

"Just over two to one," said Steganesh. "With surprise on our side, and my crystal, of course."

"Of course." I was going to have to find out where he'd found that chunk of abaston. It was almost as large as the piece the Archimandrite habitually carries around with him.

"To where did the other drivers vanish?" Batrix mused.

"Under cover, if they've got any sense." Seeing their team-mate shot had probably sent them scurrying for the fields like terrified sheep.

"I trust no one will suggest we rush them," Batrix commented drily.

The riders began to move, kicking their mounts into a fanning-out manoeuvre. I stood upright, cocking the hammer on my repeater. "We don't have to. They're coming this way."

Maybe we should have made it back to the coach door, maybe not. We'd never have made it anyway, most likely. Within two or three seconds the riders were moving past us, spreading out along the length of our short waggon-train. It left their line thin, but I don't think they were too worried. One look at what sat astride some very panicky horses would have most people surrendering out of general principle.

They weren't human, or any recognisable animal, just bits of both. Fish, dog, lizard, rat, snake: pieces of a thousand species pushed together into crude, man-shaped lumps of flesh. I found the effect disconcerting, what it would do to anyone without any experience of the more insane aspects of magic, I couldn't guess.

"This isn't Chrysomancy!" I said.

"Agreed," said Steganesh.

"Then what, exactly?" asked Batrix. The very question I was asking myself.

"Teramancy," Steganesh muttered in my ear. "The chimera principle. It has to be."

I'd heard the terms before, but never seen it in practice, or the results. Making monsters out of people, or anything that crawled, walked or flew. It was something most Chrysomancers considered primitive – the kind of magic only backward cultures practised. Very much beneath them.

Which meant we weren't dealing with Spooks, or at least not the kind you'd expect to be invited to one of the Archimandrite's parties.

The thing nearest us clumsily lowered its musket. The creature had the face of a decomposing cod, topped off with lunatic ass's ears. One arm looked like it was from a lizard, the other was vaguely squid-like. Its body was bloated like a toad, with legs that were half-insect, half-snake. Light reflected off its scales in an oily rainbow.

Batrix produced and fired his pistol. The thing reeled in its saddle, clutching at the reins with a suckered arm. Batrix fired again. The horse, pushed beyond endurance by both the noise and its unnatural rider, reared up, lashing its front hooves, its eyes flashing far too much white. The thing in the saddle toppled back, landing heavily on the dirt road. I distinctly heard something inside it burst.

Apart from the shrieking horse and the gunshot, there hadn't been a sound. The creature died without uttering so much as a squeak.

Steganesh snatched up the fallen musket. He fired the moment he'd levelled it. Something else crashed soundlessly from a saddle.

"At least they are not hard to kill." Batrix calmly cocked his repeater and fired at a creature that was charging straight at us. Thick, yellow ichor burst from its shoulder and oozed down a matted grey pelt. It crashed to the ground, just a little too close to my feet, shark teeth champing in a horse's jaw, drooling bluish saliva.

I leapt aside, firing at the elongated skull. It flew apart in yellow-flecked shards of bone and less recognisable stuff. Suddenly, I felt very sick.

All the gunfire was making us the centre of attention. The remaining four riders pulled their mounts out of the loose formation they'd been holding and closed in on us instead. A musket ball tore a groove that wasn't much narrower than my fist in the coach-work just above my head. The things could shoot about as well as they could ride, and their muskets needed to be reloaded after each firing.

I cocked and shot almost at random, for once, my pistol managing to not misfire. My vision was filled with prancing horses and mis-matched animal parts. I could fire with my eyes closed and still hit something. My ears ached with the hammer of gunfire and the screams of horses.

Eventually, there was nothing on horseback left to fire at.

I half-fell against the coach. My repeater was empty. There were seven dead things sprawled about the road-side and three dying horses. We'd been lucky.

Or maybe luck hadn't come into it.

"They were too easy." My voice shook faintly. I told myself it was suppressed excitement.

"They did seem to die with rather more ease than I'd anticipated," said Batrix. He was reloading his own pistol, ramming home the paper cartridges of ball and shot with a lever incorporated alongside the barrel. Somehow, he was managing it without even watching what he was doing.

"Are you sure?"

I looked sharply towards Steganesh, not liking his tone. He was pointing at the ground and the strange carcases. They were twitching, starting to move. For a moment I imagined they were going to make us all liars and stagger back onto their feet. The reality was somewhat worse.

Death had robbed them of whatever cohesion their components enjoyed, even though destroying the whole obviously hadn't destroyed the parts. Each individual bit was thrashing, twitching, wriggling – tearing itself away from the rest. Near my feet, the horse-headed thing with shark's teeth was trying to gnaw at my leg, even as the rest of its warped body pulled itself in every direction. Separated claws dragged their way laboriously along the ground; an arm pinioned itself forward like a huge, grotesque caterpillar; features – faces without heads – lay in the dust and gaped.

Batrix fired his reloaded pistol. Limbs flew apart, but the oozing bits continued to wriggle blindly.

"Get back in the coach." I kicked out at something vaguely snake-like. It snatched at my ankle, then slid off and rolled across the road. "There's no point staying here. They can't harm us."

"I'm not convinced." Steganesh was peering at his abaston fragment, his manner distant and distracted. I noticed the stone wasn't glowing at all, despite all the obvious magic around us.

"What are they going to do? Disgust us to death?"

"No." He glanced up at me, then back at his stone. "But I do believe they'll eventually reform and come after us again."

"Why?" asked Batrix.

"Ah. Now that, I don't know. But if there's even the remotest chance, don't you think it might be an idea to stop them first?"

"You make it sound as though each individual piece is sentient," said Batrix. He shot an over-sized toad's head that was dragging itself towards him with a bloated tongue. "As though they are following a plan of some description."

"Oh, I'm confident of that, just not one of their own." Steganesh took a step forward, raising his crystal fragment. It began to glow: a pearly luminescence, shot through with vivid yellow flashes along the veining. "Might I suggest you both look away for a moment."

I didn't need encouragement. I'd seen how bright a stone could get. I put both hands over my face, placing my forehead against the coach for good measure. I didn't see the flash, but I felt it, like a blazing Sun bursting through a cloudy day, like slipping into a hot bath. And some part of me – maybe a part that still remembered the wizard's training I never completed – responded to the release of abaston power. For a moment, I hungered for that power as much as I did for *chavet* during withdrawal.

"All gone," Steganesh called lightly. I turned round, lowering my hands. The ground was clear of the still-living dead bits. Even the dying horses were gone. The surviving animals had scattered. No doubt terrified by the past few minutes' events.

"Impressive," commented Batrix. He'd lowered his pistol but was showing no sign of pocketing it. The heteromorph's distrust of wizards was as automatic as my own, and maybe even more deeply ingrained.

"It looks remarkable," I said, "but all he's done is translocate everything. Somewhere some poor devil is going to find a heap of offal in his garden – a pile of meat without the sense to know when it's dead."

"Credit me with some decorum, Wil." Steganesh slipped his now lifeless crystal back into a pocket. "I dropped everything into the ocean. There should be enough scavengers out there to ... absorb the threat, I think."

"I hope you're right."

"Is it all over?" Romino was climbing down from the coach's door, holding a large wooden box in both hands.

"Yes," I said. "Sorry. If we'd realised you wanted an unbelievable death, we'd have left a couple alive for you."

He looked surprised. "Alive? What would I want alive ones for?" He scanned the area, disappointment briefly dampening the enthusiasm that lit up his face. "Ah well. Next time, eh?"

He vanished back inside the coach. His file didn't mention it, but I wondered if he was suffering from some morbidity of the brain.

"Let's round up the surviving horses," I said to no one in particular.

Chapter Six

WE HAD A BRIEF, wordless funeral. The driver and his boy were buried side by side, next to the road, their graves marked by two anonymous piles of stones. The boy turned out to be the driver's son and I'd had to ask to find that out. No one had been inclined to mention it.

Gosigna and *Gosigné* Echosic stood away from the burial. Judging by their expressions, they didn't even count as interested bystanders. Gen Romino twitched nearby, the curious box under his arm, but he said nothing and had the air of a man who wasn't interested much either. Rhys Ecozar stalked back and forth, irritably glancing at his watch as four waggoners laid their dead to rest. Only Sotha Ponac showed any concern for two people – one, just a child – who'd been shot down so pointlessly. She stood in silence as the bodies, wrapped in tarpaulin, were lowered into the ground. There was a definite sadness in her green eyes.

Batrix and Steganesh stood opposite her – the heteromorph rigid, his feelings unreadable, Petran swiping at the dirt with the tip of his cane, no less inscrutable. I spent my time leaning against the coach, tapping the *chavet* bottle in my pocket, try to count the number of times I'd seen child-sized bundles placed in the ground. Maybe the over-zealous tutors at Madrasaté Seminary had been responsible for the deaths to start with, but at least they'd had a belief; something to pray to, somewhere to commend the soul of a child.

What were we left with, now? Private beliefs that couldn't lawfully be spoken aloud and two lumps of clay left in the earth. No hope, no soul. Dissolution, pure and simple.

We left them by the roadside. After a mile or two, I'm sure they were pretty much forgotten.

I don't get much chance to ride. It's a pastime I'd taken up in my post-seminary years, but Bureau business doesn't leave much free time. Not that I could afford a horse on my pay. So I took the opportunity to get in the saddle of one of the four horses we'd rounded up. The other three were tethered to the waggons trailing the huge, six-wheeled coach. I'd picked out the best looking for myself: a lean, white-starred mare with an aristocratic gleam in her eye. She was skittish at first, feeling my weight on her back, but once she realised that I was perfectly human, she quietened down, walking sedately behind the coach as though she was in a presidential parade.

But I couldn't convince myself there wasn't some faint, distinctly non-horsey stink clinging to her saddle.

Batrix and Steganesh elected to ride in the coach. Petran, I know, preferred the luxury; the heteromorph – at a guess – because he couldn't ride. Even Batrix couldn't do everything. It suited me to be alone: I felt tense enough without subjecting myself to the fear and loathing presently warming up the coach's atmosphere.

The Echosics were nominally in charge of the pilgrimage, though it was pretty clear that she was the boss of that household. Rhys Ecozar, along for reasons his file was hazy on, was not popular with either of the Echosics, and I didn't think it was entirely because of his friendship with Sotha Ponac. *Gosigna* Echosic clearly loathed the younger woman, and once again, I didn't believe it was simply because the *ingosigna* was a close friend of Ecozar, or just because she wasn't Anesicci. Besides, it looked to me like her relationship was rather unbalanced, with all on his side. This just brought me right back to my original musings, as she so clearly just tolerated Rhys Ecozar's affections, and wasn't Anesicci, what was Sotha Ponac doing here?

And maybe even more important, why was Petran Steganesh with us? What possible interest could he have in some ancient Anesicci tribal site? He was no scholar, certainly never an historian or folklorist. It was hard to believe, knowing him as I did, but could he be an agent for the Chrysomancers after all? All that flamboyant hatred for them a double bluff? It seemed so unlikely, but he wouldn't be the first one to live a false life. My old friend and partner, Sanej, had recruited me while I was still at the Madrasaté Seminary; a place where he had spent many years as a tutor while simultaneously being an agent for the Philosophic Party rebellion.

So, positing that Steganesh was indeed a Spook agent, that likely meant there was something they wanted in the Anesicci Estates. Maybe something *Ingosigna* Ponac also wanted?

Risnek had sent me in half-blind. In the papers he'd given me there was nothing about either *Ingosigna* Ponac or Steganesh being along for the ride, but that didn't mean he didn't know. Why else two Bureau members? Why send us along at all? A simple pilgrimage to Qaijente shouldn't provoke Bureau interest, which clearly meant it wasn't just a simple pilgrimage. Hence Batrix and I. Hence Steganesh. For all I knew, hence Ecozar, the Echosics and Romino. But definitely, hence the things on horseback.

They hadn't been a serious threat, despite their callous murder of the driver and his son. No, they were just a warning. A message sent to make someone nervous. But which someone? Steganesh had dealt with them easily enough. Or Romino? Why had he taken an apparent interest in the proceedings, when everything was safe. And what the hell was in that box he cared for so much?

I rubbed at my head. I couldn't work anything out yet, not with so little to go on. I was going to have to wait, and watch, and hope that some answers came, before we were all too dead to care.

And meanwhile, I'd keep my spirits up by thinking what I was going to do to Risnek when I got back.

₧

Our small waggon train moved steadily south, not halting until evening came. Aurochs are fussy things, for their size. Once they can't see more than a few feet into the gloom, they unanimously declare the day's travel over by stopping dead. Not even the best driver in the world can move an aurochs which has decided to take its night-time rest.

The animals were left to forage in a nearby grassy meadow, the aurochs content to stay put while there was food within reach, horses tethered to stakes driven into the ground. They'd be safe enough with the overgrown cattle close by – nothing that hunted this part of Ramini was big enough or dumb enough to attack a healthy aurochs.

A meal was cooked by one of the waggoners: a stew consisting of some unidentified dried meat and vegetation, stirred in a pot over a fire built on the roadside. It surprised me when everyone in the coach meekly left their comfy chairs to accept a steel dish of stew and bread and stood in the open night air, eating. Even Steganesh, though he'd wrapped his cloak about himself.

The Anesicci, I could almost understand, they were supposed to be making some kind of pilgrimage to their past, after all. Maybe this was the way they fooled themselves into believing it was how their ancestors lived. Even Batrix would take a stern delight in roughing it. But Sotha Ponac? She didn't strike me as the outdoors type, though she was making a good effort at outwardly enjoying herself. And I knew perfectly well that Steganesh's idea of dining out al fresco was not bothering to lay a cloth on the table and using only one set of knives and forks.

The grouping interested me, too. The Echosics stood together, as distant from the flames as it was possible to get without losing their heat. Ecozar was several feet away from them, close to the pot. Although Sotha Ponac was with him, her body was subtly turned away. Batrix wasn't far from where I sat on the coach's steps, trying to look as though I was enjoying the food. Tension was almost making the heteromorph's body quiver. Steganesh was leaning indolently against the nearest waggon's side, spooning up his portion with elegant swoops of his wrist. We were all working so hard to ignore each other.

I finished dinner, mopping up the last drops of whatever it was with a piece of crust, and stood. I strolled towards the fire and handed my dish back to the waggoner who'd been guilty of the meal. If I'd hung onto it for too long, they might think I wanted seconds. Casually, I glanced around. Everyone was lost in their own thoughts, watching me as carefully as I was watching them. Only *Gosigné* Echosic actually met my gaze. I took that as an invitation and wandered in his direction.

"Who sent them, Bureau man?" he asked as soon as I was close enough to understand his forced wheeze. His wife looked at him once – in contempt, I thought – and spared me hardly a glance before returning to watching the distant cooking fire.

I wasted no time pretending I didn't know what he was talking about. "I've no idea. I don't even know what they were. It wasn't a Chrysomantic spell, though, of that I'm sure."

"We used to call them *ochitlac*," he rasped.

"Chato!" *Gosigna* Echosic hissed at him, her attention fully back on her husband again.

"It can do no harm," he said.

Her fingers tugged absently at her amulet. "Must all Anesicci ways be exposed to *tlanasc*! More quaint customs for them to coo over and privately laugh at!"

"*Gosigna*—" I began.

Echosic didn't let me finish. "I'm sure it's not like that, Anej."

"It's exactly like that, you sentimental fool! Take a look at this Bureau man; look into his face! What do you see, eh? Respect? Equality?"

"Anej!" Echosic's voice was an agonising rasp. He might just as well have appealed against a mudslide. His wife turned to face me. The fury filling her eyes was terrifying, simply because it was impersonal. It wasn't me she hated, just everyone who wasn't Anesicci.

"Tell me what you see, *tlanasc*. An old woman? Someone like your mother? Or is it an aboriginal? Some primitive hang-over from the crude days before your ancestors came across the sea and civilised us!"

I waited several seconds before answering. I didn't want to respond too quickly, nor in anger. And I thought she needed a chance to take a breath or two, to cool off.

"You could be just like my mother, *Gosigna* Echosic," I said calmly, reasonably. "For all I know, you might even be my mother. The Chrysomancers stole me from my home when I was still too young to remember anything about it. I don't know where I'm from, or what I am. I'm not even a proper wizard. You can hate the people of Ramini for what their forefathers did; you can hate me. It doesn't matter. Just remember, at least you've got a past to hate for."

She glared back as though I'd slapped her. Then, her mouth thin and her cheeks bloodless, she stalked away. She didn't look like someone who could see where she was going all that clearly.

"You must forgive Anej," Echosic wheezed. "She comes from a very ancient clan, one that features often in our legends. The past is often more real to her than the present."

"Living in the past's a dangerous hobby."

"The past is all many of us have left."

"And self-pity's worse..."

Echosic laughed, a strangely bird-like sound. It surprised me; I hadn't thought he was capable of humour. "You are right, Bureau man. My wife's aggression often causes me to be defensive."

"And now she's not around, maybe you can tell me what she wasn't so happy I should know."

"*Ochitlac*," he said. "It literally means man made from beasts. Our old tales are full of such things: sorcerers creating mannequins from pieces of dead animal. Until this morning, I had dismissed such tales as fanciful..."

"In a world once ruled by Chrysomancy?"

"You forget, Bureau man, since your ancestors came across the ocean, the only magic we have known is theirs. After a while, all other forms become forgotten, the stuff of myth."

"I'll bet your wife hasn't forgotten."

"No ... Anej has a long memory. One attuned to the ancestors, she claims."

"You don't sound convinced."

"I am a man of my time, Bureau man. I wear your clothes, I think your thoughts, yet I am still Anesicci. When the colonists came, there were only two choices left to the clans and kingdoms already here: become assimilated, or flow with the stream and retain as much of ourselves as we could, while aping the new ways."

"Sounds pretty close to assimilation to me..."

"I agree, there is a fine line between the two." He paused. Ponderously, he bent down and dropped his empty dish on the ground. "Most kingdoms became fully integrated into the new order. Many had no choice. But a few retained what identity they could. The Anesicci were one, the Tletlascu another. My wife, and Rhys Ecozar, belong to the branch that flowed with the stream, but never sank. I, on the other hand, immersed myself fully."

"Yet Ecozar doesn't seem to be in your wife's favour."

Echosic cleared his throat and spat. "Ecozar is a fool and a hot-head. What he advocates... Let us say it would not be in the interests of either the Anesicci or the Republic."

He got my attention with that. "In what way?"

"You will have to ask him."

"For example, he wouldn't want to go around creating these *ochitlac*...?"

Echosic's huge head slowly turned towards me. "You would suspect one of us?"

"Like you said: it's Anesicci magic. No Chrysomancer would sully his hands creating those things."

"What you are suggesting is that we are fighting among ourselves. Why should we do that? To what end?"

I shrugged. "If I knew that, I'd be a lot closer to knowing what's going on. I might even be able to take a guess as to why Batrix and I are on this trip."

"You don't know?"

"Do you?"

His face creased into a heavy frown. "If you will excuse me, Bureau man, I must find my wife." He plodded off into the darkness. Only, it wasn't the direction in which *Gosigna* Echosic had stormed away.

Feeling deserted, I swept my gaze across the campsite. Steganesh had gone, presumably tiring of the bucolic novelty once his food was eaten. Batrix still stood alone, distantly observing. Gen Romino had been cornered by *Gosigna* Echosic, and they were caught up in something like a heated, incoherent argument. Meanwhile, the lovely *Ingosigna* Ponac had been deserted by Ecozar and was presently gazing at the fire as though absorbed in either it or her own thoughts. I decided it was time I paid my compliments.

She turned before I was less than ten feet away, pulled out of her reverie by my footsteps. In the uncertain shadows thrown by the flames she looked almost angry.

"*Ingosigna* Ponac. I'm sorry if I startled you."

"*Gosigné* Scilli." Whatever illusory expression the dancing light had given her, there was no doubting the warmth in her voice. "No apology necessary, *gosigné*. Your appearance is timely. Come. Distract me from boredom I fear is about to consume me."

I raised her hand and kissed it briefly, just as Steganesh had done.

Despite our standing within a yard of what was rapidly turning into burnt stew, I could smell her perfume. "Someone has already given you my name, then."

"Your colleague, Batrix, this afternoon as we travelled together. I was enquiring why the government had sent two members of the Internal Bureau on our trip."

"Did he tell you?"

"He seemed a little vague on the subject." She paused, holding her breath for a moment as though she was about to approach a matter of some delicacy. "Is it true that Batrix is a heteromorph?"

I made a note that the next time I travelled with a beautiful woman, I'd have to make sure I didn't have some exotic companion like a Shifter along. "Absolutely true."

"And will he ... become a woman at the next Full Moon?"

"Outwardly. And considering the length of this trip, I'd say there's a good chance you'll see it, *ingosigna*."

She waved a dismissive hand. "Call me Sotha. We're going to be travelling in each other's pockets for so long, I don't think there's need for such formality."

I didn't need to be asked again. "Still, you have me at a disadvantage, Sotha. While Batrix has no doubt been busily lying through his teeth about me, I know nothing about you."

She laughed softly. "A lady never talks about herself, *gosigné*. And gentlemen never talk about ladies."

"Then I suppose I'll have to be ungentlemanly and ask why you're here. If I may be blunt, I don't think you're Anesicci, so it must be because of Ecozar."

"How delightfully direct, *Gosigné* Scilli! Is this a professional enquiry, or are you taking a personal interest?"

"Which of the two would you prefer? And call me Wilonek, or Wil."

"Oh, personal, definitely. But no, I'm not here because of Rhys, although he is a dear friend. I am a student of our history, you see. The influx of settlers from the Old Lands decimated the many kingdoms that had thrived on this continent for centuries. Once abaston stone was discovered here, and the Chrysomancers seized power, they all but obliterated what was left. Qaijente is one of the few places left in Ramini with significant traces of the kingdom the Anesicci once ruled."

Although the night wasn't cold, I felt a sudden chill. I moved fractionally closer to the fire. "Would I be correct in thinking the Anesicci object to people like you digging up their past?"

"They do place a great deal in the sanctity of their ancestor's remains, yes. Why do you ask?"

"It might explain a few things."

"Like *Gosigna* Echosic's rather obvious hatred of me?" She was sharp.

"It did cross my mind."

She laughed again. I liked it. "Anej Echosic is rather ... old-fashioned, you may call it. She still believes a woman should be married and tending the home, not wandering the countryside, single, and in the company of unmarried gentlemen."

"Like Ecozar."

"There you go again! I would almost believe you jealous, Wilonek Scilli. I admit there is precious little love lost between the Echosics and Rhys. In fact, as I think on it, everything I am and do only lowers me further in the good woman's eyes."

"And that obviously doesn't bother you."

"Should it?"

A moment later, a narrow, white-hot poker was thrust into my left arm. The pain followed close behind. I remember hitting the ground, hot ashes from the fire blowing into my face. I remember a woman's voice shouting incomprehensibly. I remember the blood flowing over my right hand, which was clamped uselessly against the wound.

Then the world shrank to a fading, echoing dot, and I lost it.

CHAPTER SEVEN

WHEN I NEXT OPENED my eyes, I was lying on my back, staring up at a glowing oil-lamp. It was hanging from a curved wooden beam and the light hurt clear to the back of my head. I was on one of the waggons. My arm was throbbing as though someone was monotonously hitting it was a sledge-hammer. In fact, my whole body was racked with tremors. I had to keep my tongue away from my champing teeth in case they nibbled chunks out of it. I'd sweated so much it was like I'd been dipped in the ocean. In all, I'd been in better health.

Batrix loomed over me. Then Sotha Ponac, Gen Romino and Petran Steganesh leaned into my sight. I was so glad they were enjoying the spectacle.

"How are you, Wil?" Sotha's voice had an unhealthy, shrill edge to it. I suspect she'd never seen anyone shot down before, especially someone standing right next to her.

"I'll ... live." It took me several moments to get those two words out; my teeth kept pinning them down before they could escape. "I think."

Batrix nodded. "You will, Scilli."

"He looks damned ill to me," came Romino's reassuring voice.

"Get them out!" I hissed to Batrix. He cocked his head on one side. "Everyone. Get them out!"

The heteromorph turned and made oddly formal shooing motions with his hands. "I think it would be best if you did as he asks."

"I could help," Steganesh tried protesting.

"Especially him..." I managed to get the words out between clenched teeth. The trembling was getting worse.

"If you would." Batrix stood – as much as anyone could in the waggon – and smoothed his tunic. They took they hint. Finally.

Once they'd all gone, I reached a shaking hand into my coat. I pulled the *chavet* bottle from its pocket. One long, deep swallow, and the shakes began to ease. I took another drink, and within seconds, the only pain I felt was my throbbing arm. I sighed.

"*Chavet* withdrawal!" Batrix was glaring down at me, the full force of his disapproval pinning me to the floor like a bug.

"Quite an opportune moment, don't you think?" I managed to pull myself up into a sitting position and look down at my arm. My coat sleeve was rigid with congealing blood, there was an almost perfectly straight tear right across it. "Close," I muttered. "And I don't have another suit."

"I thought you were seriously injured!" He sounded offended that I wasn't presently staring into the Abyss.

"Sorry. I wanted everyone to think I was hurt much worse than I am. The withdrawal symptoms helped no end."

"Coupled with the amount of blood you dripped on us all, yes." For the first time, I noticed the gory smears across Batrix's normally pristine tunic. "You have missed your calling, Scilli, I believe you should be on the stage."

"At least there they only throw rotten fruit."

"I did not think *Gosigné* Ecozar was such a jealous man." Batrix supported me as I came to my feet. I'd been shot in the arm, yet it was my legs that weren't working.

"Why? You think he shot me because I was talking to Sotha?"

"So, it is Sotha already. You do move fast, Scilli."

"Very funny." I found a bench and sat myself down. "If I said *Ingosigna* Ponac had a warm and straightforward personality, and invited me to use her name without a hint from me..."

"Then I would say she is not a woman to be trusted."

"You sound just like *Gosigna* Echosic." I began stripping off my coat, waistcoat and ruined shirt. Batrix stood by, taking each item from me like a perfect valet. "The oddest thing is, I agree with you."

"For you to agree with me is indeed odd, Scilli. Obviously, the young woman has turned your head."

"And you've been taking sarcasm lessons." Free of the bloody coat and shirt sleeves, my arm didn't look anything like as bad as it felt. The bullet had ploughed an unsightly furrow across the biceps, causing a gratifying amount of blood but little else, and even that was drying up. For all the pain, it would barely leave a scar.

"I fear you will never be able to impress the women with that," Batrix commented dryly. "A very poor duelling scar."

"You're rapidly developing a one-track mind, Batrix." I dug a handkerchief out of a trouser pocket and began to dab carefully at the wound. It hurt like hell. "Now, listen. You're to tell everyone that I've been badly hurt. Severe blood loss, muscle damage, loss of my arm, whatever you like. Anything other than it's just a scratch."

He folded his arms and gazed down his nose at me. Now I was sitting, he could just about manage it. "I trust this is not just some tawdry way of securing more sympathy from *Ingosigna* Ponac."

I didn't dignify that with an answer. "The amount of wriggling and moaning I did should convince them—"

"Petran Steganesh is a Chrysomancer. He may well have recognised the symptoms of withdrawal."

"Maybe so. If he did, I'm counting on him to be just perverse enough not to tell. Besides, he also happened to not be around the campsite at the time of the shot."

Batrix stared at me long and hard. The blue lenses turned his gaze inhuman. "You think it was he who shot you? Why?"

"Maybe he changed his mind after the last time." I shook my head. "No. Petran wouldn't use a gun. He's too proud of his skill with an abaston stone."

"Unless he wished to make it look like another."

"You're definitely getting better, Batrix," I admitted with a certain grudging admiration. "And there are two other candidates."

"Who?"

"Chato Echosic left me minutes before the shot. When I asked if he knew why we'd been sent, he got all flustered and walked off. To join his wife, he said. But she was having a frank exchange of views with Romino. Echosic went nowhere near her."

"Where did he go?"

"Ah. Now there's a question."

"And who is the second?"

"Rhys Ecozar. He was also absent at the time."

"Perhaps I should question all three, see if they can satisfy me of their innocence."

"It's called an alibi, Batrix. And never trust anyone with a foolproof alibi. It means they've been thinking long and hard. Most people can't remember what they were doing or where they were a couple of hours previously. Why should they? No one goes through life expecting to be asked what they were doing at six minutes past midnight four days ago..."

"Indeed? And what will you be doing all this time?"

"Lying here, thinking hard, and expecting at least one unannounced visitor. Maybe even my failed assassin."

"Then you are taking a considerable risk."

"If someone wanted me dead, the fact I'm still breathing is risk enough. They won't care how close to death I am, just to help me on my way. Maybe they'll even tell me how I upset them before finishing me off."

"If indeed you were the target."

That was a valid point. "If indeed. Now, are you going to stand around holding those bloody clothes, or do I get something clean? I'm getting cold!"

"Are you once again about to produce a piece of paper that shows you outrank me, Scilli?"

I grinned. After all this time, it seemed he was still annoyed by me pulling temporary rank during our last assignment together. "Not this time, no."

He tossed the clothes into a dirty pile on the floor. "Then I shall send one of the waggoners with fresh linen." He stepped over to the rear of the waggon, pushing a canvas flap aside.

"And blankets," I called. "Don't forget the warm blankets."

He disappeared without a word, the canvas flapping shut behind him.

ഇറ

Batrix found a waggoner whose build generally matched mine and persuaded him to donate a few items of clothing. I had a new shirt – a bit coarse, but at least it had two sleeves – and a calf-length coat in faded leather to replace my black frockcoat. It looked as though it would come in handy next time I was exploring Ramini's more frozen climes.

Additionally, the heteromorph had bandaged my arm so thoroughly I could barely move it. That, he'd explained, was the idea. Gravely ill patients didn't just lie around holding a dainty handkerchief to their supposedly near-mortal gunshot wound. I took his point, but it was going to make life difficult later.

Then he'd taken the oil-lamp away, leaving me in the darkness, with just my pain and a mental map of the campsite for company. So I lay there, trying to recreate everyone's position the moment I was shot. I managed to pinpoint just about everyone who'd been present, but I don't know how useful the image was. What I really needed to know was the positions of everyone who hadn't been in sight, and the type and calibre of the gun the attempted assassin had been holding.

I'd been facing Sotha Ponac, with the cooking fire on my right and her left. *Gosigna* Echosic and Romino were on the far side of the fire, pretty much mirroring our image, except for the argument. If I'd been facing roughly west, which I think I was, then the shot had come from somewhere in the south-westerly arc. A little more to the south-east, and either I'd have been back-shot, or the bullet would have struck Sotha as well. The only other angle was almost due north, and that would have meant firing between the squabbling figures of *Gosigna* Echosic and Romino. Even at close range, I'd never heard of anyone who could shoot that accurately.

But all that hinged on one supposition: that I was the target. Maybe I wasn't, and the would-be assassin was simply a lousy shot. It was a possibility, if not a particularly helpful one.

Steganesh, Echosic and Ecozar were absent. That didn't help. Ecozar and *Gosigna* Echosic might not see eye to eye, but would he want to shoot her? Gen Romino might be vaguely irritating, but I couldn't see even his odd ways sending anyone into a murderous rage, no matter how many years they might be exposed to it. And Sotha Ponac? The only person showing any dislike towards her had been standing in full view at the time.

Unless it hadn't been *Gosigna* Echosic who I'd seen arguing with Romino. The thought hit me like a freezing wave. Her husband had walked away from the camp when he'd said he wanted to talk with her. Had that been a careless use of words? And if it hadn't been the old woman, who in hell was it? Steganesh? He could perform the illusion easily enough. He was a high enough *shakrat*. But why should he? And if not him, then who? One of our party? Or the waggoners team?

I gave up; my head was beginning to throb as badly as my arm. I had a whole bunch of suspects, and not a single motive between them. Or at least, not one that I knew of. Therein lay my problem. I couldn't think of a single reason why Sotha Ponac, Romino or *Gosigna* Echosic should be a target. Whereas there are several people who might be tempted to put a bullet through me. Steganesh among them.

The canvas flap snapped; someone was getting into the waggon. I lay still, clutching the repeater that I had tucked under the blanket. My coat may have gone, but I wasn't fool enough to let that go with it. Cloth rustled, and I silently cursed Batrix for taking the lamp away.

"You needn't think you're fooling me with the fake sleeping, Wil. I can see you perfectly well."

It was Steganesh. I wondered if he could read minds.

"Come to finish the job?" I said.

Something began to glow brilliantly: his abaston stone. He placed it on a roped-down packing case: the deadliest room light in the world.

"My dear fellow! Surely you don't think I'm responsible for this?"

I laughed, remembering just in time to make it sound like a man teetering on the brink of eternity. "I don't think you've ever been responsible, Petran."

"Fancy." He sat himself on a small patch of the bench I'd left free, flapping out his cloak so that it settled like bat's wings around him. "It sounds to me like you still hold a grudge."

"Now why should I do that?"

"Some people do. Aren't your bandages a little tight?"

"Why are you here, Petran?"

"Why, to see how my old friend is doing—"

"On this trip. Who's paying you?"

He sat back, folding his arms under his cloak. His moustache exaggerated his smile, making his face into a player's comic mask. "I might ask you the same question, Wil. What possible interest could the Bureau have in a tiny bunch of aborigines off to worship some rocks?"

"Is that what they're going to do?"

"You may be naïve, my dear fellow. I have no intention of being so."

"I know nothing..."

"I have no doubt of that. They never explain the climax of a ceremony to the sacrificial ram. The heteromorph knows something, though, I'd put money on that. Why don't you ask it."

"Not demand? You're getting soft, Petran."

A hand peeked out from his cloak in an elegant gesture. "Times change." He produced a box of his brown cigarettes and took one out. "Do you mind if I smoke?"

I twitched my bandaged arm and winced. "Can I stop you?"

"No." He raised the cigarette to his lips. It was already lit and glowing before it had gone halfway. "Let me give you a little advice, Wil." He blew out a thick cloud of fragrant smoke, knowing how much I hated it. "Watch your back—"

"Not my arm?"

"Very amusing. I'm serious, dear boy. Whatever the Under-Director may have told you, these people are not simple devotees of some ancient cult."

"Work that out all by yourself, did you?"

"Very well. You've already guessed that far. Well done—"

"If they have some kind of secret agenda, I don't suppose you'd like to tell me what it is?"

He stood abruptly. "I came here to pass on a friendly warning, Wil. I've done that. I've nothing more to say." He picked up the glowing abaston crystal and turned towards the canvas flap.

The moment his back was turned, I pulled my repeater out from under the blanket. "Not just yet, Petran." I cocked the pistol, nice and slowly, so he couldn't fail to hear its mechanism. He froze, then half-turned to look back at me, face in half-shadow.

"A little melodramatic, even for you."

I didn't have to fake the trembling of my hand. If I'd fired, it was more likely I'd put a hole through the waggon's cover than Steganesh. I raised a knee and rested the pistol's barrel along it. "Some time back,

I promised myself that I was going to have my revenge," I said.

"Fancy. By killing me, I suppose?"

I tightened my finger on the trigger. "Perhaps you'd like to give me one reason why not?"

He didn't move. I wished he would. My forefinger was getting tired. If I didn't relax it soon, it was likely to jerk and fire the pistol whether I wanted to or not.

Eventually, as though he was face to face with some unpredictable predator, he turned himself fully around and stood facing me. "Well?" One of his eyebrows was raised sharply, a sure sign he was angry. And an angry Steganesh is a dangerous one.

"I'm the one with the gun, Petran," I said. "I get to do the asking, you the answering."

"I could kill you before you had a chance to pull the trigger." He waved the still blazing abaston piece to underline his point.

"You could. But then you'd have to explain why you killed an already badly injured man with magic. Those Anesicci may be frightened enough of a Chrysomancer to let you accompany them, but I think cold-blooded murder would be enough to cure that."

"You're gambling, Wil."

"I do that all the time, Petran. Put it down."

"They'll hear the shot."

"I don't think so. You wouldn't come here unless you'd cloaked the entire waggon in a glamour of some kind. I know how you hate to be disturbed."

"Then they wouldn't know if I used my abaston crystal." He sounded like a public advocate who'd uncovered some obscure but vital shred of evidence.

"Even you couldn't disguise the absence of my body for more than a couple of days, Petran. Or maybe I'm wrong, and you don't care about questions..." I twitched the pistol.

He hesitated for a few seconds longer, then he placed the crystal back on the packing case. "I don't need to touch it—"

"Spare me the lecture. I've attended them all. We were both at the same seminary, remember?"

"But I qualified, Wil, third *shakrat* by the time war broke out. You never even made first."

"Ever hear of in the field experience?" I pointed my repeater at the crystal and fired. The detonation was a hundred times louder than the gunshot, but not loud enough to drown out Steganesh's anguished howl. He collapsed onto the floor, hugging his sides. His face was suddenly very pale and moist.

The abaston stone had flown apart into several bright fragments, one landing on the floor close enough for me to reach. I picked it up – a chunk about the thickness of my thumb – and tucked it inside my bandage. Then I returned my attention to Steganesh.

He was getting off the floor, leaning on the packing case for support. His glistening face was grey and pinched.

"Hurt, did it?" I asked solicitously.

"So you've broken my crystal," he muttered, his voice thick. "The pieces will still be attuned to me."

I shook my head, re-cocking my pistol and aiming it once again at him. "I don't think so. The matrix is broken. If more than one of those pieces were still attuned to you, neither of us would be here, and there'd be a hole big enough to drop the Bureau's offices in where this waggon train is standing. I know the dangers of resonance as well as you."

He picked up a shard. Though his face didn't betray him, I knew he was willing the fragment of crystal to do something very painful and permanent to me.

"They're all effectively new, un-attuned stones," I continued. "The only reason they're still glowing is due to that last command you gave. Even the damaged matrices are committed to it. You're helpless, Petran."

"That could be your mistake."

"So you say."

"You saw those monsters today!" His voice was growing stronger, all signs of pain were draining from his face. "I was the only one who managed to save us! What if something like them attacks again?"

"Once again, so you say. For all I know, you conjured them in the first place."

"To what end?"

"If I knew that, we wouldn't be having this conversation. Now, you have some explaining to do."

"Indeed?" He was completely at ease again, his poise fully returned. I wondered if he actually had a spare crystal already attuned and waiting for him. It would be the kind of reckless gesture I'd expect from him.

"If the Echosics and Ecozar aren't, as you claim, what they appear to be, what are they?"

"Just because you showed how tough you are and used your gun to shatter a crystal, you expect me to tell you?"

"No. Because I expect you to prove you're not scared of them."

He didn't laugh out loud. If he had, I would have been certain. Instead, he contented himself with weary amusement. "Is that what I am? Scared?"

"If you find it so difficult so tell me, it's the only conclusion I can reach. Several years ago you'd have found it almost impossible to keep anything so important – even if it was potentially fatal – to yourself. If the Anesicci aren't giving you a fit of the shakes, it's someone else. But you are worried—"

"I told you that—"

"For yourself. Not me. Not Batrix."

He waved a hand impatiently. "You saw how that primitive bunch of natives reacted when you told them I was a Chrysomancer! They couldn't do enough for me. They're the ones who're scared!"

"That's what I thought at first. But there's another interpretation. Someone like you might have been just what they wanted: a tame Spook. We both blundered in with eyes wide open."

"Both?"

"Like you said, I was the one who told them what you used to be. Still are. A wizard."

"And what is supposed to have alerted me?"

"Something one of them said this afternoon, maybe. When I was riding outside the coach. Romino's a good bet; he doesn't seem all that discreet."

"It's an intriguing fantasy, my dear fellow. I'll give you that."

"Those chimera-things appeared such a short time after we left Wael Edra. I still can't see what purpose they were supposed to serve. Don't you think they were singularly pointless?"

"Tell the driver and his son that."

"Such concern, and so sudden. I didn't notice you breaking your heart over their graves earlier."

"What's your point, Wil?"

"Echosic told me such things were common in early Anesicci legends. They even have a name for such magic: *ochitlac*. If you didn't summon them, maybe one of the Anesicci did. Maybe one is a wizard in his own right. Maybe he or she wanted to see what you could do."

"You're guessing…"

"And you're still worried. That means you'll be the best ally I could wish for: one who's scared for his own skin."

"I'm warning you, Scilli—"

"No, Petran, I'm telling you. Don't worry, I have no intention of trusting any of the Anesicci, and I certainly don't trust you. Until somebody starts to come up with a few answers, the only person whose word I'll take is Wilonek Scilli."

"Not your friend the heteromorph?" The sneer fitted poorly on his urbane features.

"Not even him." Which was pretty close to true. I couldn't shake the feeling that Batrix knew a lot more than he was telling me. Either he was getting his own back for the way I kept so much to myself the last time we'd met – unlikely, knowing the way the heteromorph thought – or he'd been ordered to stay quiet. That felt about right, but it didn't feel good. Was I being kept in the dark because I needed to be? Or was Risnek twisting the knife a little more?

"For an injured man, you take too many risks."

"At least lying down I know no one's going to creep up behind me."

"But they can burn down your waggon."

That was a cheering thought. While I contemplated my mortality, Steganesh scooped up the fragments of shattered crystal. Unless, for some bizarre reason, he tried re-assembling the original, I was confident he'd never know about the piece I'd hidden.

He wrapped all the pieces in a corner of his cloak. Just before leaving, he paused. "I was sorry to hear about Sanej. I always liked the old man."

"For some reason, the feeling was mutual, Petran. Just goes to show that even he made mistakes sometimes."

Clutching his glowing fragments to his chest, Steganesh dropped through the flap.

The brief glimpse of sky I caught told me dawn wasn't far away. Pretty soon, we'd be moving again.

CHAPTER EIGHT

MORNING BROUGHT A PLEASANT surprise. Two waggoners hopped into the back of my waggon and, with plenty of apologetic noises, got me to my feet. They helped me out and down to the ground, very careful not to touch my wounded arm, and half-carried me to the six-wheeled coach. After a respectful knock, they opened the door and shoved me inside.

I almost fell, caught off-balance by the sudden removal of their oh-so concerned handling. Grabbing at the nearest chair-back with my right hand, I managed to keep upright without losing too much dignity, or making it look easy.

"Good morning, Wilonek Scilli."

I heard the throaty squeak of Chato Echosic, but didn't see him at first. I couldn't imagine how such a big man could hide in a coach that size. Then his bulk heaved up from behind an ottoman: a whale breaching. His wife was already perched on the cushions, her face drawn and pinched, ready to disapprove of someone.

Echosic gave me a brief, none too convincing smile. "I trust you spent a comfortable night."

"All things considered." I circled the chair I'd grabbed: it was empty, a well-padded armchair. Good. I wanted somewhere to rest my bandaged arm. Trussed as it was, it still ached like hell.

Barely three seconds after I had sat, the coach swayed and lurched. The driver was whipping up his team of aurochs. Echosic and his party didn't seem to have the inclination to hang around. Breakfast was definitely going to have to wait.

Batrix was sitting immediately to my left, by a window. Almost directly opposite him, also close to a window on the coach's right side, was Ecozar. Sotha Ponac was to his left, sitting just an arm's length away. She smiled at me as I sat; it looked a damned sight more genuine than Echosic's smile, but who could tell?

As with the day before, Steganesh was at the front of the coach, sitting at the table, being ignored – apparently – by everyone. If Romino was around, I couldn't see him. Maybe he was hiding away elsewhere, playing with his precious box.

They all looked tense. If someone outside had suddenly sneezed, there'd have been more than one seizure, I reckoned.

"We have decided not to wait on breakfast but rather continue ahead." Echosic lowered himself onto the ottoman with a perceptible groan. I was glad the coach's erratic sway didn't make him stumble: even if his bulk didn't drive a hole straight through the floor, it's debatable we'd ever get him back up. "After last night, I'm sure you understand."

"Do I?" I asked.

"The bandits," Ecozar replied, almost distantly. Although he wasn't looking towards Sotha, it was obvious his attention was entirely on her.

"The bandits who shot you," added Steganesh, his tone waspish. "I'm sure you remember."

"*Gosigné* Echosic and *Gosigné* Ecozar are assured that the assault you suffered last night was either from bandits, or remnants of the things that ambushed us yesterday morning," said Batrix. He looked at me enigmatically. Evidently a lot of discussion had gone on behind my back, either last night or immediately this morning.

"Bandits," I repeated. I don't think I sounded more than completely unconvinced.

"Yes." Ecozar tilted his head towards me a little. He moved as though his neck hurt. "Do you have some other explanation?"

I didn't. I didn't even have the vaguest of theories. They were all way ahead of me on that score. "I just wonder why bandits would take one shot and leave it at that. Why no raid following immediately? Or enough gunshots to take us all down?"

"He has a point, you know." That was Romino. His eager face suddenly popped above a chair-back several feet to my right; he'd certainly kept himself concealed. He looked back at me and winked, grinning twitchily.

"You simply want to record a bloodbath with that infernal machine of yours," *Gosigna* Echosic snapped. Romino laughed and disappeared back behind his chair.

So whatever was inside that box of his was a device of some description. Even though I had no idea what, that very detail was significant. It suggested Romino was no magician. Spooks hate all forms of machinery, even the ones that kill efficiently, like firearms. They think it takes all the fun out of life and death.

I didn't know how the equivalents of Chrysomancers in Anesicci society reacted to modern science, but if *Gosigna* Echosic was any kind of measure, it wouldn't be favourable. Chrysomancers simply distrusted science and engineering on principle. From the day the simplest clockwork device had been invented, they'd done their best to suppress anything they couldn't control. It hadn't worked of course, just driven science underground. The more they'd tried to bury learning and enquiry, the more a certain kind of mind wanted to dig it up.

From clocks to steam-powered engines, the principles were discovered and applied. Once it became obvious that abaston power was waning – the existing stones growing exhausted, fresh ones becoming increasingly rare – scientists began crawling out of their holes, daring the Spooks to use their precious, fading power to stop them. Even the Archimandrite had a huge clock installed at his villa at Dak Talini – an ironic acknowledgement of the imminent passing of wizardry.

For centuries, war against the Chrysomancers had been unthinkable; finally, it became inevitable. As was the outcome.

"What's this machine?" I asked. I saw Batrix out of the corner of my eye, giving me a puzzled look. Romino's head popped up above the chair again: a jack-in-the-box with a sickly grin.

"You want to know?" No one could fail to note the fanatic's gleam in his eye, or the pitch to his voice. Whatever it was, Romino was addicted to it. "But I thought you were a Spook!"

"Romino!" Echosic's falsetto voice still managed to convey a chilling degree of menace. I wondered who he thought he was warning the younger man against offending. Surely not me?

"I failed the medical," I said easily. "I couldn't conjure an egg out of your ear."

"Fancy," came Steganesh's laconic tones. I ignored him.

Romino was untangling himself from his chair. He scooped up his ubiquitous box and strode towards me, displaying its polished surfaces as though they explained everything. He placed it carefully at my feet and began to unsnap several clips around the top. "It's a helioscope," he explained, his voice reverential.

It still looked like a polished wooden box to me. "Fancy," I said. Steganesh could sue me later.

Romino slid another box from inside the outer one, just as polished and a perfect fit. If it hadn't been for a series of holes bored all around the bottom of the outer casing, it would never have come out; the vacuum would have been too strong. For a moment, I thought it was identical to the outer box – except in size – then I noticed two of the facing sides weren't wood at all, but something more like paper. Stretched rigid across the four edges.

He held up one of the paper sides, pointing it in my direction, holding the box level by the wooden sides. "Look ... see?" he asked.

"See what?" I was looking at a piece of taut paper. What else did he expect me to see?

"The image. The reversed image."

I looked again. There was nothing to see. Obviously, Romino was as mad as he acted.

Then he twisted the box, just a fraction. Something moved across the paper I was staring at. It was an image of Chato Echosic, sitting on the ottoman, but upside down. To be truthful, it was so faint, until it had jiggled across the paper screen, I simply hadn't registered it.

"Well, well," I said. "A box that casts shadows of people. Upside-down ones. Very useful."

Romino twisted the thing in his grasp: now I had the opposite screen facing me.

"And now what I am looking for here? Does it show Echosic the right way up?"

"No, no! The hole! The hole!" Despite the exasperation in his voice, there was no doubting the enthusiasm. He'd probably gone through this scenario a dozen times before.

"There's no hole," I said. The smooth blank screen stared back at me, rather smugly, I thought.

"It's just a pin-hole. You can hardly see it."

"Then why am I looking?"

Romino lowered his box to the floor. "A pin-hole in a sheet of stretched paper lets an image through, and casts it on the rear screen, inverted. You saw that."

"Image through a pin-hole? Are you sure this isn't magic of some sort?" No wonder *Gosigna* Echosic was wary.

"No, no, no! It's science! I don't know why it works, I only know it does. Leresch discovered the principle over fifty years ago, but it wasn't until the effects of the volatile fraction of quicksilver on salts of iodine were uncovered that a use was found for it."

I looked helplessly towards Batrix. "Do you know what he's talking about?"

He shrugged. "Not exactly. But I do recall hearing of this helioscopic theory..."

"Stupidity is what it is." *Gosigna* Echosic left us in no doubt of her feelings.

Romino didn't look as though he'd heard her. Maybe he was used to it by now. "It's simplicity itself! Listen..." he pointed to the screen where I'd seen Echosic's faint, upside-down image "...in use, I would replace this screen with a silver plate that has been sensitised by exposure to iodine."

"Sensitised to what?"

"Light, of course!"

"Of course." I glanced at Batrix again. His face was unreadable.

Romino was oblivious to us both. "The image projected through the pin-hole is cast upon the plate, and it leaves a permanent image. Exposure of the plate to volatile quicksilver develops that image."

I'd believed Professor Alva half mad, with his unstoppable enthusiasm for his locomotive-engine, but Romino made him look sober by comparison. I couldn't see why in hell anyone would want to do something so bizarre.

"Why?" I asked, my confusion making me sound dense.

"To retain the image." Romino made it sound the most natural thing in the world. "To keep it, a record of an event. A piece of history."

"Most intriguing," said Batrix, his tone remarkably neutral.

"Yes," I agreed, my head whirling. "Here's to a changing world, eh?"

"Now you see what we have to endure," said *Gosigna* Echosic. She was tugging at her ugly amulet angrily. "The constant foolishness!"

Romino grinned at me again; we were true conspirators, us two. He slid his helioscope contraption back into its box and hugged it. "Don't mind Anej," he confided to me in a whisper that couldn't be heard more than half a mile away, "she doesn't like change. She can't see the future the helioscope must have!"

"How short-sighted of her." I was talking to his back. He'd retreated to his chair – bent over his precious box – and disappeared behind the tall back once more, folding himself up like a crab.

"The boy is evidently a genius," Batrix commented quietly.

"He's crazy enough to be one."

"Or making an excellent pretence."

I gave Batrix a sour look. "My own sparkling brand of pessimism not enough for you these days?"

I swear that he almost smiled.

"And how are you this morning, *Gosigné* Scilli?" Sotha Ponac was leaning towards me, her face all concern. I squirmed in my seat, trying to make it look good.

"I'll live, *ingosigna*. Thanks for your concern."

"Oh, she has plenty of concern, that one." *Gosigna* Echosic must have been snacking on sour lemons all night. She was being particularly unforgiving.

"They breed them tough in the Bureau, Sotha," commented Ecozar. He was glaring directly at me, ignoring the older woman. His black eyes were cold, trying to be threatening; he didn't even come close. I've been intimidated by experts. "I have heard some of them have no blood at all."

"And others have a lot less than they started with." I stared back, not blinking, focusing on the bridge of his nose. It's easier than actually looking into someone's eyes, but it has the same effect. After several moments, he took a sudden interest in the scenery beyond the window.

"We thought we'd lost you, last night." Sotha was replying to my last words; Ecozar and *Gosigna* Echosic might just have well never spoken. "You looked dreadful."

"I think you'll find Wil is very difficult to kill," Steganesh spoke up from the end of the coach.

I wouldn't look towards him. "There speaks the voice of experience."

Sotha glanced towards Steganesh, then back at me again. She smiled, just barely. "Do I detect hostility?"

"Merely history, dear lady," replied Steganesh.

"Then you must tell me some time. I am an historian."

"I thought you said you were an archaeologist," I said.

"Aren't they the same?" Her smile was arch and provocative. I decided to direct my attention elsewhere; I was started to feel decidedly provoked.

"I think you are a little out of your depth, Scilli." I could barely catch Batrix's whisper myself, there was no danger other ears would hear it. Ten years in the Bureau breeds strange talents.

"A snack, Gen!" Echosic suddenly wheezed. "No need for us all to starve for the sake of dispatch! Eh?"

Romino uncurled off his chair, and moved – boxless, for once – behind the ottoman, where Echosic had been rummaging earlier. He reappeared, dragging a huge basket across the floor. He left it directly in front of Echosic, who clumsily bent forward and raised the lid.

"A few items I put aside," he gasped. Leaning forward was making him sound more breathless than usual.

Acting as distributor, Romino first issued porcelain plates to each of us, then began to litter the available floor space with various food items. There were two chickens, spiked all over with cloves; a massive baked ham; stone jars of pickles and preserves; a gallon jug of what proved to be porter; and eight different cheeses.

Echosic piled his own plate higher than looked safe and sat comfortably back to devour it all. It was easy to see how he'd reached his present size.

The sight of all that food reminded my stomach that it was empty. Determined to play the helpless invalid, I asked Batrix if he'd fill my plate for me. The heteromorph gave me an unreadable look before taking my plate and stepping towards the impromptu banquet. I wished I'd learned to read that face, but Batrix had always been too skilled at hiding behind a bland expression. The blue-lensed eyeglasses he habitually wore didn't help.

"I'll do it." Romino took the extra plate off Batrix, allowing him to choose his own breakfast: a few slices of fowl, along with a scoop of pickles and a discreet mug of porter.

Meanwhile, *Gosigna* Echosic had selected a few items of her own – as restrained as her husband had been greedy – while *Ingosigna* Ponac laid out meals for herself and Ecozar, arranging a selection of items in elegant patterns across their plates. It seemed a shame to disturb the simple beauty by eating any of it.

Romino was weighing down my platter with enough victuals to feed an army. "Hold it," I called out. "A light meal will be enough..."

"Nonsense," piped Echosic from around a chicken leg. "You need feeding up, get your strength back."

"I suspect my system's still recovering from the shock."

Romino handed me the plate. I could barely hold it with one hand. I placed it on my lap and was just about the pick up the fork Romino had included, when the entire coach shook as though it was about to fall apart. My breakfast slid to the floor. One of the women screamed.

I was destined not to eat anything that morning.

CHAPTER NINE

THE COACH SHOOK AGAIN. Something else crashed to the floor, joining my own food. Whatever it was, it didn't sound like it had survived the trip.

I craned my head towards Batrix's window. I half expected to see some huge giant outside, playing with the vehicle like a child with a toy. But there was nothing obvious, just the fields and the morning Sun.

I began to stand, but Batrix pushed me back down into my chair. There was another unsightly stain down the front of his tunic. Porter this time, I think.

"You are still too poorly," he said. "Remember?"

"Sometimes I forget."

"Then you should be grateful I am here." He reached for the door and pushed it carefully open, peering outside with great caution. The coach lurched drunkenly again – my chair almost toppling – and when I looked up again, Batrix had disappeared. The door was swinging emptily back and forth.

"Arm or no arm!" I muttered and swung out of the chair. I leapt through the door space, pivoting on the doorknob with my free hand. Jumping heroically about gets hard when you've an arm bandaged against your side.

Batrix was getting to his feet, dust from the road adding to his already ruined uniform. He didn't look hurt, not physically, anyway.

I turned through a circle, looking for whatever was tossing the coach about. I saw nothing, except for the coach itself leaping and bouncing on the spot, as though it had just taken on life and was celebrating its new birth with a jig.

The doorway erupted more people. Sotha Ponac, followed by the Echosics and Romino, tumbled unceremoniously out. I wasn't surprised to see Romino clutching his damned helioscope; he thought there'd be some image out here worth recording, no doubt.

"What the hell is going on?" panted Echosic. He looked all about the landscape, too. His wife was hanging onto him tightly, either worried his huge bulk would overbalance, or he'd be whisked away. Anything that could toss the coach around would have no problem, even with Echosic.

All four retreated back from the coach, eyes probing the empty countryside for the attacker. There were just more fields, with gentle hills in the distance, little more than smoky blurs in the morning light. The fear they shared was universal: I could feel it gnawing at me, too.

"It's invisible!" Romino voiced what everyone else was probably thinking. Except he sounded disappointed.

I had my doubts. Invisibility was an option, but anything under such a glamour normally becomes blind, as oblivious to the world as it is to them. Whatever was attacking the coach seemed able to see well enough.

"Perhaps it can smell us."

Steganesh jumped lightly from the coach. From his words I guessed he'd been thinking much the same as me, probably even reached the same conclusion. The result of a shared education.

"I believe it can." Batrix was pointing at the surface of the road underneath the coach. "It would have to. But neither is it invisible."

The dirt below the coach was heaving up, slowly cracking wide open. Each convulsion tossed the vehicle. So, not a giant with a toy, more like a bean on the skin of a vibrating drum.

"What's that?" Romino was pointing to something dark, its texture polished like old furniture, pushing through the convulsing dirt. Angular and smooth on one side, it was thick with arm-long spines across the other. Worryingly, it looked rather like a huge jaw.

"Maybe we ought to step back," I suggested. I looked around and saw I was talking to myself: everyone was already fanning out, their faces showing various degrees of alarm.

I limped in retreat, remembering I was supposed to be badly shot-up. I had the feeling panic just might overtake play-acting at any moment.

The coach bounced high again, thrown up as the jaw-shape thrashed against the middle axle. The vehicle landed safely this time, although much more of that treatment and we'd be walking to Qaijente.

Two more spined jaws thrust up through the ground.

"Must have called its friends in for a picnic," I muttered.

"I think not." Batrix stepped up closer and took me by my good arm. I think maybe he'd suddenly remembered I was supposed to need help, too. "It looks to me like part of the same creature."

He was right. Even before it pushed itself further out of the ground, I realised that all three jaws were acting in concert, as though sharing a common hinge. Two or three feet more of the thing were suddenly revealed, and Batrix's idea had its proof. It was like a huge eel or worm made of something like polished wood, with a three-part mouth. And it didn't like our coach one bit.

It clamped its mouth tight shut and flailed against the underside like a living battering ram. The coach was tossed higher than ever, and it crashed down again, barely keeping upright. I thought I heard one of the wheels or axles splinter.

"Rhys!" Sotha Ponac ran towards the coach. I was too slow to stop her, but she came to an abrupt halt anyway, less than a dozen feet from the coach. "Rhys!"

She turned round, looking at us all beseechingly. Her movements were erratic, close to ungoverned panic. "He hasn't come out! Did anyone see him get out?"

"*Ingosigna* Ponac!" I didn't like the way she was poised; she looked as though she was about to make a foolhardy dash for the coach at any moment. I doubted a man could have made it safely, but with her long skirts...

The worm-thing smashed against the vehicle's underside again. This time, flicking its angular head. The coach flew up and over. It landed on its side, although landed is much too gentle a word. Glass shattered, panels snapped. If Ecozar was still in there...

Like a deformed, leathery whale breaching, the worm-thing spewed out of the earth. The three-part jaw gaped from a sinuous body that seemed to keep on coming; a disgusting, sentient plant, like the jellied blossoms that grow in rocky, shallow ocean pools. Its body looked no less like ancient timber for all its flexing.

We scattered. The way the long body was questing back and forth, its thorn-lined mouth-parts gaping wide, left us in no doubt as to its next plan of action.

"I trust you're happy!" Steganesh hissed at me spitefully. "If you hadn't shattered my crystal, I could have destroyed the thing by now!"

"In a choice between the two of you, I'll take the overgrown maggot any day."

"You'll live forever, Scilli!" He lurched away from me, cloak snapping. "You're too stupid to know how to die!"

"You shattered his abaston stone?" Batrix sounded vaguely incredulous.

"Damage limitation," I said. "Do you think we could all move faster? Leaving you standing with a sudden cowardly sprint might damage my credibility just now." The worm-thing had stopped its blind groping and paused. It looked suspiciously like it was smelling us – or listening out for us.

One of the aurochs lowed nervously. When the coach had overturned, its traces had snapped, leaving the creature more or less free. Instantly, the worm-thing whipped about. It clamped its three-part jaws around the frightened animal and began to retreat down its hole. The aurochs dug in its hooves, thrashing and goring at the monster's polished flesh, but it made no impression. It was hauled across the ground and pulled brutally down into the ruptured earth like a toy. I thought I could hear its terrified lowing long after it had vanished – echoing up from some unimaginable worm-hole.

Then all went very quiet.

Sotha Ponac was the first to move. Gathering up her skirts she ran to the overturned coach. The door was open, hanging at an angle that suggested at least one of the hinges had ripped free. Bending almost double, she pushed herself inside the vehicle. I heard furniture rattling aside, the crunch of glass underfoot, and then the sound I'd been expecting but had dreaded.

The wail of disbelief. I'd heard it many times, in the moments before the mind accepts what it's being shown; that time of heartbreak when it feels like the world's finally beaten you and torn up and trampled everything that matters to you.

I knew that sound all too well.

Romino and Steganesh raced towards the coach, the Echosics following with all the haste the man could manage. I hung back. Not that I didn't want to know what had happened to Ecozar – I could picture it quite well enough – but an injured man can't move too fast. And I wanted a quick word with Batrix.

"That's the second attack this party has suffered."

"Evidently Under-Director Risnek suspected that something of this nature was likely," Batrix said. He made no attempt to hurry me into the coach. I wondered if he'd grown squeamish. "Unfortunate that he chose not to mention it to us."

"Unfortunate?" I smiled thinly at the heteromorph's turn of phrase. "The only fortunate thing so far is neither of the ... distractions chose to attack us directly. It's almost as though both have simply been attempts to delay us, maybe even stop us getting to Qaijente altogether. The coach certainly doesn't look like it's going to be heading anywhere in the near future."

"And Ecozar?"

"Unfortunate." I repeated his own word deliberately.

"I wonder if he would see it in that way?"

"He's past seeing anything, Batrix. Rhys Ecozar is dead. Dead because he didn't get out of the coach fast enough. Why was that, d'you suppose?"

"Fear makes humans react in the oddest ways, I have found."

"You think staying inside something that's been battered apart is just odd? He was closer to the door than either of the Echosics, and they got out. They had to have passed him. If he was in some kind of funk, why didn't they drag him out?"

"Neither evidenced much love for the man..."

"So much so they'd leave him to die?"

He didn't respond. I don't suppose there was much he could say, not without a great deal of thought.

"Let's get inside." I reached inside my borrowed clothes, trying to remember where I'd left my *chavet* bottle, and took a couple of pre-emptive mouthfuls. "There's another roadside funeral waiting for us."

CHAPTER TEN

AS IT TURNED OUT, I was wrong. Neither of the Echosics had any intention of leaving Ecozar's body planted anonymously by the roadside.

"He was Anesicci," Echosic wheezed with the kind of dignity reserved only for the corpses of those disliked in life. "We must bury him at Qaijente, in the shadow of the cliffs. He, of all people, would want that."

Ecozar was in no condition to tell us what he wanted. Sotha Ponac tried to protest that taking a corpse on such a journey – without adequate embalming – was much too insanitary. I could see her point; the Echosics didn't. *Gosigna* Echosic merely silenced the younger woman with a patented look, and all three Anesicci got on with planning a suitable memorial ceremony for their dead.

In all, it was no less hypocritical than I'd expected from the moment I'd seen Ecozar's body.

He'd been wedged against what should have been the coach's roof, now a temporary wall. The ottoman was lying across him, holding him in a distractingly natural position: he looked as though he was half-lying on the horizontal coach side, half-propped against the roof. If it hadn't been for his obvious injuries, I might have expected him to open his eyes and complain that one of his legs hurt. As it was, I guessed there was more than one bone snapped, and not just in the leg. His face and any exposed flesh was battered and pulped, blood was everywhere: walls, floor, roof, all the furnishings. He must have been tossed around like a ragdoll, smashing into every unsecured item the vehicle held. I hoped he hadn't suffered. It didn't look a particularly quick or easy death.

Sotha Ponac had been inconsolable at first. She'd crouched by the shattered body, wailing and moaning, blaming herself, wishing she'd been more attentive while he still lived. It had been an upsetting sight; only Batrix and *Gosigna* Echosic appeared unmoved. The heteromorph, at least, I could understand.

Waggoners wrapped the body in a length of tarpaulin and stitched it into a shroud. Ecozar was going to get an unofficial lying in state in the back of one of the waggons until we arrived at Qaijente. I hoped the irony cheered him.

Not that I was supposed to believe there was anything left of Ecozar to notice.

We cleared out of the half-wrecked coach. Waggoners swarmed over it, securing ropes and wedging eight-foot long timber levers under the roof's edge. They righted the thing, but it was a sorry sight. All of the glass was gone, two of the axles were snapped, three of the wheels had broken spokes and all of the steel tyres were buckled. Not to mention the wooden shafts for the aurochs – the survivors of which needed rounding up – and the furniture. The crew broke out spare axles, wheel spokes and shafts, but the furniture was irreplaceable.

The glass had to be substituted with sheets of isinglass – all of which had seen better days.

By nightfall, the coach may have been roadworthy again, but it was a far cry from the polished, splendid thing that had left Wael Edra only a day earlier.

Since the daylight was gone, there was no point in moving on. We made camp exactly where we were. The aurochs were gathered up and staked within sight, despite their loud protests. After the worm-thing, our confidence in the beasts' invulnerability was shaken. The waggoners handed out ancient, but well cared-for muskets among themselves and posted a perimeter guard. Sotha Ponac remarked their payment hadn't included watching over our tender persons, but it seemed they'd appointed themselves our protectors, nonetheless.

We had another quiet supper of unidentifiable stew. No one seemed anxious to say much. For myself, whatever it was we were eating, I couldn't taste it. Maybe it had no taste.

Everyone retired to sleep in the coach with almost indecent haste, leaving Batrix, Steganesh and I to stretch out wherever took our fancy. I chose my cosy shelf in the waggon again, pointing out at least I'd be dry if it rained. Batrix merely raised an eyebrow at my sudden fastidiousness, but Steganesh grunted noncommittally and strode off into the night, jabbing savagely at the ground with his cane. Maybe he was checking it for softness.

Batrix let me retire to my waggon berth without comment. I'm sure he guessed I wasn't about to sleep, but he was generous enough not to interfere or question.

I allowed just over three hours to elapse. Only a complete insomniac would still be awake after that time. Assuming nobody on this trip was an insomniac, I'd only have the guards to watch out for, and since they'd be tending to look outward – I doubt any would have the imagination to anticipate an assault from within the camp – I expected to have a pretty free hand.

I untied myself from Batrix's constraining bandages. With only one free hand, and the bindings limiting my movements, I was beginning to appreciate how trussed-up madmen felt. I've performed more difficult tasks, but right then, I couldn't remember any.

Eventually I was free and feeling several pounds lighter. The gunshot wound was still sore and vivid, but there was little stiffness, which worried me. There's nothing more certain to go wrong than something with an ideal beginning.

Much as I hated doing so, I left my gun behind, tucked under the pillow – I didn't want to start waking up the camp with gunfire, no matter what – and wadded blankets into an unconvincing shape that was meant to be a sleeping me. It wouldn't fool anyone who took more than a cursory glance, and why should anyone be looking? An assassin wouldn't be likely to go about complaining I wasn't where I should have been. In place of the repeating pistol, I removed the knife that I always keep tucked inside my boot and slid it through my trouser belt. Pausing only to take a drink of *chavet* – you never know when withdrawal will strike, it has its own rules and timetable – I stashed the bottle and exited through the waggon's back flap.

It was thoughtfully quiet outside, just the offhand murmurs of our self-appointed guardians. They were making a pretty good job of announcing their presence if there was anyone out in the dark waiting to rush us. I didn't think that likely; the danger was already with us: one of the pilgrims. Why else had Risnek sent Batrix and me? He'd obviously known there was something askew about the whole enterprise. The pity of it was, he hadn't thought to tell either of us what his suspicions were, or hand over any evidence he might have to back them up, if there was any.

I ran at a crouch across the campsite, doing my best not to get between a guard and the still annoyingly bright glow of the dying fire. Luckily, Ecozar's body was stored in a waggon less than fifty yards away; unluckily, it was open ground all the way. The unlimbered waggons and coach had been arranged with a great deal of open ground between them, so they didn't form a wall behind which anything could hide. To stop anyone doing exactly what I was doing right then. I thought I should have a word with them about their ideas of security one day soon.

I reached the second waggon without anyone raising the alarm. Now, as long as there was no one inside, I'd be in and out in short order and able to get some sleep after all.

At that moment, it occurred to me that I'd been assuming Batrix didn't know what Risnek was up to. But I couldn't know that for sure. The two of them would have had their own little chat before we'd met up outside Doctor Bezdichnij's surgery, if only for Batrix to receive his orders. Why was I assuming Risnek hadn't told the heteromorph everything he'd forgotten to brief me with? I'd already wondered if Batrix was holding something back. Nobody alive knew when my birthday was, so it would be a fair guess he wasn't planning a surprise party.

Wonderful thing, trust. Or so they tell me.

I pulled myself up onto the back of the waggon, wincing at the slow, rolling throb that woke in my arm. The gunshot wound wasn't going to be as co-operative as I'd thought.

I slid over the waggon's loading gate and flopped inside like a beached seal. As luck would have it, I landed on my wound. The throb escalated to spearing agony in an instant. It was all I could do to stop myself yelling out loud. I had to be content with clutching the gunshot, wallowing on the floor and shrieking mutely through clenched teeth.

Eventually the pain subsided to a restless ache. I stood upright – or as upright as I could under the waggon's tarpaulin – still clutching my arm. My fingers felt suspiciously warm, and a quick glance confirmed the bleeding had re-started. I would have to take care I didn't drip on anything or leave sticky red finger-marks everywhere.

I wiped my hand dry on my thick shirt – Batrix was going to love me – and wedged my left hand into my belt. Hopefully the bleeding would stop soon, and I was trusting any stray drips would run down my arm and be mopped up by my sleeve, shirt-front and trousers. No embarrassing clues in the waggon, but a lot of explaining to do tomorrow.

The inside of the waggon was cluttered with crates, boxes, portmanteaux and every kind of luggage. My own case was lying where it appeared to have been thoughtlessly tossed, on top of a wooden locker. What I couldn't see was any sign of Ecozar's tarpaulin-shrouded body.

Obviously, it was stored away from prying eyes. Most of the containers I could see were too small, or entirely the wrong shape, to act as a temporary coffin. But there was one crate, pushed up against the waggon's side, which looked made to measure. Around six-feet long and two-feet square in section, Ecozar would have fitted in there as snugly as his bed at home. Even better, there was nothing sitting on top, no heavy boxes that I'd have to move, silently, with one hand.

There was a crowbar hanging off one of the canvas supports. Slipping it gently under a corner of the crate, I heaved, carefully. The lid began to lift with barely a sound. It hadn't been nailed down any too tightly, suggesting hurried work.

As quietly as possible I levered up the lid. But as I slid it to one side, I didn't see Ecozar's face gaping blindly up. Instead it was full of salt, almost to the brim.

I lowered the lid gently to the floor and lay it flat; I wasn't going to risk knocking it over and waking up half the countryside. Then I poked a finger through the salt. Several inches down, I touched fabric, and it wasn't canvas. More like quality woollen cloth – the sort a well-to-do Anesicci would have his suits cut from.

I began scooping salt away. It was a frustrating process; the fine crystals kept running back into the hollow I was trying to create. But eventually, I had Ecozar's head and shoulders exposed, and a small mountain of salt standing higher than the sides at the crate's other end.

The waggoners had gone in for a crude form of preservation after all, despite the Echosic's specific orders to the contrary. That intrigued me. First, the crew had appointed themselves our armed guard, then I find they've disobeyed a direct order. I wondered if all waggoners acted like that, regardless of who was paying them, only following the orders they saw fit: the ones they didn't feel would endanger or inconvenience the waggon train. They must have had one hell of a strong guild.

I wondered how Anej Echosic would react when we reached Qaijente and she saw Ecozar's salt-dried corpse. It also occurred to me that if I'd waited much longer before examining the body, there'd be little to investigate. Desiccated remains aren't very forthcoming with the finer points of evidence.

Maybe the waggoners weren't acting independent of orders after all.

Dismissing speculation for the moment, I got on with the examination. Ecozar's remains hadn't begun to dry out much, despite the salt. Whoever had packed him in the crate hadn't bothered to clean him up first: dried blood still covered his face and what I could see of his clothing. Multiple cuts, almost certainly the result of crashing into just about every item on board the coach as the worm-thing had shaken it like a rattle. Blood and cuts, but curiously, no sign of bruising. Why was that? I dug deeper in the salt and found his hands. Pulling them out, I found no bruises there, either, just more blood, gashes and split nails.

You hit someone with bits of furniture, they bruise. Even if the continual battering kills them, there will still be some bruising. So, there was only one deduction. Ecozar was already dead when his body was tossed around the coach. Dead long enough not to bruise.

I buried the hands again and continued to stare at the face. Ecozar wasn't being free with any answers. If I were a *shakrat* of the same level as Steganesh, I might have been able to resurrect the dead Anesicci long enough to ask him what had happened, but even then, there may have been too long a delay after death. And all that salt wouldn't help.

I thought back. Who had been the last one out of the coach? Steganesh. If he'd killed Ecozar with some quick spell, there'd be nothing to find. The Echosics followed Sotha Ponac out and none of them had made any comment about their travelling companion suddenly turning very dead. If they'd even had the time to see, of course. In the panic, I guess everyone was looking out for themselves. And did anyone have enough time to kill in the rush? Echosic was big enough to choke Ecozar. But it took time to strangle someone to death, far longer than the few moments we had to evacuate the coach. And strangulation would have left marks: the very marks that were conspicuously missing.

Steganesh was the only one who could have struck Ecozar dead in the time available. But why? Until I could uncover his reasons for being on the pilgrimage, I couldn't even guess.

I looked more closely at Ecozar's face. The blood had a peculiar, powdery appearance to it, although that could have been caused by the salt. It could also have been a side-effect of magic.

Then I saw the faint discolouration of the lips – a greyish-purple tint that could easily have been dismissed as just another sign of recent death. Hell, I'd missed it myself at first glance, and I was looking for suspicious indications. That, coupled with the powdery blood residue, set little alarm bells ringing in my suspicious mind.

There is a ridiculously potent toxin beloved of Chrysomancers, called *kraich*. I knew it well. One that kills in seconds and leaves very little trace behind, other than an unfortunate tendency to turn blood into a fine granular powder. I never found out if that was the deadly part, or just a side-effect. Irrelevant really, the victim is dead before they even know they're dying. There is an antidote, but it needs to be administered so soon after the poison that it's usually ineffective.

So, this was not a spell, but poison. Either way, Steganesh wasn't looking any less guilty.

I began to push salt back over the exposed features. I had no decent answers, but plenty more questions. First, bizarre creatures that seemed more intent on stopping than hurting us, and now a murder. There was plenty more than a pilgrimage going on here. And Batrix and I were buried in it as deeply as Ecozar in his salt-crate.

CHAPTER ELEVEN

I NEVER DID GET any sleep that night. Once I'd made it back to my waggon, I had to tie myself up as tightly as Batrix had done originally. Not easy when you're reduced to using one hand. In addition, the re-opened gunshot wound began to soak into the bandages the moment they made contact. By the time I'd managed to mummify myself in as close an approximation as I could get, blood was smeared all across both my shirt and the bandages. I must have looked as though I'd half-bled to death in my sleep.

I lay back on my shelf-bed and closed my eyes. I blotted out all thoughts and speculations, and I was just drifting away when I heard the canvas flap. I opened my eyes, expecting to see a couple of waggoners come to take me to breakfast – full of questions about my bloody state – and saw, instead, Batrix, struggling to climb up onto the waggon floor. He got to his feet, not worried by the low ceiling, and dusted himself off, expression somewhat prissy, then he folded his arms and pursed his lips.

"I will not insult you by asking how you come to be in this

condition," he commented.

"Cut myself shaving." I pulled myself into a sitting position.

Batrix sat himself next to me. "Count yourself lucky that I decided to come to see how you were faring before your early morning escort arrived." He began to unwind the wrappings. Some of the blood had begun to dry and glue the bandages in place, but I'm a big boy now – it didn't hurt.

"Why should you want to do that?" I asked between winces.

"Because the Wilonek Scilli I met months ago would never have stayed in bed while there was a dead body close at hand. Especially after making it so clear to us all how injured you were, and how difficult you find it to get around by yourself."

"So now I'm a masochist with possible necrophiliac tendencies?"

"You have a strange cynicism that makes it impossible for you to accept, as fact, any event which you have not personally dissected, probed, questioned, deconstructed or otherwise thoroughly examined." He finished removing the bandages, the relief was almost sensual. "The bleeding appears to have stopped once more, but if you insist on taking further nocturnal constitutionals, I cannot be answerable."

"It's just a flesh wound..."

"Even flesh wounds require a little rest and care, Scilli. Moreover, this waggon-train does not have an inexhaustible supply of spare shirts and bandages."

"Yes, mother..."

Batrix reached inside his tunic and produced a fresh roll of bandage. He'd come prepared. Patiently, he began to re-dress my arm. "Do you intend to tell me what you have found?" he asked at length.

"What makes you think I found anything?"

"You are being altogether too patient and saying very little. Generally, I have found that to mean you are thinking deeply. So, of what are you thinking?"

I always make the mistake of underestimating Batrix. He's more perceptive than most humans, what often lets him down is his rigid thinking patterns. If he'd been a little more intuitive, the resultant brain would have been frightening.

"I'm pretty sure Ecozar was murdered."

"Indeed? Based on what premise?"

"That he was dead before being thrown around the coach."

"You are certain?"

"He was first poisoned with a delightful little toxin named *kraich* – or at least I'm pretty sure he was. It kills almost on contact. You've probably never heard of it, but it was one of the Spook's little toys. They didn't always magic their enemies into non-existence."

"And you have a suspect?"

"Steganesh is the most likely." I hesitated, unwilling to say what I had to say. I never like to think of my seminary days, never mind talk about them. "I told you he once tried to kill me – it was with *kraich*…"

Batrix said nothing, his face composed into neutral planes.

"He'd heard about *kraich* in one lesson or other; he was always the brightest of the two of us and took more advanced courses. There was a girl in his class, Erane Reidl, and … well, we fell out over her. We both believed we were in love…" I allowed myself a silent, hollow laugh at that. "And Steganesh thought he'd found a quick and simple way to solve the problem. He laced a bowl of sweetberries I'd stolen from the kitchen the day before with the minutest of doses. One that still could be fatal. Luckily for me he must have had an instant change of heart and given me the antidote almost immediately. Even so, I was seriously ill for weeks."

"And afterwards?"

I shrugged. "I never spoke to Steganesh again – until recently. He and Erane Reidl continued to be close, for a while, but once they both achieved first *shakrat* she was sent to another seminary, Styr Alwrœm, a centre of excellence, so they told me. When war broke out, it was a natural target, and the rebels made sure no Spooks walked out of what remained."

Batrix sat back and lowered his eyes, admiring my bandaged arm for far too long. This time, he hadn't strait-jacketed it to my body. "While agreeing with you on principle," he said eventually, "but only up to a point, as I wonder if you have not picked on Steganesh simply because of your ... past?"

"I hope I'm more professional than that—"

"I hope so, too, Scilli. But you will be the first to admit, the human predilection for emotion often clouds their rational thinking."

"And no heteromorph would be seen dead with an emotion, I suppose."

His expression was unreadable. "I did not say that, Scilli. Those few heteromorphs with whom I have had some experience do have a kind of emotional response. But feelings do not govern our actions in quite the same way; we were designed to obey and submit, not question. Passion and reason are never drawn into conflict."

"Lucky you."

"If you say so." He began handing me my shirt, then, before I could take it, he took it back and ripped off the bloody left arm. Then he let me have it.

"Not perfect," he remarked, once I'd shrugged the ruined thing on.

"There are one or two spots of blood still remaining. But I am confident you will be able to explain them away."

"Sometimes I think you expect too much of me, Batrix."

"I think not." He stood, tugging at the hem of his tunic. I could see that he'd tried cleaning off the various stains, with little success. "I will see you later, at breakfast. I would also recommend the sunrise; the sky has taken on the most remarkable colouration."

And with that enigmatic announcement, he ducked out of the waggon.

Intrigued – as he knew I would be – I got to my feet and made my way to the back. I pushed up the canvas flap and peered out at the dawn.

Batrix hadn't understated it. The sky was the colour of pearl, shading through to fresh blood in the east, which turned into molten iron where the Sun already peered over the horizon. Everything the light touched was alive with a roseate glow. Violet shadows stretched across the flat land, seeming to go on forever. The entire landscape somehow didn't look real, and for an instant I was convinced it wasn't real. That the world had become an elaborate construct, built solely for my own delight and confusion.

Then the Sun heaved itself another degree higher, and the illusion broke. The pink light was no different from any other dawn, the sky unremarkable. I felt saddened, and worse, I felt alarmed.

Something had just happened.

Strange and beautiful sunrises may happen naturally, but in a world accustomed to the weird fantasies of which many Chrysomancers were once so proud, the unusual has to be questioned. Decades ago, the bizarre and inexplicable might have been commonplace. Now, they were prohibited.

It didn't matter that I'd never become a fully indoctrinated Spook. I didn't need a slice of striated crystal and a fancy rank to smell it: someone, somewhere, was practising very potent magic. The kind that makes reanimating bits of dead animal and summoning giant leeches out of the earth look like hedge-wizardry.

I heard distant voices; the camp was waking up. Holding onto the waggons' metal frame, I leaned out a little and looked around.

I spotted several waggoners strolling across the campsite, talking among themselves. Probably last night's guards going for some rest. I was envious; my own eyes felt like the lids had transmuted into lead. Then the Echosics and Sotha Ponac appeared from the coach.

A few seconds behind them, Steganesh strolled languidly around the other waggon from wherever he'd spent the night, deep in conversation with Gen Romino. I wondered what those two had in common. They hailed the other three and joined them, both of the Echosics and *Ingosigna* Ponac tensing up the moment they heard Steganesh's voice. They made no objection, though.

Two waggoners stepped down from their over-sized cart. Echosic called something and waved a heavy arm in my general direction. No prizes offered for guessing what he was saying. They began to head my way – coming to invite me to breakfast, no doubt. I hoped it would be a little less eventful than yesterday's.

It didn't escape my notice that the strange dawn had reverted to normal just a few moments before everyone appeared. It was meant to be a secret. That Batrix had decided to rise unusually early was a happy accident. For me, anyway.

I wondered if the heteromorph had realised the significance. Was that why he'd alerted me? I doubt he imagined that I was the sort who went all wet-eyed at the sight of the Sun coming up, after all.

I pulled on the battered leather coat just as my escort reached my waggon. "Morning," I said brightly. "I trust you both slept well?"

They might just as well have been mutes. Both raised an arm, and I allowed myself to be lowered onto the ground. They weren't particularly gentle, but by the same token they took care not to jolt my wounded arm. They spotted the fresh bandages peeking through my coat's sleeve though, and the new spots of blood on my shirt. Even so, they remained resolutely silent.

I was carried to where last night's fire was revived and, once again, burning cheerfully. The Echosics, Steganesh, Romino and Sotha Ponac were already sitting around the flames on collapsible chairs, happy campers all. Only Batrix was absent.

"Good morning, *Gosigné* Scilli," Echosic wheezed. "Sit yourself down. I'm afraid circumstances rather dictate a poorer standard of breakfast than I'd prefer..."

"Never mind," I said, lowering myself onto a spare seat, no doubt put out for me and facing Sotha Ponac. "At least you're still alive." I smiled towards Sotha, and she gave me one back, but it was a forced, weak gesture, meant to convince me she was all right. I wasn't convinced.

"To be sure," Echosic agreed, nodding his ponderous head slowly.

"Not worried about bandits out here?" I persisted.

"Wil has a somewhat unique sense of humour, you'll find." Steganesh spoke from his chosen spot, just outside the general circle. "And often quite inappropriate."

"But I do admire pretty sunrises, Petran. Did you see this morning's? Seemed quite special to me."

"I missed it, I'm afraid." His face was as smooth as an alabaster statue.

Echosic pulled a silver watch from a pocket and snapped it open. "Where is the lieutenant-commander?" he muttered. "I understood he was normally a model of punctuality."

As though given his cue, Batrix appeared around a waggon. Despite his tardiness, he didn't appear to be in any hurry. "My apologies, gentlemen, ladies. I had trouble rising, and none of the crew saw fit to awaken me." There weren't any chairs left, so he contented himself by standing at my side, arms clasped in the small of his back.

I had to admire Batrix. The lie was spoken with such understated conviction, even I believed him.

"These things happen, sir." Echosic was forgiveness personified. He closed his watch, slipped it back into his pocket, and turned – as well as he could – to look at Romino. "Gen!" he snapped.

The younger Anesicci sprang to his feet and ran towards the waggons like a child blessed with some important errand. He returned with a trunk I recognised from yesterday morning, dragging it carelessly across the uneven road. Flinging it open, he spread food and drink across a printed cloth *Gosigna* Echosic had placed on the ground. You didn't need to be a detective to recognise exactly the same victuals from yesterday's abortive breakfast. Evidently, Echosic wasn't in the habit of wasting food.

I tilted my head back to look up at Batrix. "What happened to you? We were all getting worried."

"Where do you think we are, Scilli?" he asked, softly.

An odd question. I thought for a few moments, performing a quick calculation as I looked around at the dawn landscape. "Couple of days out of Wael Edra ... the fields are getting drier, becoming grassland ... landscape's growing flatter... At a guess I'd say we're in the S'Kaan

Estates by now – approaching Llawgefros. How's that?"

Romino had passed everyone a plate. Now, the twitchy smile all across his face, he was handing round the food, item by item.

"Excellent, Scilli," Batrix spoke to his boots. "However, I have just been scanning the horizon with a telescope. Llawgefros is nowhere to be seen."

Interesting. "Then we've both got our estimates wrong. All the delays..." A platter of ham was lowered onto my lap. I helped myself to a slice, before passing it up to Batrix.

"So I thought, initially." He leaned across me and passed the platter to Sotha Ponac without sampling it. "But there is also a singular lack of huts, cottages, sheds, or any sign that this landscape is occupied at all. And before you comment further, I would add I also took a reading of the Sun. Unless my watch is in error, we are at the correct latitude. However, it would seem that no one else is."

"So you also thought there was something wrong with the sunrise?" A tray of loaves came next. I took one and broke it apart. It was a little stale. Batrix also helped himself to bread. He tore off a piece and popped it into his mouth.

"Is it possible that we – the entire waggon-train – could have been transported ... elsewhere?"

"You mean you think we're no longer in S'Kaan?"

"Not in a S'Kaan that any of us would recognise, no."

A parallel world? One alike enough to our own that we wouldn't notice? At least, not at first. Back at the seminary we'd been taught about the possibility of such places, but I didn't think even the Chrysomancers had actually tested the theory. How could they? Abaston power isn't infinite. How many crystals would be drained just attempting a link with even the closest of such places?

Ever since it became obvious that the supply of crystals wouldn't last forever, and neither would their energy, the use of abaston power was strictly rationed. Nothing on this scale would even be contemplated. Even before, in the good old days of complacent certainty in a never-ending supply of abaston, I'd have thought it unlikely. Why take the risk of potentially contacting a world where rationalists have total control and might be powerful enough to overthrow you? Stick to the realm where you have all the control, all the might.

"Who could have done it?" I wondered aloud. Sotha Ponac glanced in my direction; maybe I'd spoken too loudly.

"Steganesh?" suggested Batrix.

I shook my head. "Not with those crystal fragments. Even with a chunk of abaston the size of your head I doubt there'd be enough power."

"If that was the only stone he brought with him."

The thought had already occurred to me. But carrying more than one attuned abaston stone is something at which even the Archimandrite would balk. However, by most standards, Sendivogius is sane. I wondered if the same could be said of Petran?

"There is another possibility," I said. "So far, all the phenomena we've witnessed seems to have meaning to the Anesicci. Maybe it's one of them. Echosic admitted that it would need a powerful Anesicci magician to create those homunculus-type things. And so far, none of the Anesicci has been hurt."

"Ecozar was Anesicci."

"One neither of the Echosics liked."

"You think that may be significant?"

"Significance is where you find it..."

Sotha Ponac leaned towards us. "You're not eating much, gentlemen," she commented. I shrugged, Batrix bowed.

"Thank you, *ingosigna*," he replied. "But I eat little this early in the morning. I find it sits hard on the stomach."

"And what about you, Wil?" She turned her green eyes on me, giving me a full, frank stare. "Is your stomach delicate in the morning, too?"

I looked around the campsite; at the Echosics and Gen Romino stuffing great wads of food down their throats. Watching their greasy mouths endlessly chewing. "My entire body's delicate, Sotha. I'm like a hot-house flower – the smallest thing can upset me."

She smiled. "That, I find hard to believe. Is your wound paining you?"

"Only a little. I've had worse." Honest and brave, that's me.

"Commander Batrix." She returned her attentions to the heteromorph. He bowed again. "Wil tells me that when the Full Moon rises, you will change into a woman. Is that true?"

Batrix cleared his throat delicately. I half expected to feel a knee in my back. "If that is what he told you, *ingosigna*, then I am afraid he has misled you. Certainly, on the night of the Full Moon I will change my appearance; I will take on a female shape. But I will be no more a woman than I am presently a man. Heteromorphs are neither. It is the way we were designed."

"How curious. Then why were you designed that way?"

"The Spooks did it because they could," I replied for him. Maybe Shifters aren't supposed to have feelings, but I'm sure Batrix has greater depths than he'd admit to. Besides, I couldn't help thinking Sotha's questions were a little impertinent. How would she react if I'd asked about her own, private lunar cycle? The one men aren't supposed to know about.

"How do you mean?"

"One of them discovered they could create human life, or an approximation of it. History tells us he was the Archimandrite's brother, Stenek Franni, although I've always had my doubts. But whoever it was, five hundred years ago, the creatures they began to grow in their vats were given a little extra: they transmorphed into the opposite sex every month. It gave the Spooks endless scope for exploitation and experimentation, plus it showed the world how clever they were."

She looked a little shocked by my vehemence, but what the hell. I was brought up to show the same casual disregard for a Shifter's life and body, it was a guilt I had to live with.

"Then it's a mercy the Chrysomancers were finally beaten in the war!"

"Oh, yes. So the government could outlaw heteromorph creation, incidentally making any who survived less than second-class citizens. The Philosophic Party has shown its concern numerous times, by consistently employing any surviving heteromorphs in dangerous, filthy jobs that no human would want. In the ten years since the war ended, an entire race of beings has been virtually wiped out in and by this Republic...!"

Echosic's breathless wheeze cut in. "You sound like a Liberationist, sir."

I shut up. I wasn't making a stand for President, after all. "That's me: bleeding-heart Scilli. Batrix can tell you all about my liberal views."

"Indeed." Sotha appeared unphased by Echosic's interruption. "How long have you been in the Internal Bureau, Commander?" she asked, switching her gaze back to Batrix.

"Since the war ended. But it will come as no surprise to Scilli that I believe my initial appointment was motivated by political expediency. President Thinos needed to be seen promoting heteromorphs into positions of trust and authority. However, since that time I have, by my own talents I believe, achieved a rank and position within the Bureau faster than many humans could have managed."

"You're looking at a future President," I commented.

Gosigna Echosic's harsh laugh gave away her opinion on that thought. "There are times when I rue the loss of the Spooks," she sneered. "At least under their rule there was order. Ever since the war, there's been nothing but moral decay and chaos."

"That is a rather dangerous viewpoint, if I might say, *gosigna*," commented Batrix.

"I'm sure my wife meant nothing by it, Commander." Echosic almost stammered with nerves. The heteromorph's Bureau uniform represented the government by proxy to him.

"Spineless!" hissed *Gosigna* Echosic. "I meant a whole world by it." She waved a stick-like finger towards Sotha Ponac, clutching her amulet in the other hand. "I say it again, under the Chrysomancers there was discipline; there was observation of the natural order of things. Now, what have we? Unmarried women going unchaperoned across the country ... in the company of single men!" Her finger switched to Batrix. "Unnatural spawn raised up to be the equal of man!" Inevitably, I came next. "Gutter-trash placed in positions of judgement over honest people!"

"Anej, please..." begged Echosic. There was something ludicrous in the sight of such a huge man being so abject with his thin, waspish wife. It didn't impress her.

"It's what we were warned of in the Vaticinations: the last, miserable days of sordid decadence! The Finalities! Mankind's last few corrupt years before destruction!" Her finger was punctuating each word with a fleshless jab, like some wrathfully inspired teacher. There was an unhealthy light in her eyes, her entire face bright with zeal.

"Anej!" There was desperation in Echosic's wheezing now: his eyes kept darting between his wife and Batrix.

I don't know if anyone else had noticed, but during *Gosigna* Echosic's sideshow, the air had grown colder, and the rising Sun begun to dull and gutter. I glanced up. Thick, purple clouds were congealing in the sky, blotting out what had promised to be a fair day. Worse, they were travelling in the opposite direction to the few white traces already streaked across the heavens. Even I know clouds don't normally drift against the wind.

"You sound like an Anesicci Fundamentalist," Batrix was saying.

"My wife does hold rigid, even old-fashioned views," Echosic tried to apologise.

"Merely the truth, Chato!"

"Hence your pilgrimage to Qaijente and Grémasicci Boya." I didn't know what Batrix had latched on to, but the sudden silence made me drop my gaze from the threatening sky. *Gosigna* Echosic was staring at the heteromorph with unnervingly wide eyes. Echosic looked as though he was expecting the death sentence.

"What can you know of Grémasicci Boya?" The contempt in the old woman's voice could have stripped paint.

"I know that the lake holds tremendous spiritual meaning to the Anesicci and is mentioned quite specifically in the collection of holy prophesies you referred to as the Vaticinations."

"It is central to the Finalities!" *Gosigna* Echosic snapped as though he'd missed the whole point.

"Would someone mind telling me what the Finalities are?" I asked. There was a fatalism about the phrase I didn't much care for.

"Indeed," Batrix was saying as though I hadn't spoken. "I believe the lake is the starting point for the destruction of the world."

It was at that point that the thick, blood-red rain began to fall.

CHAPTER TWELVE

THE RAIN CAME DOWN as though the black clouds drifting overhead were bleeding to death. Within moments, the campsite was sodden. A maroon curtain now shrouded the countryside. The fire must have gone out, but I didn't wait around to check. I made for the nearest waggon and dragged myself inside.

I was soaked in the blood-red water. But luckily, unlike real blood, it didn't seem to stain. In fact, rubbing my wet fingertips together, there was an almost gritty feel against my skin, like fine sand.

But the smell was real, like an overflowing midden, getting worse as my body heat warmed the stuff up. At least I was on my own in the back of the waggon; wherever the rest were huddled, it was going to get pretty rancid, depending on how many of them were together.

The constant thunder of rain on the waggon's canvas top ceased as abruptly as it has begun. I needed some fresh air anyway, so I risked parting the tarpaulin curtain and looking out. The Sun was stronger than ever, the sky was a lustrous blue with not a cloud in sight – not even the merest wisp of thistledown. Only the soaked ground gave any clue that it hadn't been a dry, bright morning since dawn. Strange wasn't the word for it.

I hopped gingerly out of my shelter, not wanting to slip in the stinking mud. Around me, the rest of our brave travellers were venturing into the rain-free air.

Batrix was scrubbing at his hair, the expression on his face telling me all I needed to know about his thoughts. "Intriguing weather in this part of the Republic," he commented.

"Funny. I was expecting frogs," said Steganesh. He shook out his cloak, his expression as fastidiously disgusted as Batrix's.

"Meaning what?" I asked. He stopped flapping his cloak and gave me a pained smile. Brushing a fingertip across his moustache, he wandered away again.

Romino was clutching his helioscope box and grinning. "Splendid fun!" he chuckled. "Don't you think?"

"There's nothing to beat getting soaked by something that smells like it poured out of a horse's ass!" I brushed at my drying coat; something like a fine cloud of red powder floated off. Carefully, I sniffed at some of the stuff that was glued to my hand: sure enough, it stank. "Not sand, then."

"At least it will clean off when dry," said Batrix, batting at his tunic's shoulders.

"That doesn't tell us what it is, though." I looked towards Echosic, who was slowly dusting himself down, like a man in a dream. "I think Steganesh knows more than he's telling – I think he's known all along. But Echosic doesn't look as confused as I feel, either."

"You believe all these phenomena are related?" the heteromorph said. "And *Gosigné* Echosic recognises them?"

"I don't know what I believe. But I'm thinking a hell of a lot!" Still beating at my drying clothes, obsessed with the thought of getting the foul-smelling stuff out of them, I walked towards Echosic. I think he was aware of my approach, but he was as absorbed with cleaning himself off as I was. It was the dreamy, almost off-hand way he did it that was so fascinating. Here was a man caught between revulsion and curiosity.

"You want to tell me about it, Echosic?" I asked. His huge head raised itself slowly. His eyes were somewhere back in Wael Edra.

"Tell you?" he echoed distantly. "About what, Bureau man?"

"The red rain, the leech, the homunculi… All very strange, all very new. Things I've never seen before, and I was raised in a Spook seminary. In places like that you get to see a lot. But you don't look too surprised, Echosic. You look like a man who's seeing his dreams come to life, or his nightmares, maybe."

His face paled, and bright, ruddy patches stood out on his cheeks. "You think you know everything?" It was the first show of temper I'd ever seen from the big man. It was frightening, I don't mind admitting. "Just because your Chrysomancers have filled your head with their little miracles, you think you understand the universe?"

"Careful, Echosic, your guilt's showing." I could feel everyone clustering behind me, eager for a show. I decided not to disappoint them. "I never said I knew everything. Otherwise, I wouldn't be asking you about the last few days. But I think you know something, or at least, recognise something."

"You're a fool, Bureau man!"

"I'm not alone there." I turned, locating his wife. Her sharp face was pinched with anger. I wondered who at.

"What about you, *Gosigna* Echosic? Anything to say?"

She remained defiantly close mouthed. But there was something about her tight expression, and the white-knuckled hand squeezing her stone and metal amulet that more than answered me.

"I don't suppose there's any point asking you, Romino." As ever, he was cradling his box, watching the proceedings with wild-eyed interest. "Or perhaps you've taken a helioscopic imprint for us?"

He shook his head rapidly. "Alas, no. There's been no time: everything comes and goes so swiftly…"

"It strikes me you've used that gadget of yours very rarely so far, Romino," I said. "What kind of enthusiast are you?"

He bobbed about, like a ferret looking for a rabbit. "As I said, everything moves too fast. A helioscope needs time to set up…"

"Very little point in bringing it, then." I rounded on Steganesh, who was standing at the back of the group, swinging his cane. "What about you, Petran? I don't suppose you know anything, either."

"I know a good many things, my dear fellow. What exactly is it you want me to explain?"

"Never mind the music hall act, Petran. Where are we?"

"How should I know?"

"Because this is why you're here, after all. Why else should one of Madrasté's brightest stars invite himself along on a simple pilgrimage? Why else would you be armed with the biggest chunk of abaston since the creation?"

He smiled, showing large, even teeth. "You have the floor, Wil. Tell us."

"To move every waggon – and person within them – into some other level of existence. To get them out of the way. I can't pretend to know what for, but there's no one else here with even a fraction of a motive, and certainly no one with the means."

"With the crystal that you so thoughtfully shot to pieces, I suppose?"

"You could do it even then, by degrees. You're the only person I know who'd be insane enough to attune more than one piece of crystal at a time, Petran. But if you bled the fragments empty almost immediately, the risk of resonant amplification would be minimal, using them up as you gradually shifted us all out of the world we know into another."

"Quite a fanciful theory, Wil. One of your best. But accepting I somehow could do a mass attuning of abaston fragments and survive, exactly when am I supposed to have shifted us?"

"And why?" Sotha Ponac was suddenly at my side, looking intently at me with those big green eyes. I began to sympathise with a cobra's victims. "You've still to supply a motive."

"The only motive Petran needs is money," I said, trying not to sound too bitter. "Or simple perversity. But as to when, at a guess, I'd say round about the times those homunculi attacked, and the giant leech."

"Diversions?" snapped *Gosigna* Echosic. She was sharp, I had to give her that.

"Exactly. We were supposed to be so busy dodging out of the way that we'd never notice any ... changes going on around us. How am I doing so far, Petran?"

"The Spooks lost an excellent brain the day the seminary was liberated." Steganesh reached into his waistcoat pocket and drew out a handful of sharp-edged fragments. He tossed them into the air. I caught a few. Despite my lack of training, I could recognise lifeless abaston when I held it.

"Delicate operation, trying to balance the Chrysomantic forces, keep them from resonant amplification, and direct them, all at once.

Any time you're tired of life, Wil, I recommend it."

I could feel Sotha suddenly tense up. "You killed Rhys!" she cried. "You summoned that creature!"

Steganesh almost looked penitent. "No one was supposed to be harmed, *ingosigna*. I assure you of that. There was no reason to believe the leech would destroy the coach before everyone was well clear. It was just a diversion."

"And the coach driver and his son?" I asked. My fingers were itching to reach for my pistol, but I resisted the urge. Out of the corner of my left eye, however, I noticed Batrix didn't have such a high opinion of Steganesh's magical ability as he produced his own pistol. I hoped it didn't come down to a test.

"Sadly, another regrettable accident. Those chimeras were damned difficult to control, especially while I was trying to appear uninvolved. I never imagined they had such bloodlust."

"You're a murderer!" Echosic moved forward a step. I tensed, waiting for the explosion. Nothing happened. Steganesh remained standing calmly, still swinging his cane.

"I repeat, I regret the deaths. But there's nothing any of us can do to change that now. And, what I did was necessary."

"Necessary!" I had to grab one of Sotha's arms to keep her from flying at the Chrysomancer. "Necessary for what?"

"Good question, Petran," I said, still hanging onto the struggling woman. I expected her to turn and lash out at me any moment, since I was the nearest target and she couldn't reach the one she wanted. "And for whom?"

"Does that matter? We're here now; we'd best make what we can with it."

"And where is here?" asked Batrix. His gun was half-raised: obvious to Steganesh, but not yet an intimidation.

"Wil was on the right track. Echosic knows. I'm sure his wife does, too, given her beliefs."

"Echosic?" The big man had his back to me, maybe trying to stare Steganesh down. He'd have had better luck with a cliff face.

"I refuse to believe..." he rasped, finally "...that this is all some elaborate illusion!"

"There you are, Wil! We're nowhere!" Steganesh was beginning to enjoy himself. It did my heart no end of good to know someone was.

"This is the Anesicci equivalent of what you would call a dream-land." *Gosigna* Echosic's voice was curiously lacking in its usual sharpness. I couldn't tell if it was wonder or fear. "A place beyond the waking world where dreams are born: hopes, fears, terror, love. The land where the Anesicci were formed before being dreamt into the mundane world..."

Echosic turned on his wife, his face a miserable combination of anger and sadness. "Must you insist on interpreting all of our past so literally!"

"And it's also the land of our myths, our legends." She faced her husband, the harsh features slamming down again, as cruel as prison bars. "Can you deny the presence of the *ochitlac*? Or the world-leech? Will you turn your back on your heritage so far?"

"It's all an illusion, woman!" he barked. It sounded as though he was tearing his throat out. "You're only seeing what you expect to see." He thrust a massive arm towards Steganesh. "What *he* wants you to see!"

"On the contrary," Steganesh said, smooth and velvety. He could have sold me snake oil for *chavet*. "This is all quite real. You will find reality is not so..." He paused dramatically. This was his big moment, he wasn't going to spare us. "Objective."

"Oh, this is excellent! Excellent!" Romino was busily taking his cumbersome heliograph machine apart. I think he expected some kind of Anesicci bogeyman to materialise in front of us any moment. I was half-afraid he was right.

"Perhaps you would like to tell us who you are working for, *Gosigné* Steganesh?" The pistol in Batrix's hand was significantly higher. A few more confessions, and it would be aimed straight at Steganesh's heart. It didn't comfort me. Even a third *shakrat*, with the sort of power Petran seemed to have at his fingertips, could beat a lead bullet.

"No, I wouldn't, as a matter of fact. It's largely irrelevant, now, anyway."

"You don't expect us to get back."

He smiled at me. I was sure his teeth were getting bigger. "Not without my help. And I don't intend to give it."

"We could make you!" Echosic snarled. His ruined throat made him sound almost feral. It was still an empty threat.

"No, we couldn't," I said. Objective or not, the admission hurt. "He's a third *shakrat*, with plenty of unattuned abaston chips, and a morbid yearning for death. Even if he couldn't throw some kind of glamour over us all, my guess is he'll happily destroy every one of us. Himself included."

"I don't want to, Wil..."

"That won't stop you, Petran. You forget, I know you too well. Your wants have always been subject to your quicksilver whims."

"How true." He dug into his waistcoat again. "But if it helps you sleep better, you can have the rest of the crystal pieces." He held out another palmful of milky white and gold-veined shards.

"They are still fully charged?" Batrix asked me.

I nodded. It surprised me he couldn't tell. Compared to the drained pieces, these scraps of crystal sang with vitality. "They still might not be all of them, though." I stepped forward, as though I had full confidence in the heteromorph's casually aimed pistol. "If you don't mind, Petran."

He raised his arms. "As though it matters," he smiled. I was about ready to smack that grin off his face. "I assure you that is all."

I found nothing in his pockets, but all that meant was that he had no more bits of abaston in them. "Echosic," I said, stepping back, "do you think the waggon-crew would be happy to search for any bits of crystal he might have hidden away somewhere. And I don't just mean where he's been sleeping."

"I should imagine so," rumbled the big man. He called a waggoner over and explained the facts of life to him, quickly. Not surprisingly, the waggoner agreed to have his men scour the campsite. I doubt he was any happier with the thought of stray bits of abaston stuck to axles or dropped into water-butts than the rest of us.

"And what do we do with him now?" Echosic asked, looking back at me.

"Destroy him!" hissed his wife. She stepped to within a few inches of Steganesh's face, holding up her amulet, and spat. Very courageous of her I thought, now he was unarmed. "Cut off his head and burn it!"

Steganesh wiped at the silvery threads of spittle hanging off his cheek. "Aren't you frightened I'll grow another one?"

"Be somewhere to put your second face, anyway," I couldn't help remarking.

"Chain him up in one of the waggons," Batrix said in his best Bureau voice. "One where he can do the least damage. And maintain a decent guard over him."

"He must suffer!" *Gosigna* Echosic virtually snarled. She didn't take her eyes of the Chrysomancer. "First the blade, and then the flames! It is prescribed!"

"So you say, *gosigna*. But until we can think of a way out of here and back to Qaijente, I think it's best to just lock him away somewhere."

Echosic nodded his agreement. Romino looked as though he wanted to record Petran in chains with his apparatus. But from the look the old woman graced me with, I was no better than the Spook. Maybe even worse.

I wondered if she was given to stabbing people in their sleep? Or shooting them at night?

CHAPTER THIRTEEN

FOR WANT OF ANYTHING better to do, we rode out across the increasingly strange landscape. No one bothered thanking me for saving the horses only two days earlier. If I hadn't, we'd all have been left rattling around in one of the waggons. Only Echosic cried off actually climbing on horseback, for which I guessed all of the horses were grateful. Instead, he chose to ride inside the coach; lying down, I imagine.

That left his wife, Batrix, Sotha Ponac, Romino and me to the horses. *Gosigna* Echosic was pretty scandalised to find both she and the younger woman would have to ride man-style, their legs either side of the saddle. But Steganesh's stitched together chimeras hadn't thought to bring any side-saddles with them. Sotha Ponac had grinned in delight, although whether that was at the chance to ride like a man, or simply because it shocked the old woman, I couldn't tell. Probably both. Whatever it was, she vanished into the coach for a while, returning dressed in a green pea-jacket, britches and riding boots. It was almost as if she'd been anticipating the chance to wear them. *Gosigna* Echosic was eventually persuaded to change her dour dress for more practical wear: a jacket and split riding skirt, also provided by Sotha Ponac. The woman must have packed clothing for all occasions and seasons. I wondered where she kept it all.

Once in the saddle, and moving, I took my time absorbing the landscape that was unfolding around me. It looked barely different from S'Kaan at first, but as the hours rolled by, it mutated subtly, gradually losing all resemblance to the world I knew. Whatever method Steganesh had used to transport us here, it obviously involved some form of exponential magic: once the initial conjuration was done, each following change became more pronounced than the previous one. It's a good way to invoke major deviations with the minimum effort, but it still takes an awesome degree of power, and there's no guarantee that the momentum will cease once it reaches the end point. Every youngster in the seminaries is given several historical examples of augmented conjurations that didn't want to stop. The great, perfectly flat expanse of the central plains is the most famous. A range of the tallest mountains in Ramini used to be there, or so the story runs. It may even be true.

I resolved to check the remaining abaston fragments the first chance I got. I had a feeling they were involved in the spell and still powering whatever Steganesh had committed them to, which meant they'd be running down without anyone else's help, becoming steadily more useless.

Or that was what I hoped. If they were being steadily drained, there was less chance of the spell running away with itself. Once the abaston crystals were exhausted, it ended. That would leave us stranded, probably, but with at least a slim chance of survival.

"The world seems to have taken on a somewhat ... baroque look,"

Batrix commented. He was perched on his saddle as though the act somehow made him undignified. Luckily, his horse – a small brown and black – didn't seem fussy.

"Yes," remarked Romino in a barely repressed sulk. "Can't we stop so I can capture it?"

Typically, Batrix had understated it. The land about us was stark and flat, the soil – if you could call it that – a deep, burnt orange. It hurt your eyes to look at it. I hoped that was just because of the blinding Sun over us. The sky was blue enough to break your heart, fading to a gentle purple near the horizon.

It should have been hot, the kind of heat that wrings you dry of all strength and thought, the mind flowing out with the sweat. But it was quite the opposite: it was freezing. Cold enough for our breath to hang in desultory clouds around our heads. Aromatic mists curled up from the horse's bodies. We were carrying our own winter haze with us.

Great chunks of red rock littered the plateau, scattered by some giant child who'd lost interest in the game. Nothing grew, nothing moved; the sky remained an unbroken blue. Only we were intrepid enough to endure this arctic cold under a harsh desert Sun.

"Did you hear about the recent, unexplained disappearances and sudden attacks from nowhere?" I asked Batrix. I don't know why I asked; maybe just to hear myself speak. Of course he'd heard of them. Most of Ramini had heard of them. The Bureau had spent every day since the first senator walked into thin air, denying it had ever happened.

"I am acquainted with the rumours, Scilli," he replied. "But I prefer not to believe in the likelihood."

He could still make me laugh. "Still a triumph of hope over

experience? Just think about our own situation, then tell me you don't believe it."

He was silent for a while, his round face solemn with thought. "Are you suggesting that the phantom attackers in the Capitol came from this place?" he said eventually. "Or that each disappearance found themselves lost in this desert?"

"Not quite. But I think the principle's the same."

"Then, whoever Petran Steganesh is working for—"

"—is probably the same group who've been orchestrating the random assaults and kidnappings. Or whatever they are."

"It's the beginning of the end!" *Gosigna* Echosic's strident voice lanced through the cold air. Ever since sun-up, she'd been acting a little odd – not quite possessed, not quite insane, but driven, in some unhealthy manner. Her face was pale, and her eyes had a perpetual glow that hinted they might be seen in the dark. She no longer looked at anyone directly – even when speaking to them – but stared at something just above their heads, seemingly an infinity away. Her amulet was now permanently clutched in one hand. "The Finalities!"

"If you say so, *gosigna*," I said.

"Not me, Bureau man, not me. The Vaticinations."

"Naturally. How stupid of me."

Romino leaned towards me from his saddle. He looked like he was about to fall flat on his face. "She's mad, you know." His confiding whisper could be heard halfway across the orange plateau.

"You'd know, of course."

He smiled his conspiratorial smile; we were both still in on the secret. Privately, I thought Romino's mental state a deal more unstable than the old woman's.

Batrix came back to the point. I could tell he still wasn't convinced.

"Accepting, for the moment, that the phenomena you describe are genuine, why should this waggon-train be treated on the same level as senators and government ministers?"

"Good question. Maybe you should ask Steganesh."

"Assuming he would answer."

"Which he won't..." I looked across at *Gosigna* Echosic. She was still sitting rigidly in her saddle, alight with her convictions – or insanity – whichever it was. "Do you have an explanation, *gosigna*?" I asked.

She turned her luminous gaze on me. I knew how a mouse felt, face to face with a starving wolf. "Of what?" Wherever she'd been the last few moments, it obviously wasn't with us.

"Why should your waggon-train get whisked off to this nowhere land? What's so special about it?"

"Perhaps we are to be saved, Bureau man. Have you thought of that?"

The end of the world again. "That's comforting. Still doesn't tell me why you're all so special that someone should want to save you."

Romino sniggered. I ignored him, it was getting easier.

"Leave her alone, Wil. Can't you see she's sick?"

Sotha Ponac had nudged her grey pony in beside mine. She rode as though born to it. I wondered if there was anything she couldn't do well... I had to drag my mind back from the murky thoughts it pounced on.

"Somebody has to know why we're here!" I was tetchier with her than I wanted to be. Maybe I was getting edgy, or something.

"If *Gosigna* Echosic ever did, I doubt she's in any condition to remember it now. Leave it, Wil. Ask her husband. Or Steganesh."

"Not much of a choice. Neither are very forthcoming."

"Better than none at all."

"You think so?" I shut myself up. I was getting nowhere, and the cold wasn't easing my brain. I rubbed at my arm instead, as though a sudden twinge had reminded me it was still there.

"Hurt?" Sotha asked.

I shook my head, truthfully. "Maybe the cold's getting into it." I made a play of rubbing it once more, then dropped my hand. "I don't think I was the target, Sotha," I said, just loud enough for her to hear.

"How do you mean?" She drew her pony in closer and leaned towards me, almost touching shoulders. It felt good.

"You were talking to Ecozar shortly before I joined you, and we were standing between whoever fired the shot and the flames, if my calculations are correct. It's possible our mystery marksman wouldn't notice Ecozar leaving, and if so, they'd probably not be able to tell the difference between me and him. Not from a silhouette..." I waited to see if she caught up with me.

"You mean Rhys could have been...? Oh, no. No. I refuse to believe it!"

"Which of us is dead now?" I persisted.

"That was an accident—"

"I don't think so. You all got out of the coach safely. Even I managed it." I could hardly tell her I'd been poking around his dead body and already knew the truth. But I sounded very reasonable to me. "If Ecozar was in any condition to move, he would have."

"You're saying he was already dead, or dying?"

"It's a thought. I have them when I'm lying awake at night."

She looked around, trying to act casually. It was as subtle as a stage whisper. "Then which of us...?"

"The Echosics didn't like him..."

"...only because of his beliefs. He wanted full repatriation for the Anesicci people and the return of all their ancient lands."

"So does *Gosigna* Echosic."

"Not through bloodshed."

"Ah, the patriotic type. Fight to the last drop of everyone else's blood, eh?"

"Not at all! Rhys would have given his life for—" She clamped her jaw shut just a little too late.

"Seems you knew him well, Sotha. How well?"

"That's a little impertinent, don't you think?"

"Maybe. But you'd be surprised how many murders are committed by those closest to the victim."

"I've already told you, we were good friends. Nothing more."

Gosigna Echosic muttered something I didn't quite catch, but from the sudden tension in Sotha's facial muscles, I could guess what it was. The old lady was pretty free with character assassinations in her native tongue.

"Maybe that was enough." I pulled on my horse's reins, putting a little air between it and Sotha's pony.

"Meaning what?" There were two livid patches on her cheeks. Something had gotten to her, and I doubted it was me.

"We've been assuming the would-be sniper had a good aim. Maybe he was a lousy shot, and this hole in my arm and Ecozar's death are accidents. Maybe you were his target all along."

The patches on her cheeks drained of colour. She couldn't have looked more shocked if I'd told her I was her long-lost brother. Her pony wheeled away, dragged aside by hands that were clutching the reins tighter than was needed.

I wondered if we were still friends.

My horse side stepped. I looked down at the ground, but there were no rabbit holes or snakes. It pranced again, getting pretty damned jittery. I looked around, but I couldn't see any reason for its nerves: no approaching riders, no storms. As ever, the land and sky were empty.

It wasn't until I was shaken for a third time that I realised it wasn't my horse, it was the ground bucking like a shy mare. A ripple passed across the orange earth as though it was thin mud, horses and riders rose and fell like toy boats. I looked up again, taking more notice this time.

The waves were flowing across the landscape, and they were coming straight for us, a few seconds apart and growing marginally higher each time. In less than a minute, I was no steadier than I'd be on a storm-tossed ship. I'm a lousy sailor.

I jumped off my horse. If I was going to get seasick, it wouldn't be from the saddle. I could barely stay on my feet. The waves were now almost a yard high and coming more and more frequently. The ground was shrieking: the dying howls of some old earth-god. If the other riders and their horses were making any sound, I couldn't hear it.

I fell heavily and couldn't get up again. The heaving earth tossed me about like I was a leaf going over a waterfall. I couldn't get my breath.

Then the sky began to change. Deep violet streaks blotted out the blue, waves of darkness sank the daylight. As the ground writhed and howled, I began to think old lady Echosic was right: it was the end of the world.

The ground stilled abruptly and silence fell. So suddenly it made my ears ring. I dragged myself up onto my knees and looked around.

It was dark: night had fallen. That almost made me laugh: fallen was too gentle a word for what night had just done on us.

We were still all together, picking ourselves off the sly ground, dusting ourselves off, calming the horses, checking waggons for damage. Above us, the inky heavens were full of twinkling lamps. It was a calm, clear night.

I rolled back off my knees and sat heavily on the ground, arms clamped tight around my legs. I still wanted to laugh, but was scared that if I did, I'd never stop.

"Scilli!" It was Batrix. I wondered what blindingly obvious observation he was about to make. "Have you noticed? There appears to be no Moon."

CHAPTER FOURTEEN

ONLY A HETEROMORPH WOULD notice something like that, I thought. I guess it's no odder than us looking up at the mid-morning sky and wondering who stole the Sun. But the Sun's always somewhere about during the daylight hours, otherwise it wouldn't be daylight. I've never been told the Moon has to be permanently visible in the night sky.

"Maybe it hasn't risen yet," I said, looking around at the stars, just in case there was the faintest hint somewhere. "Or it's gone down ... or even in its dark phase." I sounded as though I thought normal time had some kind of meaning here. In a place where night rode in on an earthquake, what sense would a planet's normal progression mean?

"There is no Moon." He said it as though he was explaining to me black wasn't white.

"You sensitive to it, or something?"

Batrix shrugged – the most human gesture I'd ever seen him make. Or maybe he'd quivered with the chill. Now the Sun was gone, the air was cold enough to freeze a beard.

"If there is no Moon, what will happen to my change?" If I hadn't known better, I'd have said he was panicking.

"What makes you think it's the Moon that triggers the change?" I asked. "And that it's not periodic, just happening to coincide with the Full Moon?"

He shook his head. "I do not think so."

I didn't, either. Cycles in nature might continue, regardless of how the world changed, but there was nothing natural about heteromorphs. Franek Stanni – or whoever first had the bright idea – would have made sure the male-to-female shift linked with something as traditional as a Full Moon. It gave the metamorphosis a mythical touch no self-respecting Spook could resist.

"Is that such a bad thing?" I said, not sure I believed it myself. "Staying in the same shape for a little while longer can't be harmful, surely?"

Batrix looked the tiniest bit worried, which probably meant that inside fear was tearing him to shreds. "I am unaware of such a thing ever happening. There used to be rumours that heteromorphs require the lunar change, that it is somehow essential for our wellbeing. But since it has never happened, such a speculation must remain simply that: a rumour."

"Put about by who, though? And why?" The Chrysomancers, probably. But because it was true, or because they wanted their Shifter slaves to think it was? Spooks often placed control mechanisms into their creations and servants. Look at the use of *chavet*. I had no problem imagining some kind of destructive obsolescence built into heteromorphs. Though what the hell use it would be, only some probably long-dead wizard could tell me.

I heard my name being called, and recognised Echosic's high rasp.

He was rolling towards me from his waggon, while all about, waggoners were dashing about in some sort of mindless frenzy. There was lots of running and shouting but no obvious progress. Maybe I should have been more unnerved by events as well.

"What is it, Echosic?" I said.

He brought his huge girth to a halt just under a yard away from me. Even in the poor light, I could see his face was almost purple, while starlight glittered faintly on a thick coating of sweat. His breathing was something less tuneful than a holed bellows. "This is intolerable!" he gasped at me.

"I couldn't agree more. Maybe you should write a letter to the President. We could all sign it."

"You were sent to guard us, sir!" He cleared his throat noisily and spat. "What are you going to do?"

"Lieutenant-Commander Batrix and I were assigned to represent the Ramini Government, Echosic," I corrected him. I don't suppose he believed it any more than I did. "What exactly are we supposed to be guarding you against?"

"All this!" He waved a heavy arm at the world, his voice failing him.

"Since neither of us is a Spook, that would be difficult."

His wife chose that moment to benefit us with her wisdom. "Perhaps they are the cause! Perhaps they are the ones who brought us here!"

"I thought we were all being saved from destruction," I said. "If you're going to rave incoherently, at least try to be consistent."

"She is my wife, sir!" Echosic drew himself up in indignation; it was an awesome sight.

"I'm well aware of that, Echosic. She's also trying my patience." Before he could bluster on, I raised my voice over his reedy anger.

"Under the circumstances, I suggest Commander Batrix take control of this trek. He's the closest to military we have, and this is now clearly a military matter."

"How very thoughtful of you, Scilli." The heteromorph's voice was as dry as ever. "I never thought I would hear you espousing the military cause."

"Who's espousing it? We need someone with a logical brain taking command, and you do have some government authority."

"And you will be much too busy, I expect?"

"Me? No one would take orders from someone like me, Batrix."

"You see, Chato. They're dividing us between them already." *Gosigna* Echosic was beginning to really get on my nerves. I wondered, if I ignored her, would she disappear like this world's Moon.

"D'you think the waggoners would make an acceptable militia?" I asked Batrix, making myself oblivious to the Echosics' growing objections.

"If they can accept a heteromorph commander, I imagine so. They are already remarkably well-disciplined."

There didn't seem to be much evidence of that in the moment. "You can always shoot a couple if they get funny."

"Do you think we're all going to die?" Romino was wandering through the chaos as though in a charmed dream. His ever-present box was under an arm, a dazed smile stretching his face.

"Does nothing depress him?" I muttered.

Echosic wheezed a sigh. Now that command had been taken away, he looked deflated and spent, barely half his size. "Ever since taking up his infernal hobby, Gen has become more and more – what can I say? – distracted. He always carries the device with him, but he hasn't attempted to use it once in the past two years. All he ever does is dabble with his chemicals. I can't understand it."

Batrix leaned close and whispered. "It is an effect of the volatile quicksilver, I have heard."

"What happens?" I asked, equally softly.

"The mechanism is unclear. But over a period of time it appears to damage the mind. Eventually, it is fatal."

I looked at Echosic: he was watching Romino drift aimlessly. It was almost fatherly. I wondered if he knew or guessed. It would explain several things.

I felt the ground begin to vibrate again through my boots. I glanced at Batrix: he felt it, too. Were we about to get another violent change of daytime?

"Somebody is coming!" Echosic's voice was down to a subdued whisper.

His wife's sharp face snapped up. She sniffed the wind like some half-starved dog. "Yes!" she hissed.

I nodded at Batrix. "Time to get those men behind you, I think."

Without a word, he turned and headed towards the waggons. Difficult to tell in the dark, but I'm sure I saw him produce his pistol.

I returned my attention to the two Anesicci. They both seemed to be in some kind of trance. "What exactly is coming?"

"I'm not sure." Echosic's harsh voice was loose with uncertainty. He looked worried. That didn't bother me half so much as the look of predatory anticipation on his wife's face.

The vibration grew stronger. But it wasn't like last time. This felt more like the throbbing of a drum as someone beat their hands across it, or the pound of marching feet. A lot of feet. Thousands.

"An army?" I said. Echosic turned to look at me as though his neck was broken.

"*The* army."

"Now you're getting as crazy as your wife."

He tried to shake his head, managing just a painful twitch. "I can't explain it, Bureau man. It's as though I am attuned to this place through my blood, through ancestry. I feel it. But I cannot understand it..."

"We've been away too long!" crowed his wife.

He managed a shrug. "I just know that the army is on its way. A voice ... words..." He tailed off, unable to explain.

I could sympathise. Once, I'd managed to attune myself to an abaston crystal. It resulted in a rapport that I couldn't put into words either.

The underfoot throbbing was slowly resolving itself: no longer a homogeneous vibration, but definitely the tramp of hundreds of feet, maybe even hooves. In daylight we may have stood a chance – even if it was just spotting them in time and running like hell – but in the dark, lit only by the stars, there was no way of telling where this army was, or how close.

There was a bright yellow flare from the direction of the waggons. For a moment, I thought they'd been set on fire, but it was the waggoners, no doubt with Batrix at their head, lighting torches. They spread out, marking our stand with a circumference of fire. The torches threw a little more light in all directions, but it also made the night beyond even darker.

I hoped that at the same time, it didn't make us easier targets.

"They're here!"

For a wild moment, I thought *Gosigna* Echosic was going to drop to her knees. Just who the hell was she expecting? Some Anesicci god?

A moment later, I had my answer.

An impressive figure rode into the radius of torchlight on the back of a slab-muscled chunk of horse meat. The animal needed to be big: its rider was a giant, made all the bigger by black armour that reflected red highlights from the torches. His head was totally encased in a smooth conical helm that sported ludicrously ornate wings, or horns, or some other over-stylised crest. The helm's eye slits were alive with a gentle, greenish luminescence that reminded me of something that I couldn't quite place. Although hidden in dancing shadow, there seemed to be a huge sword hanging from the rider's belt, or saddle.

Everyone inside the circle of torchlight grew quiet and tense. All I could hear was the snap of flames and the muted creak of the horse-borne giant's harness.

"You will deliver to me the one known as Petran Steganesh."

The giant's voice was surprisingly soft and gentle. He sounded more like a servant announcing luncheon was served.

"Yes, lord," sighed *Gosigna* Echosic.

"Shut her up!" I barked at her husband before turning back to address the armoured figure. "And if we don't?"

He raised a hand in an apologetic gesture. "Then we must take him by force."

"Why?"

The giant leaned forward in his saddle a fraction. The horse fidgeted. "I do not know who you are, nor do I particularly care. I simply ask you to accept this fact: I have no strong desire to harm either you or any of your entourage, but there are eight hundred men beyond your lights, mounted and on foot. I do not see you putting up more than a token resistance to such a force. Therefore, I ask again that you deliver Petran Steganesh to me."

"Why?" I repeated.

"That is not your concern."

"I think it is. Petran is not only our prisoner, but probably our only escape from this place. Personally, I don't care if you want to free him or flay his hide inch by inch over a lifetime, you can't have him."

"We will have him, sir, whether you wish it or no."

"And we've only your word that you have anyone else back there. How do we know there's nothing but a collection of roped-together nags carrying a few empty pots?"

"Most have found my word acceptable in the past." His voice still hadn't risen above a polite murmur. I wondered if he ever got mad.

"So you say. An odd boast for someone hiding like a turtle, though."

"Very well, if it is so important to you." He took his helm in both mailed hands and raised it. Underneath was a noble, grey-haired face, but the eyes were still unreadable glowing slots. "I am the Grif Ditya of Meijtloaca: Conqueror of Anesicci and Scourge of Cotechatlu."

CHAPTER FIFTEEN

THIS TIME, *GOSIGNA* ECHOSIC did drop to her knees, holding up her amulet in both hands while chanting to herself. Not surprising, she'd just come face to face with someone claiming to be the greatest figure from her own mythology. And he did closely resemble a painting I'd once seen, purporting to be of the Grif, if that could be any kind of proof. The sitter may have been the artist's grandfather, for all I knew.

Echosic was torn. A war between his personal convictions and generations of native belief was clearly raging across his broad face. Eventually, the modern man won: his knees locked, and he took one tiny but very telling step away from his wife.

Romino had reappeared. He stood just behind Echosic, fiddling with his damned box. At least the look of awe of his face was a change from the usual happy grin.

I felt a grab on my arm. It was Sotha, gripping on tight, as though she thought I was her anchor. I hadn't the heart to tell her I was floundering just as much. Her expression of thrilled disbelief was too fragile to disturb.

"What is going on?" she whispered.

I found myself laughing. "Better ask your friend old lady Echosic," I said. "I'm just visiting." I returned my attention to the mounted figure. "You're asking us to believe a lot, *gosigné*. We all know that Grif Ditya – if he existed at all – died two thousand years ago."

"In that, you are manifestly mistaken," he replied equably. "For here I am."

"*You* obviously are, but is Ditya?"

Batrix appeared at my side, the one that wasn't being monopolised by Sotha Ponac. "All the waggoners are willing enough to fight," he said. "Each has at least one firearm. Unfortunately, they are all either fowling pieces or squirrel guns."

I'd expected no better. The waggon-train hadn't set out expecting to fight a small war, after all. "Shouldn't matter. That museum piece and his band – if there is one – don't look as though they've ever had anything bigger than an arrow fired at them. I'll bet money that gunpowder will scare them half to death."

"It is a popular misconception that cultures more primitive than our own will be terrified by displays of modern engineering, or that they will worship it," Batrix muttered, pedantic to the last. "It is my guess they will simply accept it as a new form of sorcery."

"Are you trying to cheer me up?" I muttered. "Get back to your troops and be ready for whenever ironsides up there decides to charge."

"As you wish, Scilli. But I would caution you: this world is not ours, whereas the creature calling himself Grif Ditya is perfectly at home. He may be able to throw us off guard even more easily than you plan to throw him."

"When you're president, remind me to never miss your annual State of the Republic speeches. With your obsessive attention to the truth, I'm sure they'll be fascinating." I was talking to myself, of course: Batrix had already flowed silently back into the darkness.

The man calling himself Ditya spoke again. "If you have finished with your discourse, I would be grateful for your decision. I confess that the night grows chill and I bored."

"You've already had our decision, my lord Ditya, or whoever you are. We keep Petran."

"A rash choice."

I shrugged. "My life's been lacking in excitement lately."

"And do you speak for you all?"

"He does not!" *Gosigna* Echosic flailed her twig-thin arms, waving her amulet as though it were about to ignite with purifying flame. "Whatever you command, my lord, I will do it. That man is nothing. He has no position in life or on this pilgrimage!"

"If you don't shut her up, Echosic," I said, as politely as I could, "I'll have one of Commander Batrix's new militia put a ball through her head."

I never took my eyes off the mounted figure, so I've no idea what Echosic did, or even if he did anything. But his wife ceased bleating, and that's what counted.

"Very well. This has taken far too long already." Ditya replaced his grotesque helm. He pulled his massive horse around, drawing his equally impressive sword. He waved it at whatever was out in the darkness.

"Here we go," I said lightly. I pulled out my repeater and checked that all five chambers were loaded and capped. I hoped no one saw how much my hands were shaking.

"Choose your targets!" I heard Batrix call from the darkness. He was instructing the waggoners, but I decided to take the advice to heart anyway.

Ditya bellowed something incomprehensible. He wheeled his horse about and charged straight for the ring of torches. From somewhere behind him came a strange rustling noise, but there was still nothing visible. He hit the circle of flame and ploughed on through. Not one of them so much as twitched at his passing.

He didn't pass through them as though he was just a ghostly image, they didn't float to one side, let him pass and drift back into position again. Somehow, and even though I was watching I couldn't see how, he rode between them, or around them, although it was patently impossible for him to do either.

Then things got more confused. I had an impression of the massive horse thundering past, and Ditya's swinging sword, but I could neither hear nor smell anything. And a horse that big had to smell. Someone fired. If it was meant for the Grif, it missed. Or seemed to.

Ditya's army swept through. They were even worse. They didn't look hideous or frightening; I could hardly see them at all. Like black-draped figures in a dark room, they were little more than impressions. Something was there, but after they were gone, it was impossible to remember what it had been.

It was like some dream or unremembered nightmare. I was buffeted by things I hardly saw, fired point-blank into a shadowy thing as it flowed past and didn't see it react. I stood my ground and kept firing, swinging the pistol like a club when it was empty, because I was scared to move. An irrational fear had swept over my reason and left it drowning. If I began to run, I'd never get away. I would be stuck in the same spot, fleeing endlessly, but never moving.

All about me were shouts, swearing, gunfire. I saw many people knocked to the ground, but none of Ditya's shadow army faltered.

We were fighting visions. Echosic had said this was a land of dreams, and he was right, much too right. We were living a dream. This was a world where lamps won't light, and even when they do, they don't illuminate the dark. This was a world where whatever was stalking you would always be behind you, just out of sight.

This was a world where logic didn't exist, only the crazed reasoning of a fever. And with the same helplessness of dreams, nothing I did would make any difference to the outcome. I was fighting clouds, wide-eyed but blind. The whole unreality of it all drove me to panic before I had begun to fight. Even life in Madrasaté Seminary hadn't prepared me for this.

The half-visible wave broke over us and moved on relentlessly, leaving us flapping and gasping on the orange sand, like so many stranded fish.

After an unmarked time had passed, I got to my feet. I was old and dying, nothing but a dried-out husk. I'd hate to be young and feel the way I did. It'd be so unfair.

A dirty, red-smeared mannequin that looked a little bit like Batrix trudged out of the darkness. He wiped dirt from his blue lenses and fussily adjusted the eyeglasses on his nose.

"That, if I may say so, was not our finest hour."

"That was a fiasco!" Angrily, I smacked dust off my coat. It didn't improve its appearance by much. "Steganesh has gone, I suppose?"

Batrix simply nodded.

"Anyone hurt?"

"Strangely enough, no. Whatever that army was composed of, it had substance enough to knock us all flat, but not enough to harm."

"Maybe they simply couldn't be bothered."

"Let us hope not."

I gazed about. What I could see in the torchlight was encouraging, in a downbeat way. Everyone was alive, apparently unharmed, and already on their feet, dusting themselves down. Only *Gosigna* Echosic stayed on the ground, her face still enraptured as she talked constantly to the amulet pressed against her lips. She certainly picked the strangest things to worship.

"Where's Sotha?" I asked, alarm tugging at my pulse-beat. She'd been right next to me when Ditya's army hit, now I couldn't see her anywhere.

Batrix frowned, looking about the torch-lit area with greater precision than my panicky stabs. His eyeglasses sparked black and gold in the flames. "I do not see her." He glanced in my direction, and not for the first time, I wished I could see his eyes. "I rather fear that she, too, has been taken."

"Why?"

I was pacing out a narrow path alongside an arc of torches, staring at the rut my boots were slowly wearing in the dirt, anything other than imagine where Sotha Ponac was.

"That question might be aimed at many events of the last few days." Batrix stood close by, arms held behind his back, watching me worry. Maybe he wanted to learn how to do it. If so, he'd come to a master.

"All right, why Sotha? Steganesh I can accept. He got us here. Maybe this was all part of his escape plan. Whatever. He's involved. But Sotha? Why?"

"Walking back and forth snapping your fingers like that will not help."

I stopped and glared at him. "I do not snap my fingers!"

"You do, and it is very irritating. I wish you would stop."

"And I wish you'd learn to worry!" I resumed my pacing. My fingers could take care of themselves.

"My concerns are not for general viewing. Rather, I direct my energies towards the problems at hand."

I pulled myself up, jamming both hands into my trouser pockets. "Yes, you're right," I admitted with a sigh. I directed a sidelong glance at the heteromorph. "Don't you get tired of that? Always being right?"

He matched me with an ironic expression. "Am I? No one ever listening to you would think so."

I let that one go. I've found that arguing with a heteromorph – especially this particular heteromorph – is a pretty pointless act. Their brains aren't wired up properly. Everything's too black and white, too logical with them. No nuance. Sometimes I think they're more like machines than people. Maybe I should start checking for the steam and smoke exhaust.

I looked around at what was left of our camp. Strangely, all of the waggons were intact, Ditya's army had made no attempt to wreck anything. All of the horses and aurochs seemed fine too, if their obvious nervousness was ignored.

Men and animals were both jittery. Just what was it about those shadowy things? Unable – or unwilling – to damage property, they could still knock beasts and humans about and leave them glancing anxiously over their shoulders.

"Find out if anyone has the faintest idea which way Ditya and his hoard disappeared. At least a direction will give us a starting point."

"If direction means anything in this place," Batrix commented.

"You noticed it too, eh?"

"The sense of unreality? *Gosigné* Echosic did say this was a place of dreams. Perhaps that is even more literal than he realised."

"Well I'm convinced."

Batrix left me to worry. I don't know what other people dreamed about, but my dreams never make much sense. Scenes change without warning: one moment you're talking with an old friend, the next he's become a three-legged milking stool. How can you fight that?

The night erupted suddenly into glorious day. The Sun – already high in the sky – filled the frigid air with heat. The sky had become a deep, perfect summer blue. Sadly, the land remained sterile and orange, and nothing flew in the brilliant sky.

I stretched, spreading myself out to catch as much of the warmth as I could.

Night fell again, equally unexpected.

This time, not only wasn't the Moon dangling in the heavens, but the stars were also missing. It was as close to absolute blackness as I've ever known. If it hadn't been for the ring of torches, still guttering in the faintest of breezes, I wouldn't have been able to see the end of my pallid nose.

"Someone's nightmare..."

I knew I hadn't died of fright: my heart was hammering away far too painfully. When I could breathe again, I turned to see who'd sneaked up on me. Romino.

In the stark lighting from the torches, he didn't look half so mad. Even if the crazily shifting glow did make him look as though his expression was constantly changing, it also added a gravity that wasn't normally there.

"You damned near scared me to death!" I hissed at him. No reason to tell everyone I was frightened of the dark. "What do you mean, 'someone's nightmare'?"

"Can't you feel it? That's how this place works: it makes dreams and nightmares feel real. Anej Echosic has long had a dream about the Grif Ditya, how she'd like to meet him. It came true."

"It came true for all of us…"

He shrugged. "Perhaps it's more accurate to say aspects of our thoughts and dreams are plucked out and made solid. Or as real to solid as you can get here. Of course, the powers that rule here will tend to use whatever shapes you dream of to their own advantage. Anej got Ditya – as urbane and gentlemanly as she might desire – but it wasn't her he rode off with."

"You mean she had a girlish desire to be taken away by a knight in armour?" Somehow, I couldn't square that image with the sharp-faced, cruel-tongued woman I'd become familiar with.

Romino giggled. It felt like someone was trickling iced water down my spine. "Mad, isn't it?"

Not as mad as you, I thought. "So you're saying the sudden change from night to day and back is also someone's nightmare?"

"Or fear. This place is feeding on their morbid dread of the dark, I'd say. A dread strong enough for the powers to think it useful enough to be a weapon."

Fear of the dark? Or someone's fear there'd be no Moon? Was Batrix so terrified the Moon would never rise that he was spreading his fear far and strong enough for the magic here to react? The heteromorph's exterior was always so controlled, it was hard to believe he could be hiding such emotions.

A single blob of flame approached, resolving into Batrix carrying a torch. I felt guilty, as though he was able to divine what I'd been thinking.

"Most of the crew are agreed that the Grif's army kept moving straight ahead." He pointed out into the utter darkness. "Were we in our own reality, that would be to the west."

So Ditya had just ploughed through us and kept on going, if direction meant anything at all here. That was a thought I needed to keep well buried, especially if there really was some way it might come true.

"Then that's the way we're heading."

Daylight spread over the scenery once more. A Sun the colour of old blood burned sullenly in a sky that shifted from lilac to bruised purple. The orange earth looked black; with a little more effort, it could almost look like ordinary soil.

I glanced at Romino, and he winked back. "Someone round here has a sick mind," I muttered. Batrix frowned in confusion. "I'll explain one day. Get the waggons moving. Who knows how long this light will last."

A vast winged shadow swept across the land. For a moment, it enveloped us all. I smelled something like sulphur. Up in the broody sky there was nothing to cast any kind of shadow.

What kind of nightmares do you have? I wondered as I watched Romino trot towards his horse. If I were a praying man, I'd have prayed we weren't already finding out.

CHAPTER SIXTEEN

TIME DIDN'T EXIST IN that place, but that didn't stop it weighing heavy on me. We trudged on, hopefully in the direction the waggoners had indicated. Even more hopefully, it was actually the way Ditya had taken Steganesh and Sotha. Daylight – such as it was – came and went sporadically. The Sun was red, and yellow, and green, even blue for several, by my watch, memorable hours. Nights were sometimes star-lit, sometimes not; the only common factor was the lack of a Moon. Batrix tried not to let it show how much that bothered him, but during the dark times, when there was enough light to see him, it was obvious his eyes were frequently gazing up at the sky.

Seasons, of a kind, came and went, too. Days and nights could be cold, unbearably hot, far too humid for the desert landscape, or mild. Occasionally there was rain – normal, clear, odourless stuff this time – or sleet, or snow.

During a six hour period – measured again by my watch – we suffered three periods of sunlight, two nights, a winter, and four deadly summers. I don't know how everyone else was feeling, but I found it generally depressing.

Strangely, the horses and aurochs didn't seem to be particularly bothered by all this meteorological insanity, except for the extremes of temperature. Maybe animals don't have much imagination, or they don't dream. Or maybe their dreams are so different to ours that what they were experiencing was kinder and less extreme.

I guessed Echosic would be the expert on this place, since it was supposed to be some kind of Anesicci myth-realm. But he was hidden inside the coach, not talking to anyone. And his wife, now riding up beside the coach driver, was in no mood to let anyone try. I should know. Several attempts to speak with her had been turned aside by the kind of featureless denials you'd expect from a religious convert.

Anej Echosic was enjoying herself. She'd found home. All it would take to make her time here complete would be some kind of apocalyptic disaster to overwhelm every one of us.

After the last supply of a year's weather in half a day, I decided I was going to give it another try. This time *Gosigna* Echosic could go hang; I wasn't going to ask for her permission.

I left Batrix riding stoically along with Romino and waited for the coach and waggons to pass. The coach was still moving, drawn by the remaining aurochs, but the repairs had left it slightly lop-sided. It limped rather than rolled. I dodged around the back waggon, blind-siding the woman who was perched on the coach's roof like some starving vulture. My horse and I were partly masked by the dust and poor light from a watery Sun that seemed to have lost interest in the game. I trotted up from the rear, approaching the coach from the back.

The column wasn't moving fast – not much more than a man's

fastest walking pace – but as I swung out of my horse's saddle and in through the coach's rear door, I felt like some dare-devil rider at a travelling circus. The ground looked much too far away, and skating by too fast.

I stepped carefully through the coach's interior. It was a mess, furniture left where it had fallen, nothing tidied. Chato Echosic sat in a brooding pile, propped against a crate, his massive head bowed. He looked as though he was carrying the coach, instead of the other way round.

He turned to look at me. Nothing resembling recognition moved on his broad face. But he still nodded and spoke. "Bureau man."

"You and your wife trading places?" I asked. He looked at me dumbly. "The more chipper she gets, the lower you act. Care to tell me why?"

"So you can report back to your superiors?" He shifted his feet, I'm sure I felt the coach's abused suspension lurch. "You are a spy, after all?"

I tried to look hurt. "Spy?" I said, in the most aggrieved voice I could manage. "Who's been spreading gossip?"

"You and the heteromorph are employed by the Bureau. He is part of the uniformed branch, but you are in civilian dress. It is well known that non-uniformed members of the Bureau are spies."

"How d'you know I'm not on holiday?"

"You are a spy, sir. Or an agent, if that offends you less. Rhys was correct in that, at least."

"I don't get offended. It doesn't suit my wardrobe."

He almost laughed. Something like a smile wriggled on his mouth for a moment, before it got too uncomfortable and fell off.

"What do you want, Bureau man? Not to swap quips, that's for sure."

"I want to know more about this dream-realm of yours. Romino told me you're a shaman: some kind of expert."

Echosic looked pained. His black eyes probed my face for a few uncomfortable seconds. I wondered if he could see past the pallid, red-haired façade.

"I was once, Bureau man," he wheezed eventually. He sounded embarrassed by the confession, as if I were in some kind of position to denounce him. "But age and..." he paused, apparently in indecision, finally pointing at his ruined neck "...other things changed that." He straightened his bulk for a moment, as though he'd rediscovered something he's forgotten. Pride, maybe.

"Yes, once I was the greatest shaman of a generation. Perhaps for several generations. The worlds of spirits and dream were as familiar to me as the waking world. I foresaw this pilgrimage back to Qaijente forty years ago!"

He didn't seem to want to say any more. "So what happened?"

His eyes fixed onto mine. For a moment, I saw real anger. Not the petty annoyance and rage the world in all its glory kicks out of us. The real thing. The sort of fury that could consume a man.

"Your war happened, Bureau man. I was just a simple milliner, respected by both my own people and yours, and not even so young, but the army had no respect for trade or age. I was impressed into the local regiment, given a musket and sword, and marched off." The rage faded, he was just a man again. "At Drsitu Forek, we were met by a brigade of Chrysomancer forces. Heteromorphs, to a man. The wizard commander was killed almost instantly – even their damned stones can't stop musket balls – but the Shifters fought on to the last. Glamoured, I suppose. Do you know how damned hard to kill those things are?"

His voice crackled to a halt. It was the longest speech I'd ever heard him make. He fumbled a bottle out of his jacket and took a swallow. It could have been water, it could have been liquor. Whichever, I knew it wasn't *chavet*.

"I took a bayonet in the throat. With immediate treatment, perhaps I would have been fine, but the army sawbones were three hours march behind us. By the time I was examined by some half-drunk surgeon, there was little he could do. He packed out the wound with maggots, gave me a bottle of cheap whisky, and put me out of his mind."

It didn't take much imagining: an army first-aid post, crammed with the wounded, dead and dying. Even officers receiving only the most basic attention from over-worked and usually under-skilled men – most of whose talents lay in pulling teeth. Someone like Echosic – a simple infantryman, and Anesicci with it – would be lucky to get any treatment at all.

"It destroyed your voice."

"It destroyed a damned sight more than that!" Some of the fury was back, his entire frame quivered. "I lost my skills, my talents! The spirits would no longer converse with me; their lands were barred to me!" His face, bloated with anger, wrath and anguish, appealed to me. "What good is a shaman who can no longer read his dreams?"

That was a question I couldn't answer. Much the same as: what good is a Chrysomancer who can't do magic? It was one I wasn't even prepared to consider.

"Can you tell me nothing about this place, then?"

"Only what I've observed. Much of which I imagine you've already worked out for yourself."

"I've done a lot of guessing, Echosic. That's not the same."

He paused for a moment. "It's a constructed world. Not one of the realms that naturally exist beyond our own."

"*Gosigné* Romino seems to think there's a presence, or power, behind it."

"That's true. When I say constructed, I don't mean in the sense a human would think: not some engineering miracle like a steel bridge, or an Alva locomotive engine. There is some kind of power behind it, certainly, but not even the Chrysomancers in their prime could forge something as complete, as vital as this. The creation aspect comes into play only when humans are brought into the void occupied by this power. You might call it a demon, or a god—"

"If such things exist..."

"The higher beings take no account of your laws, Bureau man. They will continue to exist whether the President says they are legal or not."

I permitted myself a smile. "I'd like to see it come to court. So, what happens when people like us get sucked into this void?"

"You must remember that only the human mind can conceive of form. The gods are as reliant upon us to give them purpose and shape as we are on them for our beliefs. Such power as exists here will be nothing but raw potential: creativity without imagination. It relies on the mind of man to provide that imagination and form."

"Hence the shapes taken from dreams."

"I detect Gen's ideas again." He took another sip from his bottle. Just so he wouldn't feel alone, I pulled out my *chavet* and had a drink.

"What you'll experience here are not simply dreams or hidden thoughts given life, but a recreation of the common memory pool that all humanity can dip into. Most are unconscious of its existence, but it is there nonetheless – the preserved memories and experiences of the entire human race."

"And the local power, or whatever, is using that to create all that we see? Not just our worst nightmares or fondest dreams?"

His massive shoulders sagged, he seemed to be growing tired of our interview. "There will be a large element of such things, yes." His voice was becoming increasingly more laboured. "People will find themselves experiencing some aspect of what they might wish for most, or dread the most. Such things are nearer the surface – more accessible, if you like."

"Romino also seemed to think such hopes and fears will be used for this local bigwig's own purpose."

"That would presume there was some purpose to this realm. Action other than reaction."

"Wouldn't you say so? Steganesh brings us here for whatever purpose, then both he and Sotha Ponac get dragged away by something in the form of your wife's childhood hero... Doesn't that sound like planned action to you?"

"Someone, or something, would need to be in control for that to happen. I told you, there is no control in such a place as this, only the aimless logic of a million unconscious minds."

"I doubt that. Otherwise, why bring us here? There has to be a reason. Why not just kill us all and burn the waggons?"

"Why do anything? We're only on a pilgrimage to Qaijente..."

"Somebody doesn't think so. And I doubt the Bureau does, either. This goes a bit further than protecting you from anti-Anesicci sentiments."

"A spy who has no remit or orders." He almost smiled again. "That is unusual, don't you think?"

"Bothers the hell out of me." Even Risnek wouldn't send us out without a full assessment of the situation and orders to cover anything foreseeable, which probably meant Batrix did know more than he was saying, and that made me feel very bad indeed. Not that Batrix wasn't telling me everything. Hell, there was plenty I wasn't telling him. We worked for different departments, after all; our private, little secrets are guarded assiduously. What gave me a cold chill and restless nights – as well as sneakily gnawing away at my self-confidence – was the thought that I was being staked out and left as juicy bait for someone. My beloved Under-Director could make himself doubly happy: complete whatever covert operation he was running and sacrifice me in the process. Nothing personal, just another seminary boy, of dubious loyalty, out of the way. Llyscu Deynah all over again.

Echosic had almost transformed himself into a shapeless hump again. Before he slipped back into whatever reverie he was after, I asked him one more thing. "Do animals have dreams?"

He looked surprised by the question. "A shaman expects to meet animal spirits during his trances," he breathed out quietly. So softly you'd be forgiven for thinking his voice wasn't a raw, painful rasp. "But whether they derive from the beasts themselves, or are a manifestation of a human need, I can't say."

I shrugged. It wasn't important.

I was backing towards the coach's rear door when he spoke again. "I have seen shadows."

"Shadows? Of what?"

"Creatures. Things other than human shapes that might exist here."

"You mean vague shapes? Like the things composing Ditya's

army?"

Echosic shook his head impatiently. "They were nothing! Just the dread that invades your bad dreams, the sense of terror that never becomes visible." He wasn't doing much for my peace of mind. "No. When the light is just right, look out into the desert. You may see them. You have some training in wizardry I understand, it may be enough."

"See what?" I had the feeling he was trying to get all mystical on me: throwing his shamanism and ancient racial memories into my eyes to make me blink.

"As I said: shadows. But not ones cast by anything visible."

I suddenly remembered the vast, winged shadow that had swept over us shortly after Sotha and Steganesh had been seized. There hadn't been anything in the sky to throw it.

There must have been something in my expression, since Echosic nodded with a peculiar look of satisfaction.

"Exactly. Let us hope they never become visible."

Chapter Seventeen

OUTSIDE, THE LIGHT HAD changed again. Now the whole sky was a luminous, bilious green: no stars, no Moon, no Sun. The orange ground had become virtually black, while everything else had assumed an unhealthy green pallor. The entire world looked sick.

But at least the scenery had changed a little. Tall, smoothed-sided, stocky minarets of rock dotted the otherwise flat land. Their sharply vertical sides flowed into the ground through a smooth transition of crumbled debris around their bases. They looked as though the surrounding land had been worn flat over the centuries, leaving indestructible plugs of rock as memorials. It also looked familiar.

I managed to drop off the back of the coach without breaking any part of me I couldn't live without. My horse was still nearby, trotting along happily with the rest of the train. Obviously, the kind who got lonely easily. I brought him to a brief halt and vaulted back into the saddle. He suffered my crude handling nobly.

The green illumination was unnerving. More than any other

change in light or weather, it was truly nightmarish. It reminded me of the shades Echosic mentioned, and I found myself looking across the landscape for them. I didn't have to wait long.

They appeared and disappeared, stretching across the darkened earth, even blacker smudges that stretched and shrank, almost as though whatever was casting them kept ducking out of the light, although it was a pretty strange light that threw shadows of things that were invisible. But I took Echosic's meaning, if the outlines of some of the shadows I saw could be taken as representative, I didn't want to meet them in the flesh.

I had no fear of them, as long as they were unseen, provided they didn't violate too many established laws in this realm. Invisibility was an easy and commonplace glamour among Chrysomancers, except its use was somewhat limited by one overwhelming factor: the invisible wizard couldn't see, either. Light doesn't care what your circumstances or needs are, make yourself transparent, and it passes through your eyes, unremarked. For short distances, or over memorised terrain, it was fine; but I wouldn't want to be an invisible man in a strange land.

But that only held as long as whatever laws governed here were much the same as back home. I guess if someone's deepest desires involved invisible, unstoppable monsters, if there was anywhere they could exist, it was here.

Romino appeared from among the waggons and guided his horse towards me. He did it all one-handed, the ever-present wooden box occupying the other arm.

"We're almost there," he called. He looked delighted about something. Maybe he thought he was finally going to use his helioscope.

"And where's that, exactly?"

That made his smile falter. Maybe I'd just dropped in his estimation. I'd try not to be too disappointed.

"Don't you recognise where we are?"

"Should I?"

He dropped the reins and gestured with his unoccupied arm: a sweeping motion that included the entire landscape. "Grémasicci Boya! We're almost there!"

I thought his delusions were growing wilder all the time. Even if we could travel all the way to Qaijente in such a short time, we weren't in our own world anymore. I was about to make some comment, when my brain finally caught up.

I'd thought the rocks looked familiar, and that was why. Grémasicci Boya. We were riding along what would be the lake floor. The familiar rock formations were almost identical to the dead volcanic plugs that towered above the water's surface like tall, unclimbable islands. The real lake was just a drowned valley, and we were riding through someone's dream of what it may once have looked like. Or maybe it was the valley's own dream. I was beginning to think anything was possible. And that meant travelling thousands of miles in a day or two.

Of course, time here meant nothing.

But there were encouraging signs. The landscape here bore more than a few resemblances to our own. Maybe that meant we could return home, if we could get Steganesh and Sotha back and figure out some way of crossing back to our own reality. That wasn't too much to ask.

I spotted Batrix riding towards us. Romino saw him, too, and spurred his horse away. Curious. The young Anesicci hadn't shown any particular dislike of the heteromorph before.

Batrix reined in beside me. "One of the waggoners has spotted something ahead," he said in a voice that sounded abrasive and forced, almost as if his own throat had been slashed. In the bilious light, he looked like a man who'd died a month earlier and was only just getting round to noticing. Was the lack of a Moon having such an effect on him?

"Such as what?" I asked.

"He is not sure. But he thinks it looks like some kind of fortified structure."

"A castle?" Ditya's stately pile, maybe?

Batrix shrugged, a second one. He was almost getting blasé "I confess that I have been unable to see it, despite having the site pointed out to me. Perhaps the man is merely delusional."

"You'd better show me."

He turned his horse and began to walk it back the way he had come. I followed at his side.

"Have you noticed where we are?" I asked, wanting to show off how observant I'd been.

"If you mean the landscape has a startling resemblance to the lake close to Qaijente – Grémasicci Boya – then, yes, I have."

So much for showing off.

"We may have another crisis on our hands," he continued.

I looked around, but I couldn't see anything outside the rocks and the sourceless shadows. "What?"

"The crew of the waggon-train are becoming increasingly restless. It appears some have a little Anesicci blood, and they have recognised this dream realm. They have convinced nearly half of the remaining waggoners that we are trapped in some kind of afterlife. Panic is only another ugly surprise away."

"You have a very poetic way of phrasing things, Batrix." I took another look at the shades drifting across the dark ground. My imagination kept insisting that a few of the shadows were gradually solidifying, or whatever was casting them were. I hoped none of the twitchy waggoners hadn't spotted them; that might be just enough to light their fuse. "You think they'll run?"

"It is an illogical move, considering that wherever they go, they will still be trapped, but, yes, I imagine that is likely."

"Frightened men don't stop to think, Batrix."

"I am uncomfortably aware of that, my dear Scilli."

"Speaking of comfort, how are you feeling?"

He turned to look at me. His face looked desiccated, the features surrendering to gravity. Only his eyeglasses remained impervious. "I am perfectly well," he lied.

"Horse shit! You look like you haven't slept for six months!"

"I will be fine."

"You don't have to be the pride of what's left of the heteromorph race, you stubborn bastard!" I hissed. It had been almost impossible not to shout it.

He shrugged again, turned away, but said nothing, not even reminding me that, technically, no Shifter could be anything other than a bastard. If I knew him at all, he never would. I sighed, loudly and irritably. It made no difference.

We reached the front of the waggon-train in silence. I was uncomfortably aware of the stares of the waggoners as I passed them: too many eyes were fixed and staring from hollow sockets, lips were sucked thin against teeth. I could smell the fear.

"There," Batrix abruptly broke the silence. He was pointing at a bizarre formation of jagged rock that clashed with the regular, eroded buttes all around us. It rose up out of the valley floor in sharp angles and abrupt lurches that looked distinctly unnatural. I could almost imagine it had been formed from massive slabs of rock, thrown together with no pattern or order, managing to stay standing despite reason and experience saying it should collapse.

Then it seemed to shift – or maybe my eyes adjusted to a new perspective – and I saw what the waggoner had seen. It was a fortress, of a kind, but one made from discarded bits and pieces from a million buildings that had been around hundreds of years, maybe even hundreds of realities. Stone walls rubbed shoulders with wattle and daub; thatched roofs alongside tile and slate; even parts that looked like they were sliced from sheets of metal. What made it so unique was the way every element had been added. Nothing was where it should be. One vast wall was constructed from scores of towers and chimneys lying on their sides. There were crazily leaning towers of small buildings – or parts of larger ones – stacked one upon another. Buttresses were tangled together into a distinctly rickety-looking bridge over a chasm that was obviously meant to be a moat of some kind. In the strange light, it seemed to glow with its own, internal light.

It was a castle of spare parts, assembled by someone who had no idea what a building was. Or, it occurred to me, in this place, it was more likely assembled from the collected thoughts and memories of everyone in our waggon-train.

"What a baroque, collective imagination we have," I remarked.

"I suppose I will have to wait for an explanation of that comment."

I waved at the ludicrous construction. "It's that thing," I said. Batrix looked in the direction I was pointing, and back at me. He didn't need to tell me he saw nothing: it was all over his face.

"You don't see it? You can't see that crazy fortress?"

He shook his head. "I see a rather ... unusual rock or crystal formation. Perhaps even an unnatural one. But nothing else."

I looked back, just to make sure I hadn't been imagining it. No, the impossible thing was still there. Which meant what, exactly? Something about Batrix prevented him from seeing what at least two humans could see? Some heteromorph peculiarity?

"How's your imagination?" I remarked.

"I was under the impression heteromorphs have no imagination." It was good to see something like the old Batrix was still active under the pallor.

"Which, if true, might explain a few things."

"Such as?"

I ignored the question. Turning in the saddle, I spotted the driver of a waggon close by. I waved towards whatever construction was sprouting from the ground. "What d'you see over there?"

The waggoner squinted, habitually shielding his eyes from some imagined Sun. He pulled the waggon to a halt level with us and dropped his arm. "Some kinda castle?" he said, not at all sure.

"Some kind of something," I agreed. "Thanks." The waggoner sketched a half-hearted salute and flicked his team back into action. Castle or not, he was determined to get there: it was where we were headed, after all.

"Well, he could see it, but does that make it real?" I said.

Batrix gazed at the departing waggoner, expressionless. "It is a sobering thought, that I might have less imagination than that man."

"Don't let it worry you. His imagination's probably reserved for more earthy things."

"As you say. However, I suppose this suggests there is something ahead that I cannot see. Perhaps."

"As much as anything in this place is real." A thought struck me; it felt right. "Echosic reckons this place somehow reacts to the collected dreams and thoughts of the human mind. You're not human—"

"How astute of you..."

"Don't get bitter on me... What I meant was that this place isn't attuned to the heteromorph mind, any more than Petran's crystals are attuned to me. Whatever you've got hidden away in your brain, it won't register..." Another thought surfaced; it was a good day for them. "Which means the lack of a Moon isn't a manifestation of your fears..."

He looked at me hard, then laughed shortly. "You thought that was my personal nightmare? That the Moon was failing to appear because of my fears?" He laughed again. "I must hand it to you, my dear Scilli, it is a fascinating concept."

"But wrong. Which means there's some other reason it isn't around."

"Perhaps this dream realm simply has no Moon. Have you considered that?" He didn't sound overjoyed at the thought.

"Yes. But the place resembles our own world more than it doesn't. Down to the landscape. Something as fundamental as the Moon to be missing... It feels wrong."

"The valley in which we are presently standing is flooded by hundreds of feet of water in the ... should I say real world? Which suggests the correspondences are not as close as you think. The differences are subtle, but marked."

"Is there something wrong?" Anej Echosic's predatory voice ripped through our conversation. She was staring down from her eyrie on the coach roof.

"Nothing, *gosigna*," I called. "Just admiring the view." I didn't need to indicate where I meant: her eyes seemed to be drawn to the bizarre fortress. The sharp edges of her face almost blunted as she lit up.

"Ditya's Castle!" We were forgotten. She cursed and bullied the coach driver into whipping up the aurochs. She wasn't going to keep her childhood idol waiting.

"Is Ditya going to be there, d'you think?" I was speaking to Batrix, but Romino replied.

"Of course he will!"

"You're very certain."

He made his patent grin and spurred his horse in the wake of the coach. "He'll be there because we expect him to be!" he called back.

"He acts right at home, here," I muttered.

"Why not," said Batrix. "His poisoned brain must be permanently in such a state as this."

"Poor bastard." Knocking heels against the flanks of my horse, I urged it to keep up. I didn't want to be late for whatever party the Grif Ditya planned for us.

The sudden scream – coming from right behind me – panicked my horse. It reared, almost throwing me clear. I stayed in the saddle purely through luck.

The screaming hadn't stopped. But it didn't sound human. Fighting to keep my panicked horse still, I chanced a look back.

No wonder the horse had reared: one of the aurochs on the waggon, only a dozen feet away, was being torn to pieces and eaten alive. One of the shades had become solid.

CHAPTER EIGHTEEN

THE WAGGON-DRIVER SPRANG to his feet, his face twisted with anger and fear. He raised an ancient flintlock musket to his shoulder and fired. A second later, he was ripped in half for his trouble.

It was a bird, or it had the shape of a bird. But not even the most vicious eagle looked anything like this. Standing over ten feet high, it seemed to be all beak, a heavy, curved double-bladed weapon that needed no help from the equally deadly looking talons on the end of its powerful legs. The rest of it was covered in matted feathers. Its wings were tiny and useless, but there were stiff hooks growing forward from each vestigial wing's leading edge, hooks it used to snare its prey before the guillotine beak could do the rest. It was as though somewhere back in time, the thing had changed its mind about being a bird and tried to become something much more savage and primeval.

There were several more shots. Aside from a shriek that could cut through steel, the bird didn't react. With an insolent disregard for us and the waggoner it had killed, it finished disembowelling the aurochs. The animal's screams stopped.

All around, waggoners were reloading their tired weapons. I drew my Alva repeater and emptied all five chambers at the creature. This time it didn't even flinch.

Another five shots. Batrix was trying his luck – with no more effect.

"What a time to need Petran!" I muttered, running across the ground and taking shelter under a waggon. It might not stop the thing, but it should slow it down.

I began to reload, watching through the wheel spokes all the time. Chaos doesn't begin to describe it. Waggoners were running about in blind panic, pausing only to fire uselessly at the bird. For its own part, the monster had lost interest in the dead aurochs, and was stalking back and forth, watching the men scurry. There was something deliberate and cruel about its eyes, the way it seemed to be enjoying the terror it was causing, or maybe I was just imagining it. But there was definitely calculation there.

It spun about suddenly, snatching a screaming waggoner up in its beak. It dropped him, pinned him to the ground with a talon, and ripped him open. All in a moment.

Another waggoner got too close. One of the creature's rigid fore-claws snagged his shirt and the hooked beak clamped shut over his head before he could even begin to scream.

Something as big, as fast, and as impervious to lead as that bird was more than all of us, even acting together, could handle. It was a nightmare, quite literally, somebody's worst nightmare.

There was another, jarring shriek behind me. I turned around and peered out from under the waggon: another bird had solidified out of the green murk. Automatically, I emptied my gun at the thing; it reacted much the same as the first.

"We're all going to die!" I muttered, hoping no one was close enough to hear me.

The second bird stalked forward at a leisurely pace. It hunched its neck, the heavy beak swinging from side to side: a senior clerk measuring up his rows of secretaries. It snapped at one man, but he rolled to the ground and scrabbled out of reach. Another, probably thinking himself safe on the bird's other side, wasn't so lucky.

Someone dived under the waggon beside me. It was Romino – still clutching his box and dragging a battered carpet-bag along with it.

"Ever wondered how a worm feels?" I reloaded my repeater as fast as I could. Both times, all five cylinders had fired, the odds of it doing so a third time were definitely no longer on my side.

"Try this." Romino pushed his bag towards me.

I looked first at it, then him. "What's in it? Lead bricks?"

"Flash powder."

It took a moment or two to sink in. When it did, I almost kissed him. Flash powder – fine magnesium dust. When ignited it burns very hot and very bright for an instant. It wouldn't kill or even harm the birds, but it would give us a few precious moments of blind confusion.

"Who's going to be the mouse tying this particular bell to those two cats' necks?"

Romino grinned back. He wanted to be a hero. Maybe he'd even let me record his noble sacrifice with the helioscope contraption.

"It's your neck," I muttered. I'll admit the thought of letting Romino risk his life didn't sit all that well. He wasn't in full possession of his faculties and probably didn't even know how big a risk he was taking. But he likely knew more about flash powder than I did – it wasn't something you picked up in a wizards' seminary – and I wasn't about to argue with a volunteer.

"Did you have anything in mind?" I asked him. Beyond our haven, a scream was cut brutally short. I tried not to think about it.

"The waggon above us," he said, opening the bag and pulling several sacks out. Each one was tied off by strong thin cord. The flash powder, I assumed. "If we can lure both creatures to it, I can detonate all of this powder in one go. It should blind them long enough for you to get in close enough for the kill."

"Me?" How did I get elected?

He shrugged again. "You ... anyone... I'll be upstairs lighting the flash." He continued to produce sacks of magnesium dust from the carpet bag. He was enjoying it – enjoying it too much. He reminded me of Fochs, just before we'd gone into Mawinnek's house back in Scan Feta.

And Fochs had gotten himself killed.

"Maybe you'd better let me do it," I said gently. "Just tell me how the powder's set off..."

"I want to—"

I cut him short. "It's not your job to get yourself killed!" And it's not yours either, a little voice nagged from the back of my head. "What I need you to do is round up as many waggoners with decent guns as you can. Talk to Commander Batrix, he'll have the best idea. When the birds are blinded, I want concentrated fire at their heads. The eyes, preferably, as close as possible. Point-blank, if anyone can manage that. Understand?"

He nodded enthusiastically, but some of the manic light had faded from his eyes. I didn't care, I was more worried about his life than his good opinion.

"Good. Now, explain this flash powder to me."

He briefed me quickly and clearly. Mild insanity or not, he knew his subject. As I listened closely, I watched the destruction outside and wondered if it was going to be enough.

Everyone seemed to have disappeared. For a moment, I thought they were all dead, torn up and swallowed by the two overgrown parrots. Then I spotted silhouetted figures under the other waggon and coach. My particular style of hiding place had become fashionable.

The birds were stalking around the emptied waggons with grim purpose. I noticed none of the horses were still alive – although the remaining aurochs were more or less unharmed – but they hadn't been eaten. Those birds weren't hungry, at least, not for animals. The obvious pleasure they took in killing was unnatural, almost human.

They weren't fooled by the hiding places, either. Only the weight of the waggon and coach kept them from either being kicked over by the occasionally probing talon or upended by a beak wielded like a lethal plough. I wondered how long it would be before the birds thought of taking a waggon apart plank by plank.

Romino finished his explanation. All I had to do was get up inside the waggon without either of the patrolling monsters noticing. It was the first time I'd ever wished I could throw an invisibility glamour.

What I needed was a diversion. I doubted I'd be getting one.

One of the birds began to pay rather too much attention to the waggon's canvas roof. It nudged at the metal frame with its beak, making the whole, fragile assembly quiver. Even I could hear the sounds of terror coming from inside. Some damned fools had tried hiding in there. How long did they think canvas would keep one of those things at bay?

The second bird's interest had also been raised. It strode casually towards the first, then walked slowly around the waggon's far side. All the while its hooded eyes remained fixed on the canvas.

Regardless of whoever was inside that waggon, we were never going to get a better chance.

"Out! Now!" I hissed at Romino. A moment later, he'd vanished. I should have hoped he knew what he was doing, but I had enough to worry about already.

Fixing my eyes on the birds, I slid back out from under the waggon. They were pacing round the other vehicle; if I hadn't known better, I'd have said they were enjoying the torment.

I was out in the open. Not daring to drop my gaze, I grabbed the side of my waggon and began to pull myself up towards the rear opening. I've seen minute hands move faster than I did. One clumsy move, and I might just as well be standing out in the open, shouting, dancing and waving my arms.

The birds tired of their game with gut-wrenching suddenness. One of them halted in its tracks and stabbed at the canvas with its beak, ripping it more easily than I could a scrap of thin paper. It shoved its head through the tear.

The screams began.

The second creature imitated its companion, taking the opposite side of the waggon. Like huge, grotesque ostriches, they stood with their heads buried in canvas.

The screams stopped.

I dragged myself inside my waggon, hoping those massive beaks didn't also include an acute sense of smell. If they did, I'd soon be as dead as whoever had been in the other waggon.

Luckily, the inside of this vehicle was pretty clear. Romino had said I'd need a smooth, flat surface to rest the flash powder on, and nothing to shield the white-hot flash when it came.

Gently, I untied the sacks of powder. I poured them, one after the other, into a growing mound in the centre of the floor. Outside, there wasn't a sound: no screaming, no shouting, no thump of massive feet on the ground. That worked on my nerves; not knowing what was going on beyond the canvas was worse than watching.

I wondered where Romino was. Had he found Batrix? Or anyone else competent? If he hadn't organised a slaughter-party by the time I ignited the powder, we'd all wind up as chicken feed.

The last of the sacks dribbled empty. There was a pile of magnesium dust in the centre of the waggon, over a foot high and a yard across. If that didn't give the things spots before the eyes, nothing would. If I were too close when it went up, losing my eyesight would be the least of my worries. I wondered if the things outside would enjoy a roasted dinner for a change.

I slithered towards the canvas, pulling my knife out of its boot-sheath. Slowly, I cut a tiny slit in the waggon's covering and put an eye to it.

I could only see one of the birds, strutting confidently about like some schoolmaster on Speech Day. I chewed my lip, realising just how dry my mouth was. I needed to be sure both creatures were within a few feet of the waggon before I lit the powder.

As silently as drifting thistledown, I moved to the opposite side of the waggon, cut another slit and peered out. My vision was filled with the sight of untidy, matted feathers. The damned bird was right on top of me!

I jerked back. I'm sure I cried out. Whatever, the thing still heard me. An instant later, the canvas parted as a scything beak sliced it like a hot knife through butter. The head arced straight towards me, a red, stinking mouth gaping.

I raised my pistol and fired. Directly into the throat. Two shots, and the gun misfired. Half-insane with fear, my hands feeling like slabs of pork, I cocked and fired again. Nothing happened.

But the head was retreating. I felt blood spraying across my face. I'd hurt it after all.

Throwing the useless pistol aside, I grabbed my box of lucifers from their pocket. Snatching several, I lit them all and turned towards the pile of flash powder.

Everything seemed to happen at once. The canvas above me was torn aside; the second bird coming to play. I tossed the lighted matches towards the pile of magnesium, threw both arms across my eyes, and dived for the waggon's rear.

I hit the ground, hard. Pain erupted along just about every nerve I had, and I'm sure I heard something snap. An instant later, the world turned agonizingly white, the light blindingly powerful even through tightly squeezed eyes. I don't know where my arms had gone, I couldn't feel them anymore.

There was heat, two awful shrieks, then consciousness lost patience with me and walked out.

CHAPTER NINETEEN

I WAS OUT FOR only a few seconds. When I came round again, the world was still a noisy, flame-lit hell.

I tried to sit up, but my arms wouldn't hold me. They were numb, as useless as two balloons packed with gelatine. Blood was soaking my sleeve again. Unsurprisingly, the gunshot wound had reopened. But it occurred to me slowly and stupidly, I was still alive and still intact. Wherever the birds might be, it wasn't standing over me arguing about who gets a leg.

Like a dying man, I flopped onto my stomach, then painfully hauled myself up onto both knees, with no help from my arms. In a supplicant's pose I gazed up at my handiwork.

The waggon was in flames: the magnesium had probably torched its few contents. Both birds were snared with lariats: two looped tightly around each neck. The ropes were staked to the ground with hastily chopped pegs that looked as though they'd been waggon-planks a short while ago. Neither of the creatures could move much, other than slackening the nooses around their necks by sitting. So far, that hadn't occurred to either of them.

Most of the noise was coming from the things: high-pitched, enraged keening. They weren't impressed with their imprisonment. And judging by the way their heads jerked about, the flash hadn't blinded them for long, either. I had to admire Batrix's efficiency: the ropes bore all the hallmarks of his mind. I doubted Romino's brain was up to it.

As I watched, four waggoners shuffled warily up to the birds, two per beast. All had pretty recent and powerful-looking muskets. They cocked their weapons, raised them and, at a distance or no more than a yard, fired directly into two pairs of raging eyes.

The keening stopped. The birds dropped to the ground like marionettes whose strings were cut. They didn't even twitch.

Batrix was suddenly in front of me. He stooped, looping both arms under my armpits, and lifted. For such a little man, he was strong.

"I think both arms are broken," I whispered. It was hard to do anything else against the agony that engulfed me the moment I stood. Even my finger nails throbbed.

"Let us hope not, Scilli. We have quite a distance to go yet, I think."

"Anyone else left alive?" I said, trying not to gasp. It was bad for morale. Mine, at any rate.

"Romino, of course. Both Echosics. Four waggoners..."

"The rest killed?" It didn't seem possible. Efficient slaughter machines those birds might have been, but I couldn't imagine them killing so many in such a short time.

"No." Batrix's tone was neutral. "The rest fled."

"You were right, then." The birds had been the final goad that set them running.

"It gives me little pleasure." We'd reached one of the waggons still more or less intact. He lowered me gently to the ground, my back propped against the vehicle's rear wheel. My arms still flopped like strips of rag. I wished they'd lost their sense of pain along with everything else.

Batrix wiped at my face. Until then, I hadn't realised how much I was sweating.

"Are you in pain?" he asked.

"Nothing a good night's sleep won't fix."

"And then you will be leaping around like a newborn lamb, I suppose."

"Naturally." I tried not to scream as he helped me slip off my leather coat. For two things with not much go in them, my arms were certainly tender. "Shouldn't you be tending some of the others?" I glanced at his drawn features. "And you look like you could do with a little help yourself."

"Those still with us are remarkably unharmed," he commented, ignoring my reference to himself. "Those creatures seemed to have a very polarised viewpoint: they either killed you, or they did not."

"Very black and white." I winced as he probed along my arms. Even though Batrix was probably being very gentle, it still felt as though both limbs were being threaded through a mangle. One studded with steel teeth.

"Very swollen," he said, pointlessly. Even with my non-existent medical training I could see that: two huge, smooth-skinned sausages, turning a little red around the edges. "But neither are, I think, broken."

"Are you sure?"

"As sure as I can be. Can you move your fingers?"

Expecting agony every moment, I flexed both hands

experimentally. It did hurt like hell, but they moved, after a fashion.

"Try to bend your elbows."

I did. It hurt even more than the fingers: as though someone had packed the joints with slivers of glass.

"Now rotate your wrists and forearms."

I came very close to yelling out loud. The pain was excruciating, and my arms were so stiff they barely moved. But Batrix seemed happy; maybe he was enjoying my discomfort.

"No. Too much movement for any breakage. But you have severely bruised all of the joints, landing on your arms when you jumped from the waggon, I imagine. Arms were never designed to take such a degree of impact..."

"Spoken like an expert on body design..."

"But after a day or two, you should have most of your freedom of movement back. I wish there was some ice, to take the swelling down."

"Careful what you wish for round here, Batrix. You'll probably get a hailstorm that will wreck what's left of the waggon-train."

"My dear Scilli, there is nothing left of the waggon-train. Without something to pull them, the vehicles must stay where they are."

"The aurochs?"

"Alive, but too shaken to be of much use, at least for a day or so."

"Wonderful." I tried getting to my feet without using my arms. I was about as elegant as a newborn buffalo. Batrix helped me again, although judging from his expression, he didn't think I should be moving at all.

The piecemeal castle was no closer. It loomed against the strange light, taunting us with its nearness, whatever that meant in this place. We might walk towards it for the rest of our lives and get no closer.

I cast my eyes around, looking for those sourceless shadows. I could say I wasn't disappointed; there were plenty to see. A damned sight more than there had been before the giant birds had attacked. I had an uneasy feeling they were gathering. Defenders of the castle, or were they naturally denser this close to the bizarre construction?

Naturally. That was a strange word to use here. Especially judging by the bizarre shapes suggested by the shades flowing across the earth. The birds were bad enough, I didn't want so much as a glimpse of what cast some of the shadows.

"Get everybody together," I said. "I don't think it'd be wise to hang around in the open too long."

"You intend to continue to that rock formation?"

"No, I want to go mineral prospecting! Just do it, will you!"

"Yes, *Gosigné* Scilli!" Batrix actually saluted. He turned smartly on his heel and marched away. I wanted to call after him, to apologise. Explain the pain was making me cranky, but I didn't do any of it. The heteromorph's rigid back was too intimidating.

Slowly, I bent and hooked up my coat. I slid its sleeves over my arms as though both were kegs of powder with lighted fuses. It was a painful, protracted operation. No one offered to help.

Eventually, I was formally dressed in the dirty, torn and blood-stained coat: an elegant representative of the government. The hole in my arm had stopped bleeding, at least, but it ached abominably. Even so, the pain was nothing like the agony burning along my arms every time I tried to move them. I sighed like one of the damned, tried to make my spine as straight as Batrix's, and strode forward.

It was not going to be easy, crossing the last few – what ... miles? feet? lifetimes? – between the abandoned waggon-train and the castle.

ↈ

We'd been walking for little more than fifteen minutes when *chavet* withdrawal hit. Glacial cramps ripped my guts apart, and I felt the shivers beginning to spread out towards my limbs.

I groped for the bottle inside my coat with fingers that alternated between unfeeling clumsiness and painful spasms. Half the time, I couldn't even feel what I was trying to lift.

I managed to get the bottle out of its pocket. Forcing an arm that was almost too stiff to move, the difficulty of which it reminded me in the strongest terms possible, I lifted a *chavet* bottle that seemed to weigh several tons towards my face. Halfway between pocket and lips, my fingers betrayed me. A violent shudder tossed the bottle from a numb hand.

All the symptoms of withdrawal, all the pain in my abused arms, seemed to hold back as I watched the bottle in disbelief. It arced, much too slowly, across the darkened ground, glowing pale blue despite the green light. It seemed as though I could still catch it before it hit. Even in pain, I could move faster than the bottle.

It struck the ground and shattered. As the *chavet* splashed in every direction, it seemed to sparkle with an extra degree of attraction. Pale blue stars danced momentarily against the almost black earth and, one by one, blinked out.

Agony returned in a triumphant explosion along every one of my nerve endings. I could hear withdrawal laughing in triumph: it had me this time. I was going to end in an agonised, drooling, filthy pile. If I were lucky, it'd kill me.

I collapsed to my knees. I could no longer tell what hurt the most: the agony of withdrawal or my throbbing arms. I was pain incarnate. The outside world was gone, the pain was too selfish. It had no

206

intention of sharing my attention with anything else.

I lay curled on the ground, for what felt like forever. The agony was the only reality. Slowly, it was taking my brain apart. I couldn't think, I couldn't speak. I could just experience.

Then, there was a change. Something subtle, something I wasn't consciously aware of, something I could just sense. Gradually, the pain of withdrawal faded. I could distinguish cramp from the shakes; the dull, corrosive throb in my arms. There was something hard and cold knocking against my teeth, a familiar hint, a taste across my tongue.

Chavet?

It was Batrix; it must be. He'd brought extra *chavet* with him. It was the sort of thing he'd do.

I was human again. The constant ache in my arms was nothing in comparison. The agony of serious *chavet* withdrawal put such things in context. I uncurled from being the pathetic creature lying in the earth and managed to get up onto my knees.

The first thing I noticed was the sky, it was blue, a pale, luminous blue: *chavet* blue.

The second thing was that it wasn't Batrix holding a bottle to my lips; it was *Gosigna* Echosic. She looked closely at me, nodded in brusque satisfaction, and stood up. She almost smiled.

"Better, Bureau man?" she grated. She looked at the bottle in her hand as though she'd never seen it before and pressed it into my hands.

"Thank you..." I began.

She waved a claw-thin hand irritably. "Don't thank me! I'd rather you weren't beholden to me. Just be thankful I will not abide suffering, even in one such as you!"

I couldn't help reflecting that such an admirable sentiment didn't seem to extend as far as her husband.

I raised the bottle and peered at it. The genuine article, even down to its distinctive shape. "Where did you get it?"

"Being a shaman's wife is an avenue to many things, Bureau man." She waved her turquoise and silver amulet over me in some bizarre form of blessing before striding away. She'd dismissed me as completely as had Batrix.

I got to my feet. Several yards away, the remnants of our party was standing, watching me. The four waggoners were plainly disturbed. Maybe they thought I was suffering from something brought on by the dream-realm. Gen Romino's expression was halfway between abject fascination and his usual fixed grin. Chato Echosic was staring at something enthralling on the toes of his boots. Batrix's expression showed nothing at all.

I had a sip of *chavet* to show I didn't care, stiff arms or not.

Then I took another glance towards the fortress. Even in the new light, it looked no less bizarre; in fact, the new clarity made it appear even more like some lunatic's vision of a castle. The light also made it look a lot more real, more solid. I wondered if Batrix could see it yet.

Pocketing the *chavet* bottle, I began limping towards the group. I don't think they were exactly impatient to be moving on, but I got the impression that my little performance on the ground had embarrassed them in some way. Maybe I'd broken some waggoner or Anesicci rule of etiquette with such an abject display. I knew exactly what Batrix thought of *chavet* addiction and the spectacle of withdrawal.

"Show's over," I muttered when I was close enough. "You want a repeat performance, next time I charge."

Echosic raised his large head. I was shocked: he looked shrunken, as though his huge frame was just a thick, deflated skin over a dwarf's skeleton. "I think we're not the ones paying the price, Bureau man." The look he gave me was so frank it made me nervous.

"How are you, Scilli?" Batrix asked. In the better light, it was obvious how grey his face was. He was gaunt and lined. Although I couldn't see past his blue lenses, I had the impression there were black circles around each eye.

"I'll live. How about you?"

He just shrugged, his new, all-purpose answer. I felt even more guilty about my bad-tempered outburst earlier: it was obvious he was hurting a whole lot more than I was.

"We'll get out," I said, just loud enough for him to hear. "And when we do, dinner's on you." The words were out before I'd had time to consider them: the last time we'd dined together had been in a restaurant named Grif Ditya's.

I don't tend to believe in coincidences. When one rears up and kicks me in the teeth, I start looking for the marionette strings.

I was about to make some smart comment when the light started to fail again. I looked up: the sky was darkening rapidly, turning to a rich indigo that was dotted liberally with stars. A beautiful summer's night, the kind you don't get in Wael Edra.

But there was still light, and lots of it. The kind of clear, silvery glow that comes from a Full Moon on the clearest night, except there'd been no Moon up to now. I'd started to look around for it when the collective gasp from the rest of the party dragged my eyes down from the sky and towards the castle of oddments.

It was that which was glowing: clear and brilliant, with a soft, silvery shine. No wonder the Moon was never visible in the night sky – it had been down here all along.

CHAPTER TWENTY

THE SIGHT TRANSFIXED US all, Batrix more than any. In the forgiving glow from the moon-fortress, he looked calm again, all the lines and pain eased from his features.

Which was in marked contrast to the fortress itself. The glow seemed to come from deep inside the jumble of stone and brick, and now every scar, carved line, joint and abutment showed up like dirty marks across a lamp. Just like the Moon it was imitating, its own light revealed an aged, pocked surface.

"I see it now," Batrix whispered. His own face was beginning to glow with its own inner light: with wonder, delight, maybe even relief. "You were right, my dear Scilli: it is indeed a wondrous sight."

I wouldn't have said wondrous. Strange, maybe; unearthly, certainly. But it didn't fill me with confidence.

"It's done you a wealth of good," I remarked.

Batrix smiled. "Indeed. Until this moment, I had not realised how much I missed the Moon. If we get back, I will see what there is to discover about the phenomenon. I cannot believe it is not deliberate."

Neither could I. Create a being that outwardly flows from one gender to another each Full Moon, but, presumably, is at its weakest at the New Moon. I could smell Spook deviousness there, but for what, I couldn't guess. I hoped the motive, if Batrix ever got the chance to uncover it, wouldn't be too hard to take.

"Never mind the ifs, we'll make it."

"Such optimism from you is most refreshing, Scilli." From the tone of his voice, it didn't sound as though he believed it any more than I did.

"This world gets better every day, eh, Scilli?" Romino nudged my arm with his elbow. I managed not to turn round and kick his legs out from under him, shrieking in pain as I did so, but it was a close-run thing.

"How do you measure days!" I growled through gritted teeth. He drifted away, oblivious. How had he managed to live so long, I wondered.

"We're wasting time!" snapped *Gosigna* Echosic. I saw the looks the four waggoners gave her; I didn't blame them. Maybe she thought she was going to be reunited with her girlish idol, all I could think of was an invisible army and giant birds, both of which had swept through a much bigger force than our present one without stopping. Just what could we expect to find in a castle that glowed in the dark?

Echosic cleared his throat noisily. He sounded like a man about to rattle his last. "Please, Anej. No more..." His hoarse whispers faded into nothing. His wife glared at him, contemptuously.

"You're weak, Chato. You were always weak! Without me you'd be nothing!"

Odd little thoughts crept into my head: thoughts about a silver and turquoise amulet, thoughts about someone hell-bent on meeting their childhood hero. Was *Gosigna* Echosic a shaman, too? She was certainly handy with that little totem of hers. Yet somewhere underneath all my half-formed ideas, I'm sure there was a remembered detail of the Anesicci never allowing female shamans. Anej Echosic was too traditional to flaunt such an ancient rule. Wasn't she?

However, she was also pretty determined to get her own way. Maybe hard-core beliefs could be sidelined for the sake of ambition.

Steganesh had claimed he'd been responsible for bringing us here. Had he lied? If so, why? What could he gain?

I started getting lost in my own theories. It only made sense for Petran to volunteer himself as the villain of the day if he knew something, and hadn't he tried to warn me? How would the real culprit react if he thought Steganesh knew a bit too much than was healthy?

Maybe the plan was to get him kidnapped and out of the way before he could reveal anything else. There'd already been so many deaths, I might start getting suspicious if Petran also wound up as another corpse.

Which left us with what? Rhys Ecozar murdered, someone taking pot-shots at me, Petran and Sotha Ponac carried off.

I almost swore out loud – continually and inventively. What was the common factor running through all that? *Ingosigna* Ponac. She'd joined the trek through Ecozar's intervention and may even have been the last one to see him alive. She was standing next to me when I was shot. The Ditya imago took her, although it was only Petran he'd demanded.

Just who the hell was Sotha Ponac?

"Historian be damned!"

"Excuse me?" Batrix was staring at me. This time, I'd obviously spoken out loud.

"Feeling a little foolish, Batrix, that's all. Irritation got the better of me." Maybe it was the light, but the heteromorph looked taller. I was sure I wasn't looking down at him so much.

Anej Echosic had already started towards the glowing citadel, amulet held aloft, Romino following dutifully in her wake. Chato Echosic was standing motionless, watching his wife stride across the flat ground. He looked more than ever like a deflating balloon: there was no longer any vitality in the man, the larger-than-life image gone.

And then another thought struck me; it was a good time for belated realisations, or maybe it was the light. Echosic was dying.

The trek to Qaijente was more than just a journey of faith: it was his last gesture. He probably even planned to be buried there, make everyone promise to wait until he was gone before they returned to Wael Edra. And now he didn't think he'd make it. He believed death would overtake him long before we stood any chance of escaping this dream-world.

I've never had any faith, so I can't imagine what it's like to have everything you believe in shattered. But Echosic's faith was more than shattered, it had been betrayed. And worse, by a part of his own ancient religion: this dream-world. It must have felt like a saviour he'd followed all his life ultimately turning out to be a fake; or even more painful, the very antithesis of his teachings.

I walked quietly up to him. He struggled out of his torpor and almost found a smile.

"How long have you got?" I asked.

He blinked at me, about to bluster. Then his shoulders drooped: the entire world was dragging at his arms. "A month, perhaps a little less, but no more."

I wanted to tell him that we'd get back, that he wasn't going to end his life trapped in a nightmare. But I couldn't, and he wouldn't have believed me. I doubt I'd believe me, either.

I took his shoulder and gently pushed him towards the shining tower. After a moment's resistance, he began walking. He had the air of a condemned prisoner heading towards the gallows.

I passed the knot of waggoners. They still hadn't made a move towards the castle, muttering angrily among themselves. I allowed Echosic to continue without me; he plodded on, like an automaton.

"Problem?" I asked the waggoners. They all eyed me sullenly.

"We ain't goin' in there!" one of them muttered.

"Afraid?" I said. Maybe they were, I wouldn't blame them. But it was odd, considering how they'd appointed themselves our guardians shortly after the trek had begun. I didn't think they were the type to scare easily – the ones who'd run away notwithstanding.

"Sort of," the waggoner replied.

"It ain't just fear!" another one butted in. "We don't know what we'll find in there. I ain't scared o' no man, but you can't fight nightmares!"

"You don't have to. This place just gives life to your strongest emotions. Everything here is symbolic, that's all."

"Them birds warn't symbolic!" another muttered.

"They weren't out of somebody's mind either," I said, wondering if it was true. "They didn't belong here anymore than we did."

"Then what they doin' 'ere! Somebody musta brought 'em ... summoned 'em... Whatever you call it."

He had a point. "Then standing around here waiting for it to happen again isn't very bright." I pointed at the increasing number of shades drifting across the ground. They were clearly visible in the light from the castle. "Want to be around when some of them break through?"

They took my meaning. "Kinda trapped, ain't we?" said the first. "Wait and see if any more o' them things get solid or come with you and face what's in that tower-thing."

"Ain't no choice at all!" another said.

I shrugged. "Probable death against possible escape."

"What about our mates what ran away?" said another. He was frowning heavily, as if trying to imagine what could happen to a lost man in a place like this.

"I don't know. If you die in a dream, do you die in real life?" They all looked blankly at me, the abstraction lost on them. I shrugged again; I was getting lots of practise. "Forget them, they're dead." And I found myself hoping they were as the alternative was too awful.

There was a pause. All of the waggoners were staring off into places only they could see. I let them. Eventually, one slung his battered musket across a shoulder.

"What the hell! We all die sometime!"

"I was kinda hopin' it'd be in bed," the one standing next to him said.

"With a whore!"

"Sixteen years young and me eighty!"

They all laughed, far too heartily. Weapons were shouldered and they began to trudge in the wake of Batrix and the Echosics. I watched them go for a while, not thinking about what I'd just talked them into.

Maybe I'd make a general yet.

The moon-glow fortress seemed to grow out of the earth as we got nearer. Either that or it was getting larger or drifting towards us.

There was no way of telling. The ground was so flat and featureless – any other rock formations hidden in the dark – we might just as well have been stationary, with the world moving under our feet.

We reached it much too soon. One moment it was a towering, crystalline streak of madness, illuminating the landscape for miles around, the next it filled the sky, and we were all gathered round an irregular oblong that must have served as a gate, or a door. It didn't glow; it was simply a dark gape in the opalescent surface of the wall, a wall that seemed to be made from a hundred different styles of roof. Maybe it wasn't as black and ominous as it looked, maybe it was just the contrast against the bright glow. Nobody seemed to want to find out, not even *Gosigna* Echosic. We all stood and looked at each other, waiting for someone else to brave the unknown.

Gen Romino was the first to lose patience, the mad grin twitching in annoyance for once. "What are you all waiting for? An invitation?"

"You don't call an open door an invitation?" I remarked.

He muttered something that I didn't catch, clutched his box tighter, and strode through the doorway. He vanished into the dark.

We waited. There was no scream, no warning shout. I would have settled for his annoying laugh of delight.

"Who's next?" I said, stepping forward.

Batrix placed a restraining hand on my chest. "Together, Scilli."

"I was hoping you'd say that."

There was a brief commotion as the waggoners arranged themselves into an escort: two in front and two bringing up the rear. They'd found new purpose in life.

I glanced at the one immediately behind me. "Can we go now?"

He nodded shortly, not even meeting my eyes, on purpose, maybe, but it was also helping them to not think about whatever frightened them most.

We all stepped forward, ambassadors to the court of Grif Ditya with their escort. Somehow, we all stepped through the gateway together, despite the fact it had only been wide enough for Romino a moment earlier. Everything went dark for a moment as we moved out of the silver glow, then brightened again.

I don't know what I'd expected. Anything, I'd thought. But not the central dining area of the Grif Ditya restaurant back in Scan Feta.

CHAPTER TWENTY-ONE

THE PLACE WAS PERFECT, right down to the last woodworm hole. Only the all-pervasive silvery glow marked it as an illusion sucked from someone's dearest hopes, or fears.

The real restaurant was the most exclusive outside Wael Edra, its clientele almost solely drawn from the art world that now dominated the town of Scan Feta and frequented by the worst aspects of that clique's tawdry entourage: vampiric critics, parasitic hangers-on, acolytes – the whole circus. Such people always need a place where they can be seen, be heard. Somewhere to air their second-hand opinions of what's good, and why it's good. Grif Ditya's filled that need admirably.

While the Spooks were still in charge, it had been nothing more than a nameless chocolate shop: a place where the real talents of Scan Feta could buy themselves a decent meal for just a few coppers. But once the war was over, and the wizards reduced to an ineffectual political party with little hope of ousting the elected Philosophics, things changed. Travel betwen the new Estates and Territories was no longer actively discouraged, and Scan Feta's permanent population rose accordingly.

In the ten years since the war, Grif Ditya's had risen from a lowly shop front to a lushly appointed restaurant, where simply getting through the door cost over ten *dinari*. Naming it after the legendary knight-champion of the vanished kingdom of Meijtloaca had been a final, symbolic act. Artists are fond of symbolism, I believe.

"Were we not in this very place just a few days ago, Scilli?" said Batrix.

"The real one, yes."

"Then the menu must have impressed you mightily."

"I don't think this has been conjured up just because I was thinking about their creamed courgettes." Maybe artists aren't the only ones with a fondness for symbolism.

I looked around. Despite the many tables laid out ready for the evening's diners, there wasn't anyone else in sight. And that included the Echosics, Romino and the waggoners. All seven had vanished.

I was about to point that out to Batrix when the surrounding light began to dim. Only a central spot – like a stage-light – remained bright. We were going to be treated to some performance or other.

Several brilliantly costumed figures drifted into the light. In their long, garish robes, they looked as though they had no feet or legs, and they swirled smoothly across the stage. Clearly, with all the checkered patterns and stylised feathers, they were meant to be native Cotechatlu dancers of some kind. But every one of them was pale and fair: obvious descendants of the colonists who had fled the Old Lands across the ocean and settled in the continental mass of feudal kingdoms that eventually became Ramini.

"A floor show," I said. "We didn't get that in the real place."

"Perhaps they did not have enough imagination."

That was, I'm sure, meant as a joke. Not only was the moonlight glow making Batrix look healthier, but it was also doing wonders for his sense of humour.

The dancers went through their opening paces. It meant nothing to me; all of the gestures and postures were just abstract patterns. Maybe that's all they were meant to be. But after a while, even I could tell that something was beginning to unfold.

Each dancer had adopted a role, no longer an identical facet of a chorus. They were obviously telling a story, but with my limited grasp of the arts, it took several minutes before I made any sense of it.

As far as I could make out, there was a king who ruled his lands kindly, if not particularly wisely. One day, a magician came to him, and judging from the bizarre and faintly ludicrous costume the wizard-dancer abruptly transformed into, the magician was meant to be none other than the Archimandrite himself. I began to watch more closely.

The mock-Archimandrite was beguiling the King with his magic: an egg, painted with crude streaks of gold across it, was obviously meant to be the magician's abaston stone. He laid out increasingly seductive wonders before the dim King: beautiful women, riches, empires, fame, glory – the usual roll-call of temptations. And like the fool he was, the King fell for it.

"What is the purpose of this?" asked Batrix. "Are we being given some simplified version of the fall of one of the original kingdoms?"

"Never had a history lesson before? I hope you're paying attention, there may be questions later."

The King was duly rewarded for his stupidity, he was bound to a molten rock and tormented by demons. It looked pretty bad for him.

I expect the illusionary actor was glad this wasn't for real.

Then there was a sudden shift in the dancers' mood. They all started looking over their shoulders. I don't know what they were expecting, but from their attitude, nothing short of a chief demon would have satisfied me at that point.

Sadly, all we got was Ditya, or the thing that copied him. He wandered into the spotlight in much the same distracted way he had ridden through us before kidnapping Steganesh and Sotha. I found myself smiling; he looked too much like an aging player who's wandered accidently on stage, oblivious of his part or what his lines should be.

He strolled up to the chained King and stared absently at him. Then he reached for the mask covering the figure's head. It crumbled like paper that had been dipped in acid. Underneath was a girl: a woman. Masses of rich red hair tumbled free. She looked as though she was meant to be laughing, but there was still no sound.

"Allegory," Batrix muttered. "The King is freed but is no longer what the rescuer expected."

"All very pretty. If this was a theatre in Wael Edra I'm sure I'd be impressed, but like you, I wonder who, or what it's all for."

"Perhaps the citadel is trying to tell us something."

"Then it had better get on with it and forget the fancy parables. Come on."

I led the way towards a door I'd seen before the lights had faded. I wondered that if I hoped hard enough it'd still be there. It was. I silently congratulated my unconscious mind's powers of persuasion.

I stepped through another brief darkness, and outside again, or some kind of outside. In a normal, sanely designed castle I guess it would have been the central keep, surrounded on all sides by walls and the main bulk of the fort. Not here.

I was standing on the lip of a ragged opening in an ancient tower. Several hundred feet below was the ground, clearly visible in the citadel's bright glow. Vertigo hit me instantly.

I didn't feel Batrix's hand on my collar; I was too preoccupied with all the swooping and spinning the world was indulging in. Only landing on my back with an impact hard enough to stop me breathing for a moment put things right again.

I lay there for a while, staring up at what looked like the roof of a grass hut – scores of feet above me – feeling like I was about to be sick. Had appearing on a ledge far above the ground just been an accident? Or did whatever controlled this world know all about my fear of heights? Or was it my fear of heights that had dropped me so close to the edge?

Trying to think it through made me feel even more nauseous. I decided to be tough and stand up. My next-to-useless arms had the last laugh, and I made it to my feet with all the grace of a beached whale. Batrix was standing near the edge, looking down. I sat back down again, quickly.

"Would you mind getting away from there?" I was no longer watching him, so I wouldn't know even if he did step back. Or off.

"Ah, my apologies, Scilli. I quite forget your ... affliction."

I dared to look. He was standing close by me. His expression – as much as he ever wore one – was contrite.

"Affliction. That's a good word for it." I tried to raise a hand to brush away the sweat coating my face but gave up on the idea. I tried blinking it free from my eyes and looked back at Batrix. "Would it be impolite for me to comment you look different?"

He nodded. I think you could still refer to him as 'he', but probably not for much longer. "I seem to be undergoing the transmorph processes. I imagine it is an effect of this citadel. As far as this realm is concerned, this is the Moon."

I couldn't take my eyes off the heteromorph. He was distinctly taller and slimmer, his tunic was beginning to grow much too short and loose. His moustache looked like one a fourteen-year old boy had been trying to grow all year and failing. His hair was thickening out and growing paler.

"The last time I saw you 'morphing, you looked like hell."

"As I recall, that was a premature shift. Painful, and not a little dangerous."

"And normally it's all as simple as this, of course." I managed to stand, still unable to take my eyes off Batrix's face.

"No. I admit the process is usually a little traumatic. There is some discomfort."

I couldn't help thinking he was understating the whole thing. Changing shape, gender, coloration – and all the other details that mark out men and women on the surface – must be a damned sight more than uncomfortable.

"On the whole, I much prefer it this time."

I wanted to tell him that I wouldn't, it made me nervous. There was something much too easy and convenient about his change. I've never been a great believer in the concept of an easy life.

There was a hoarse cry to my left. I turned and saw Chato Echosic lying flat on the uneven floor. He looked as though he'd just been dropped from a height much too far for me to think about. I glanced up at the odd thatched roof. Maybe he'd fallen?

Batrix was already helping him up. The heteromorph made it look as though he – she – was picking up a doll. The moonlight round here was potent stuff.

"I thought I'd lost you all," Echosic was gasping. "I found myself all alone in a grey place that seemed to go on in all directions. It was..." Words obviously failed him. He spluttered to a halt, reduced to fluttering his hands.

"Didn't your shamanic experience help?" I said, as consolatory as I could be.

He just gazed at me. He'd been shrunken-looking earlier, now he looked as though he'd taken up haunting himself. "All shamanic visions are of something – even if the most obscure symbols. This was..." he spread his hands again "...nothing. Literally nothing. I was nowhere." His gaunt eyes dropped away from me and stared dismally at the floor.

I think he knew where he'd been. Even I could take a guess. He'd been given a glimpse of his future, and we both knew he didn't have one.

Abruptly, his head snapped up again. His eyes were focussed once more, something akin to panic filling the void in them. "Where's Anej?" he breathed. "Where's my wife?"

"Neither of us have seen her, *Gosigné* Echosic," Batrix said calmly.

Away getting her own vision was all that I could think. I guess Echosic didn't want to hear that, though.

"Have you given any thought as to how we escape from this ... whatever this is?" Batrix said. He gestured to the peculiar niche we'd landed in. Obviously, from the distance above the ground, we were several hundred feet up a tower, with one side open to the elements. Above us was the giant straw hut, or the thatched roofs of a dozen houses. The three enclosed sides seemed to be made from the flattened remains of thousands of dwellings, shops, kiosks. Even the uneven floor showed traces of windows and doorways, brickwork and stones. It was almost as if a vast hammer had pounded a countrywide collection of cities and towns into sheets and used them as a stone veneer.

"Not only no Moon, but no towns, either."

"What?" Echosic glared at me. I was going to have to stop thinking out loud; one day I might say something I didn't want anyone to hear.

"This citadel. It seems to be a compression of every town or city we never passed. It's a concentration of everything missing from the landscape beyond."

Echosic frowned, then nodded thoughtfully. "It's a focus. This is the dream-realm."

"Then might we expect some difficulties?" Batrix asked.

"Perhaps. But if there is any part of this world where we might hope to break out, it's here."

"Take note, Batrix," I said. "Somewhere there's a door with a sign reading Ramini Republic printed on it. Let's hope it's not locked, eh?"

"It won't be so simple, I fear." Echosic looked at Batrix as though seeing him for the first time. He rubbed at his lips with a forefinger. "You are changing," he observed. Glad to see I wasn't the last to notice.

"I trust everyone will not find it necessary to comment on the obvious," said Batrix. He sounded a little touchy. "It will be quickly become tedious."

"Be thankful they care enough to notice," I muttered. "And we still haven't decided which way to head."

"I think it'll make little difference." Echosic was already heading towards one of the mosaic walls. "I suspect that from hereon in, all ways are the same."

"I hope he's not going to get all mystical on us," I said, trailing after him.

"If he does, I promise to leave him to you, my dear Scilli. That is more in your department than mine, I believe."

"Promises, promises."

As we walked, I kept looking up towards what, for want of a better name, I called the roof. I was half expecting to see Romino, *Gosigna* Echosic or the waggoners walking along it, upside down, as though it was the most natural thing in the world. Either that or strolling across the walls at right-angles to the rest of us.

The wall towards which Echosic was walking didn't seem to be getting any closer. I turned round: the opening through which I'd almost fallen appeared to be miles away. I decided I didn't like dream-worlds; they acted too much like some of my own dreams. Even the good ones.

Traditionally, dreams have been seen as signs or omens for the waking world, and a good many Spooks had made a living out of interpreting them. But that view was becoming unfashionable these days, with some brave thinkers claiming dreams were nothing more than the mind sorting out events from the past day, filing them away as coded references. That sounded an insane concept to me, but it was not surprising. Most of the ideas, which had been cherished by the Chrysomancers, were being re-examined or overturned, often out of sheer perversity. Anything regarded as true by the Spooks must naturally be suspect.

They lost the war, after all. That makes them wrong in any victor's book.

Something flung itself up from the floor immediately in front of me. I halted, hands reaching for my pocketed repeater, until the pain flaring up both of my arms reminded me it wasn't such a smart idea. A moment later I realised it was a door: a plain, ordinary half-glass door, the kind that went between just about every room at Bureau headquarters in Wael Edra, except this was coming out of the floor.

The other bit of wrongness was Gen Romino stepping up through it as though he expected the ground to be under his feet, instead of empty air.

It's hard to describe what happened next. Romino shouldn't have been able to just walk up, into space, away from the floor, with the door slamming behind him. But that's almost how it looked: stepping out through a door in a horizontal wall, which an instant later became the floor.

Needless to say, he hit the ground, and lay there like an overturned beetle, a comical look of total confusion on his face. It was all too much, even for his addled senses.

His box lay several feet away, where it had fallen. Somehow, it was still in one piece.

Echosic must have heard the commotion. He turned, saw Romino spread over the floor, and hurried back towards him, as fast as his bulk and general condition allowed. He caught the younger man under his arms and hauled him up.

"Gen! Have you seen Anej?" He dusted Romino down as though he was a valet cleaning down his master after a riding fall. Romino stared back at him stupidly.

"My wife, Gen!" Echosic's coarse voice grew urgent. I expected him to start shaking the other by his lapels any moment. "Where is she?"

Romino blinked twice. Gradually, I saw whatever passed for his mind crawl back behind his eyes and start looking out again. "Your wife?" He frowned, smile quivering uncertainly around his chin. "Isn't she here?"

Echosic dropped his hands with a groan. He stumbled away, watched by the younger man, his expression baffled and upset.

"Chato?" Romino's voice was tiny and pathetic. I had the feeling I was watching some family drama, not the interplay of friends, even the closest type.

The huge Anesicci trod heavily back onto course, towards some destination only he seemed aware of. Romino shuffled over to his battered box and stooped to pick it up, his face constantly turned towards Echosic's back. Once he had the box safely huddled in his arms, he began to follow. I had the impression he wanted to run, but something was holding him back.

"We are almost reunited, Scilli," commented Batrix, his expression arch. "I expect *Gosigna* Echosic will miraculously appear next, followed by the waggoners. What do you think?"

"Did you notice," I said, not answering him, "Romino said nothing about what he's just experienced?"

Batrix cocked his head at me. He was growing more handsome by the moment. "Should he have?"

"The three of us experienced something..."

"A something that neither of us bothered to mention to *Gosigné* Echosic."

"And you think it's likely that Romino – someone who enthuses about every unusual aspect of this trip – wouldn't take the first chance to tell us about whatever it was he saw before appearing here?"

"It occurs to me that Echosic barely gave him the chance."

I had to grant him that, but I was still troubled. More than troubled. I was certain, and in the worst possible way, that Romino was lying, that he had seen Echosic's wife, and that we wouldn't see her again, not ever.

And the worst of it was, I had no idea why I was so certain.

CHAPTER TWENTY-TWO

WE PASSED THROUGH DOOR after door. Behind each was another wonderland: bright gardens crammed with flowers, vivid with colour and stinking of death; city streets lined by tall, beautiful buildings, the pavements caked with every kind of filth; pylon-mounted cities dominating the horizon, beyond gentle alpine pastures that were strewn with millions of bones. Vista after vista. I don't know if they were from people's dreams, or somehow symbolic of the real world beyond. All I know is that in every single one we found not so much as a single living soul.

There was plenty of indications life had been there once – rotting carcasses and stale ordure –but no longer. No matter how serene or debased the scene, each was sterile.

Echosic grew more driven with each visionary world. He pushed himself harder, increasingly eager to throw open the next gate and enter the next world. I imagine he believed his wife would be in one of them, if not the next, then the one after, or the one after that. He grew more haggard, his flesh like cold tallow hanging off a spent candle. He began to limp, his breath growing harsher and louder with each disappointment.

"We've got to slow him down!" I hissed at Batrix.

"Do you have a suggestion?"

I didn't, of course. If I stood in his way, I had as much chance of halting him as I had an Alva-patent locomotive-engine. The frantic search for Anej Echosic drove the man as relentlessly as any amount of steam.

"Perhaps Romino might persuade him?"

Batrix glanced at the young Anesicci. He was close on Echosic's heels, clutching his wooden box to his chest as though his life depended on it. He didn't look as though he wanted to stop any more than Echosic did. "I do not think he wishes *Gosigné* Echosic to halt, either."

"What is going on!" It was as though we'd become infected with a kind of insanity that is normal only in nightmares. No one was thinking anymore, just reacting. We were driven as mindlessly as anyone who's dreamt they're fleeing something terrible down a dark, endless road, but can't seem to move.

Even I could feel it: a dread, a crawling between the shoulder blades. Either that, or Echosic and Romino were giving me the creeps.

Echosic had found another gate: a florid, rose-strangled thing half-hidden in a wall of yew. He fumbled with it, catching his hands on rose thorns. Batrix and I reached him before he could break through again. He was mumbling to himself, but I could only hear snatches of it.

"It's continuous ... flowing ... to another ... no breaks, no boundaries ... eventually..."

I laid my hands across his, trying to halt his frantic scrabbles. But his skin was slippery with blood, and my own were still pretty useless. He wrenched himself free with little effort, nudged me aside, and yanked the gate open. He glared my way once – a wild-eyed, possessed man – then vanished through the gate. A moment later, Romino followed him.

I looked at Batrix, happy to see a still sane face. "I feel like a man chasing a rabbit through a maze. You can see it, but never quite get your hands around its scrawny neck!"

"An interesting analogy. And not too far from the truth, I think."

"Meaning?"

He waved a slim, elegant hand. "This citadel, even more than the dream-world it dominates, is a maze. It can be anything you – or anyone – wishes. It can change shape faster than a blink. Can you think of a more subtle web?"

"And if Echosic's right, it's entirely passive. We're not even fighting some bad-tempered Spook with a vivid imagination!"

I kicked at the gate as I passed through it. Some of the rose vines reared and hissed at me. I wished I had a bottle of kerosene handy.

I didn't get much beyond two steps through the gate. The scene beyond made me forget how to move my feet.

The ground sloped away before me, dropping gently towards what looked like a vast, shallow crater. The sky glowed a sullen maroon, shot through with wriggling yellow swirls, almost as though it was on fire. An uncomfortable red light soaked everything, making the whole panorama look like some half-mad painter's vision of hell.

There were figures moving across the crater, busy as ants. At first, I thought they were the remaining waggoners, but these were thin, smoky things that didn't look any more substantial than the shadows cast across the sands beyond the citadel. I wasn't surprised to notice they didn't seem to cast a shadow of their own.

In the centre of the crater, like a bright thunderstone, sat an enormous slab of rock. It pulsed with an internal white light that was almost painful against the overall red glow. The stone dominated the landscape with its size, its brilliance. Under normal circumstances, I would have said the impact crater suggested the stone had fallen from the sky, the shallowness indicating it had happened a long time ago.

But our circumstances were far from normal, time meant nothing here. An aerolite sitting in an eroded crater was an image, what we would expect to see. If there was one thing I'd learnt it was that this world only showed things in a manner which we could understand: solid parables, fairytales with flesh.

That the glowing stone represented huge power, I didn't doubt. It was in all likelihood the core of the citadel, if not the dream-world itself. But for some reason I was seeing it as a stone, long-fallen out of the sky. That didn't make it any more powerful to me – so the image had to be there for someone else's benefit.

I looked around. Echosic was striding awkwardly down the shallow crater towards the stone, Romino in tow. The old man didn't even seem to be seeing the aerolite; he was just driving blindly forward. I doubt Romino was paying much attention, either.

Batrix stood a few feet away from me, gazing as raptly at the stone as I no doubt had been. The light was glazing his face, flashing off the lenses of his eyeglasses. There was no doubt now: he was taller, his hair longer and flowing. His face was becoming more heart-shaped, with high, delicate cheekbones. He wasn't female yet, but he was certainly no longer male.

Which made me feel better, because – despite the ridiculous fit of his too-short, too-wide uniform – as I looked at him, the only thing I could think was: he's beautiful. Whatever that stone might have been, it was certainly agreeing with him.

What had he said, months ago that were really only a couple of days ago? Heteromorphs don't dream? Maybe so, but they still have needs and desires just like you or me, and Earth's softly glowing night-time companion revolved around a hell of a lot of those needs.

I'd been right all along: this place was interpreting itself for Batrix's benefit. But it wasn't his fear of no Moon that was driving it; rather, it was a convenient way to demonstrate the heart of itself. The Moon was at the nucleus of his universe, so it was with this one.

"Moonstone," Batrix murmured. He was still gazing, almost in adoration, at the bright chunk of rock.

That confirmed it. "You mean that's fallen off the Moon? Or is the Moon itself?"

"You are being too literal again, my dear Scilli." He began descending towards the huge lump of stone, virtually in Echosic's and Romino's tracks. I stepped forward, too. I was damned if I was going to miss any of this, whatever this turned out to be.

"It's you, isn't it?" I said to his back. "All the Moon symbolism and references, it's your mind that's supplying it."

"You think so?" He was quiet for a moment; thinking, I suppose. "Perhaps you are correct. However, I have little upon which to make an assumption."

"What's going on, Batrix?" I was getting close to losing all patience. The heteromorph's answers weren't evasive, but in his pedantic manner – and my mounting temper – it sure sounded that way. "Risnek might have sent me in blind, but I doubt he'd do it to both of us. Especially you: you're the government's monument to equality."

"What do you mean?" Maybe I imagined it, but his voice sounded slightly hesitant.

"You know more about this job than I do. That's fine. I'm not the competitive sort. But if you have any idea why we've all been whisked off to dreamland – and who's behind it – now's the time to tell me."

"I know no more than you, Scilli."

"I'm sorry, Batrix, but I don't believe that. Risnek didn't send us just as government representatives, or as a hands-off signal to the anti-Anesicci lobby. An ordinary waggon-train on its way to Qaijente doesn't get waylaid by chimeras or over-sized worms straight out of Anesicci legend. It doesn't have a mercenary Chrysomancer simply attach himself for the duration of the trip. It doesn't involve me getting shot or other members of the trek being poisoned, their bodies very conveniently lost along the way. And it doesn't have chestnut-haired historians who seem to be present every time something dangerous or fatal happens, then promptly disappears with our prime suspect!"

Batrix stopped and turned to look at me. Despite the ruddy glow, his expression was hard to see, contrasted against the moonstone as it was. His eyeglasses were entirely black. "So that is it: you are chiefly concerned for the safety of *Ingosigna* Sotha Ponac."

I took a deep breath, angry at myself for such a drawn-out tirade. "I'm concerned with everyone's safety, Batrix. And, yes, I don't like to think of Sotha getting hurt, but she manages to be in too many places when bad things happen for my peace of mind. She's involved, Batrix. She's involved up to her pretty green eyes, and I want to know just what the hell she's involved in!"

He didn't say anything for almost two minutes; it felt like two hours. Eventually, he sighed and gazed up at the shifting sky. "Yes. I also believe *Ingosigna* Ponac is at the centre of some of the unfortunate events on this journey. However, I do not think she is fully responsible for our present condition."

"Then who is?"

"I do not know."

"You?"

"I give you my word, Wilonek Scilli, that I have no more idea what this world is, why or how we are here, or what the significance of that moonstone is."

"But you admit it is significant?"

"I admit to strongly believing so, yes. It is easier than thinking we have been brought to this world, allowed to come to this very spot, for no reason. That radiant piece of stone is too impressive to be a mere street-lamp."

"You'll be saying it's magical, next."

"I can barely deny the existence of magic, Scilli, merely that I find it personally distasteful – and unlawful."

"Then you're presently engaged in unlawful activity, wouldn't you say?"

He didn't answer, which was no more than I deserved. Batrix couldn't help his nature any more than I could mine. The paradox of a creature created by magic actually hating the source of its being wasn't lost on him, but it didn't make any difference. And it didn't help to remind him, either.

He turned back to face the colossal moonstone. "It calls to me, Scilli. And although I hate myself for it, I long to answer that call."

"Then maybe you should," I said. He cocked his head partly back, pointing an ear in my direction. "It's central to this whole puzzle. We need answers. The only place we're going to find them is down there."

Besides, I added silently, Romino and Echosic are already well on their way; maybe we'll find Sotha, Petran and Anej Echosic enjoying the light-show, too. I wanted to believe it. Some of it, I did believe. But I knew we wouldn't find all of them, not alive, anyway. I couldn't convince myself otherwise. I've seen too much of how the world works.

Batrix gave a peculiar sigh and resumed walking towards the bright rock. He looked like someone heading towards their execution, an image that clashed with what had sounded to me almost like a gasp of pleasure.

I dropped into step behind him, carefully taking out my repeater. It wasn't that difficult – no more so than picking up that moonstone if it was also white-hot. Maybe I wouldn't be able to fire the pistol – at least, not accurately enough to hit a stable door at three paces – but having it in my hand made me feel better. Damned if I knew why. What good would a pistol be against a mansion-sized lump of glowing rock?

As we came closer to the stone, the smoky figures also grew clearer. They were whirling around like almost-invisible dancers at a ball, spinning to music only they could hear. They made me jittery, especially when they swept by, too close. It was difficult telling what was dangerous around here and what wasn't. Ditya's invisible army hadn't hurt anyone, but these things were more visible. Maybe they were a touch more lethal, too.

But they still didn't seem to be aware of us. Maybe we were as insubstantial to them as they were to us. Maybe they weren't sentient things at all: just smoky wisps attracted to the glow like moths, slowly unravelling as they orbited, mindlessly.

Alternately, they could have once been people just like us, now dancing eternally around the moonstone until this was all that remained. It wasn't a thought to take to bed.

As Batrix and I grew closer to the glowing rock, the wisps seemed to grow more numerous. Their dancing grew faster, too. I began to feel like I was threading my way through a field of spinning weeds. I dodged left and right as the things whipped past me, seemingly oblivious. I still dreaded the thought of one touching me though.

Then three came at me, abreast. The two on the outside would have passed me front and back, but I couldn't avoid the one in the middle. It collided and passed straight through me. I was no more a barrier than if I'd been a mild breeze.

But I felt it go through: a bitter, agonising cold that was gone almost instantly. Even so, it felt as though a moment longer and it would have frozen my heart solid.

Perhaps they were guardians of a sort. Having that awful cold lancing through your body once too often – even if it did last for less than a second – could stop anyone eventually.

I looked around and spotted Batrix. Strangely, he seemed to be having no problem getting through the dancing wraiths. Indeed, it looked to me as though they were weaving around him, doing their best not to so much as brush against him.

I took several steps forward, and three smoky shapes slid through me. It was over in an instant, but I couldn't help crying out loud. That cold was capable of freezing the soul that I don't believe in.

"I don't think I'm going to make it!" I said. My voice shook from the cold. Obviously. Batrix stopped and looked back. The wraiths eddied around his legs, tiny moons circling a small moon heading towards a large moon.

I couldn't get moons out of my head.

"Is there a problem?"

"Every time one of those things touches me— *Hell!*" One brushed my leg, as though to underline the point. If ice could burn, that's what it did. *"That's* what happens!"

Batrix tilted his head. I decided I was going to have to start calling him her soon, for my own piece of mind. "And yet, so far, none have even come close to me. Curious."

"I noticed."

"Evidently I am to be allowed up to the stone, while you are not."

"Doesn't that make you just a little nervous?"

He paused, frowning. "It certainly intrigues me. But yes, it does trouble me that I am so obviously intended to reach the moonstone. I would like to know why first."

He took a step back towards me. Instantly, a thick barrier of smoky shapes slid in his way, blocking his retreat. They weren't dancing anymore, and there was something distinctly still and menacing about them. Batrix tried to push through them; the immediate spasm that wrenched his face told me all I needed to know.

He backed off. The barrier stayed where it was.

"That was quite an experience," Batrix gasped. I had the feeling whatever they'd given him was much harsher than any pain I'd felt so far. "There is little chance of their point being missed."

"Better keep going forward. I'll join you if I can."

"Is that wise?"

"They've tried to stop you getting away a lot harder than they've tried to stop me getting closer. I'll keep going." Brave, resourceful Scilli. Get enough of those wraiths wrapped around me, and Risnek wouldn't even need to bury what was left.

After a moment, Batrix resumed his walk towards the moonstone. The smoky wall gradually broke up, as though not entirely trusting the heteromorph's actions, and danced away.

I waited a while, wanting to give Batrix plenty of time to get nearer to the stone. I figured that if whatever was running this show thought it was getting its own way, it wouldn't care enough to try and stop me. The encounters I'd had so far with the wraiths appeared to be purely random – if anything in this place could be considered entirely random – but I didn't want to provoke an all-out defence.

Batrix was some fifty feet from the moonstone when I began moving again. Now that he was so close, it made me realise just how big the chunk of rock was. The 'morphing Batrix was now taller than I, but against the moonstone he was insignificant, an ant walking towards a mountain.

A wraith brushed my leg, the pain distracting me for a moment. When I looked up again, I'd lost sight of Batrix altogether, his silhouette swamped by the rock's brilliance. I began to hurry, dodging the swirling shapes as best I could, which isn't saying much. Luckily, they seemed to be slowing down, less frantic in their dance. Maybe now their prey was so close there was no need to be careful.

I upped my pace again. I felt like a man weaving through a field of randomly flocking black sheep, galvanic sheep at that, although the wraiths didn't show any inclination to scatter out of my way. And they were getting more tightly packed with every yard. It didn't matter that they'd virtually stopped moving, and hung in the air like semi-transparent bushes, threading my way through them without touching was nigh-on impossible.

The agonizing cold was coming every few seconds. I was beginning to wonder what would happen first: my legs collapsing from the constant abuse, or my heart deciding it couldn't take the strain any longer.

Then it became totally academic. The moonstone erupted into a ball of light thousands of times more brilliant than before. It drowned out the landscape and the ruddy background glow; it pierced my hands, thrown up to shield me from the glare; it filled my tight-shut eyes. I knew I was blinded.

Then it was gone again. The world seemed almost black in contrast. Through the tears and dancing purple smudges that left my eyes almost useless, I could just about see that the moonstone had vanished. In its place was a tiny figure: Batrix. Alive.

Without thinking, I began to run forward, then stopped, gazing around. The wraiths had vanished with the rock, there was nothing to get in my way. I started running again.

I was about thirty yards from Batrix. He was standing as though dazed, gazing down at the ground. His hair – or was that her hair? – was pure silver: a metallic wave that flowed past the shoulders of a ripped tunic.

"Batrix!" I called. "Are you alright?"

The heteromorph heard me, raised her head and turned, and the lenses of her eyeglasses ignited like brilliant headlamps.

CHAPTER TWENTY-THREE

FOR SEVERAL MOMENTS, I couldn't move any more than Batrix seemed able. She simply stood, cold fire roaring behind her lenses and dripping past her face to the ground, her mass of silver-white hair floating with a life all of its own.

I don't know what a god is, only that the law says all worship of whatever they are is forbidden. But for a moment, it was like watching the birth of one, and I sorely wanted to drop to my knees and worship her. It was wonderful, and I was terrified.

My trance ended. I was about to rush forward, ask Batrix if she was alright, when something hard-edged cracked against my wrist, waking up the raw pain I'd half forgotten. Thick-fingered as I was, I couldn't hang on to my pistol. But the rest of my body still had feeling, and I couldn't mistake the cold, tubular feel of another gun pressed delicately against my neck.

"I think we'll all just stay where we are, don't you?"

For a moment I didn't recognise the voice, and I didn't feel up to risking a quick peek. Then it slotted into place: it was Gen Romino's, but sounding harder, more controlled than before.

I suppose I should have guessed. "That damned box!" I muttered.

Romino tittered into my ear. "The box indeed, Scilli. A little late, perhaps, but an excellent guess, all the same."

"It was your slightly demented guise," I admitted, willing to give him credit. Why not? "Go for the sympathy vote every time. It always works for me."

"You overestimate your shop-worn appeal, Scilli." The muzzle of the gun lifted off my neck, leaving an itchy spot. Romino circled around me, working his way towards a still immobile Batrix. He never once took his eyes off me.

"Then I'm not going to make you feel better by asking what we're doing here."

"Isn't it obvious?" He was an arm's length from Batrix now but still had eyes only for me. I wondered if the heteromorph was suddenly going to spring into action and save us all.

"Whatever power that moonstone symbolised, you wanted it. But you obviously couldn't tap it yourself, not directly anyway. So you needed a third party, a go-between. How close am I so far?"

"Try taking up writing those one copper pocket actioners; I'd certainly give you a job." Batrix hadn't responded to his presence in any way. He was standing right beside her, intimately close. For a moment, I thought he was going to caress her face.

"So you experimented on a few others first. All those senseless disappearances that have plagued the Republic over the past months."

"Indeed? And what did I do with them?"

"The same as you did with us: set them loose in this place, drawn to its power by their own secret thoughts and dreams, however they perceived it. But none of them was any more able to contact it than you could."

"Excellent, Scilli."

"What happened to them, by the way?"

"Can't figure that bit out? Never mind!" He moved around Batrix and grinned at me from behind her head. I began to think his madness wasn't so faked after all. "You've already met." He waved towards the crater's downward slope. "You could say they were burned to a crisp."

"Those wraiths?"

"Cinders. Drained of everything. All they can do is stay close to the thing that destroyed them, existing on the crumbs of power which leak away. You probably noticed how effective they are as sheepdogs."

"Keeping out what the stone didn't want; making sure what it did want doesn't escape..."

"Absolutely. They're hungry, you see. Do anything for a meal." He tittered again. "If you stayed around long enough, you'd be just like them in the end. You wouldn't need to touch the thing at the core."

"How did you know Batrix would be the one?" I watched him as carefully as he was watching me.

"I didn't. That was just excellent luck! But the power certainly knew. Did you see the way it herded him. Or should I say her." He ran a hand over her hair in a way that was almost tender. His expression, however, was more lustful.

"So, you brought us here, and had the image of Ditya take away Steganesh and *Ingosigna* Ponac. Care to tell me why?"

He looked scornful, and he snatched his hand back from Batrix's hair. "Steganesh was a threat, naturally. I don't know what he was up to – all that obvious nonsense about being the one who was transporting us through the realms – and I certainly didn't want him around."

Obvious nonsense maybe, but why? "And what about Sotha?"

He laughed again. His confidence irritated me as much as the slightly crazy personality he'd affected earlier. "You mean you haven't work that out? Well, I won't spoil it for you. Neither of you is going to be leaving here in the foreseeable future; maybe you'll catch up to her at some point, and she'll tell you."

"Gen!" It was Echosic's throaty rasp. I glanced in the direct of his voice. He was trudging heavily towards us, his sagging features looking fogged and baffled. Romino had probably left him stranded among the wraiths, to be drained and frozen into another of their number.

"I can't find Anej!" The big man's misery was pathetic. I couldn't figure how anyone could love such a shrew of a woman, but it was obvious his heart was breaking.

"Oh, I think she's around somewhere," Romino smiled. "Along with the last of the waggoneers." He grinned at me, obviously delighting in the old man's pain. I suddenly realised he was holding up a familiar silver and turquoise amulet.

"You killed her," I said, not too loudly. I had no love for Romino, but I didn't want Echosic finding out the truth, not yet. There was no telling what the dying man would do, and the situation was uncertain enough already.

"Not I." He gently tapped Batrix's shoulder with a forefinger. "The power."

He'd sacrificed others, even though he knew it was certainly hopeless. I wondered what Anej Echosic had seen at the centre of the crater. Had she even seen a crater? Grif Ditya, maybe? Sitting in grace at the centre of a majestic halo. Had she rushed to him, regardless of the things whirling around her waist? Maybe the power had let her. And the waggoneers...?

I just hoped it had been quick, and that whatever still survived, it wasn't suffering.

"So now what?" I asked. "You've got your power incarnated. How do you intend to get it back to the real world? I take it that's the plan."

"The same way I brought you all here, with my little box."

"How does that work, by the way?" I wasn't all that interested, but Echosic was edging closer all the time, none of the bafflement leaving his face. I was banking on him finally coming out of his head and realising the truth. A little unrestrained chaos would be very useful, right now.

And besides, the longer I delayed Romino – even if it meant letting him crow a little – the more chance there was of Batrix coming out of whatever fugue she was lost in.

"So you haven't worked it out?" The news didn't seem to upset him too much. "The outer case is fully lined with pieces of spirit-chants taken from holy Anesetl tapestries, faced towards the wood so they look like simple cloth lining. The concentration of all that, plus my own unique touch, has given me a perfect tool for moving myself and others between the flesh and spirit worlds."

"So you're a shaman, too?" It was turning into quite a conference.

"You don't think I hung around that fat idiot and his foul-tongued wife just because I liked her cooking? Over the years, he was more than happy to tell me everything he knew. Weren't you, Chato?"

Echosic opened his mouth, then closed it again, frowning ponderously.

"I think he had some idea of his skills living on in me. An adopted son, of sorts."

"And you showed your gratitude in the time-honoured manner of all sons, by betraying him."

"Not at all! This pilgrimage to Qaijente was Chato's own idea..."

"One you were only too happy to go along with, since it gave you the chance to show just how good you were with that magic box – transporting the entire waggon-train in one go."

"Impressed, are you?" He looked more smug than ever.

"Maybe. I just don't understand why Steganesh claimed responsibility for that. Unless he was providing the distraction while you sweated over your magic..."

I was gratified to see his smug mask slip a little. "That faker has nothing to do with it! This – all this – is mine alone!"

"Then you tell me why he claimed it was his doing."

"He wanted the credit—"

"Even though it meant he was also implicated in the deaths of three people?"

Romino threw his hands up impatiently. "How should I know! For some time I thought he was working for the government, along with you two." He tenderly stroked Batrix's arm. "He certainly had some very official-looking papers on him."

Papers? Who the hell from? Was the Bureau getting even more devious? "How did you know that?"

"I looked, naturally. That night you got yourself shot."

"Which you didn't do, of course."

"Why should I want to shoot you?"

"Who says it was me you were shooting at? Sotha Ponac was standing right next to me, and your creatures rode off with her."

He laughed. "Good of you to make them mine, Scilli. But I don't control what goes on here any more than you."

I didn't believe that, either. But it left me no closer to finding where Petran's papers came from. I checked Batrix and Echosic with a quick glance: she didn't look any less entranced, and neither did he. How long did I have to go on talking before someone woke up?

"Indulge me. Say you're granting a dying man's last request—"

"Not so far from the truth."

"Tell me whose signature was on those papers you saw."

He cocked his head to one side. "Why? What could be so important now?"

I started to shrug, and a cold spasm clenched my spine. The first hint of *chavet* withdrawal. I ignored it. There was time enough before it became too rough. "I'm just incurably nosy, Romino. It's how I got this job."

His smile widened. "There was no signature, just a scribbled initial. And before you ask, no seal, either. I'm sorry to disappoint you, Scilli."

"I'm sure you'll learn to live with it." Something sharp and cold grabbed a handful of my gut and gave it a squeeze. I wondered why withdrawal always picked the most inopportune times to pay its respects.

"Gen!" Echosic chose that moment to get involved. "What exactly are you doing?"

Romino waved his pistol in my direction. "He's a dangerous criminal, Chato. Wanted by the government. When we get back, I'll hand him over." As he spoke to the old man, he used that irritating tone so many people adopt with the very young or the very old: high-pitched and condescending, as though talking to a simpleton. I think it was that more than anything that finally brought Echosic back to something approaching reality. Romino had overplayed it.

"Gen! Put that damned gun down at once!"

"Be quiet, old man!"

Echosic stiffened. In a few moments he seemed to re-inflate, regain most of his old bulk. His dark face grew redder. "How dare you talk to me in that tone. I..." He faltered, eyes fixed on something in the other's hand: Anej Echosic's amulet. Romino had neglected to put it back in his pocket.

"Where is she?" Echosic's ruined throat added an undercurrent of threat to his quiet voice. In that moment, I could see the man as he'd been as a young, powerful shaman: ruthless, dedicated, not one to trifle with.

"Who?" Romino's voice was light and mocking, but his eyes were flickering uncertainly.

"Don't be a fool. And don't treat me like one! What have you done with Anej?"

"What do you think?"

"You murdered her! A woman who treated you as a son!"

"She treated me like a half-witted slave! And so did you! 'Fetch this, Gen', 'Carry that, Gen!' She got exactly what she wanted. And you of all people know how fatal getting what you want can be!"

Echosic launched himself. Rage gave him a speed and grace I would have thought impossible. He bridged the gap between himself and Romino in a moment; the other didn't have time to even aim his pistol.

They collapsed to the ground in a swearing, thrashing mess. Echosic had one massive hand around Romino's throat, while he beat uselessly against the old man's skull with the pistol-butt. I couldn't see Echosic's face, but Romino's was turning a very satisfying shade of purple.

I dropped to my knees to try and scoop up my own dropped gun, but a withdrawal spasm unbalanced me. I ended up half-sprawled across the ground, adding to the generally foul language as both arms throbbed hideously. It was high time I took a sip of *chavet*.

I rolled to my knees, fumbling for the bottle. I had it clamped between both hands, bringing it slowly and painfully to my lips, when two things happened. I don't know in what order.

There was a pistol shot, and the *chavet* bottle blew apart in a shower of luminescent fluid.

Echosic heaved Romino up, shook him like a doll, and slammed him to the ground again – straight onto the heliograph box. It came apart even more completely than my *chavet* bottle had.

It was hard to decide which was potentially the most fatal.

CHAPTER TWENTY-FOUR

IT FELT LIKE TOTAL insanity broke out during the moments which followed.

I reached down and managed to pick up my pistol this time, holding it in one numb set of fingers. I cocked it with my free hand, ignoring all the protests from my arms and the growing cramp in my guts. I watched Romino, hoping he'd give me an excuse to shoot him.

Echosic grunted as Romino drove a knee into his groin. Even through all that padding, he'd found a vulnerable spot. The older man pulled away, face even more purple than Romino's, clutching himself and croaking. Romino staggered to his feet, crushing the half-destroyed box even more. He glanced down, his face twisted, and turned to lash a foot at Echosic's doubled-over form. The bigger man crashed to the ground, his legs giving way.

Kicking an older man, I thought. That'll do it. I raised my gun, already squeezing the trigger. Romino's head aligned itself perfectly around the sight on the end of the barrel.

Batrix chose that moment to come to life.

She straightened, almost as though waking from a refreshing nap. Radiance seemed to spill out of her. Romino stopped beating Echosic and gazed up in wonder; the old man looked as though he'd forgotten what pain meant; even I forgot about spreading Romino's brains all about the dreamworld's landscape.

"Yes! Oh, yes!" Romino took a pace towards Batrix, looking as though he wanted to embrace her.

I remembered what I was about to do to him and raised my pistol again. "One more step, Romino, and you don't get back!"

He froze, looking at me. I was some kind of peculiar specimen; a rabbit that had raised itself up on hind legs and spoken. "Don't be absurd, Scilli!"

"Absurd is this place, Romino. Absurd is your bizarre ambition. This gun is rather more prosaic, but not half as mundane as the lead ball aimed at your head."

"Pretty speech, Scilli. You definitely missed your vocation." He took another step. I began to squeeze the trigger again.

"Stop this! Now!"

It was Batrix speaking, but not her voice. Nor even the voice of anything vaguely human. It was the voice of the sky, as if all the planets had spoken together: their arrogance, their timbre.

Maybe it was the voice of the Moon.

Romino reacted first. Maybe he was half-prepared for it. "Batrix! You did it! You did it for me!" He stepped closer. I still wanted to blow his brains out, but I lowered my gun. I needed to see what Batrix's next actions were. If the power, or whatever it was, had corrupted her – sent her as mad as Romino – it wouldn't matter a damn what I did.

"How does it feel? Is it painful, agonising? Is it blissful?"

"Romino. What have you done to me?" She raised her hands and turned them over slowly. I got the impression she was inspecting every pore.

"Don't worry. It's the power, just the power. You'll get used to it." He kept edging closer to the radiant figure.

"Stay back." Batrix turned her face full on to him. I couldn't see her eyes, but I didn't need to. I could imagine how they were flaring behind her eyeglasses. "Keep your distance, or I cannot answer for the consequences."

Romino skipped back a little, but the overconfident smile never left his face. "Yes. Yes. Quite right. We don't know the effect of such power on a human—"

"The warning was not due to concerns for your wellbeing." Batrix turned to me. Her face was as devoid of expression as ever, but I'd heard the undertone in her voice, or whosever voice it was: *And because I am not human, we do not care whatever the effect may be.* "Scilli?"

"Batrix. Are you alright?"

"That is a question I can no longer answer, Scilli. I do not understand the feelings that threaten to overwhelm me..."

"Naturally!" crowed Romino. "You are no longer human. Or heteromorph. You are beyond mortal!"

"I will not tell you again, Romino."

He went very quiet and very white. The uncertainty was back in his darting eyes. I bet this wasn't going the way he'd imagined. In his mind, he'd been the one in charge, the one giving orders. He'd never thought the creature he'd have a hand in forging could have a mind of her own.

Batrix stepped closer to the crouching Echosic. She dropped to her haunches at his side, running a long, elegant hand over his face. She was something divine, deigning to concern herself with human suffering. "*Gosigné* Echosic? Can you hear me?"

He nodded, quite beyond talk, for one reason or another.

"Good." She stood again and gazed at the sky. I hadn't noticed – drenched in the light first from the moonstone, and now Batrix – how dark it was growing. Beyond the light cast from her body, I couldn't see a thing.

"We can't return," I said, wondering if I was telling her something she knew perfectly well. "Romino's box was the..." My voice trailed off stupidly. I don't think she was listening to a word.

"Petran Steganesh is nearby," she said.

I looked around, expecting him to be wandering into the light. All I could see was the stark black and white landscape caught in her flame. "How can you tell?" Despite the question, I don't think I wanted an answer.

"Here, everywhere is nearby." Which wasn't the answer I'd expected; I'm not even sure it was an answer. Not to any question I'd heard, anyway.

Then he was lying at my feet, from nowhere, and there was no question that he was dying. Even in the absolute contrast of the Batrix-light, his face looked grey and sunken. I can't say I felt particularly bad about it. I was hurting, too.

I dropped to my knees. His eyes, half-open, fluttered a little, and he tilted his face more in my direction. Somewhere, under his ridiculous moustache, a smile loitered.

"Someone beat me to it, Petran?"

"Had the last laugh, didn't you, Wil?" he breathed. "It's always the women."

"Where is she, Petran?"

He tried to shrug but ended up wracked by coughing. "Here..." he gasped, once the fit had passed. His throat was clogged with phlegm.

I looked around; there was only Batrix. Even Echosic and Romino had vanished. No, we were the ones who'd vanished. We were no longer at the bottom of some vast, shallow crater, but in a tiny, windowless room. A cell, almost. The eroded bricks stood out in harsh relief. I gazed back down at Steganesh.

"There's no one else about, Petran."

"Don't be so ... damn literal...!" He half-rose, but the effort left him white and shaking. "Echosic must have taught you something by now..." His failing voice was so quiet I could barely hear him.

I tried to think back to what the old man had said, but nothing came. Nothing connected.

Then I glanced up at Batrix, still motionless and serene, a beacon to a lost man. She'd said Steganesh was near, and that in this place everywhere was near. And during his half-ravings, Echosic had been muttering something about somewhere being continuous with everywhere else.

The dream-world! It was separate from the place I knew as real, but it was just as much a part of the waking world as I was. We created the dream-world, formed its images, its symbols. Which meant what? That there was no end to the living world, no beginning to the dream-realm? They merged, overlapped.

I'd already seen that, and the significance hadn't struck home. The landscape that was identical to Qaijente back home, except for the lake. Overlap. A real landscape aped by the dream-world.

Was that what Steganesh meant? Was this cell also an echo of a place in the real world? Was that where Sotha Ponac had gone? And if so, how had she managed it?

"Petran!" I raised his head – despite the throb in my arms – just about stopping myself from shaking it. He wasn't going to die on me yet! "Sotha Ponac! How did she return? Tell me!"

His eyes barely opened. He looked up at me with very little understanding. "She isn't what you think, Will," he mumbled. "She's on to you ... knows what you are..."

I wasn't sure I liked the sound of that. "What does she know, Petran?"

"You're a spy ... Yosec's little sneak... She's probably going to tell, y'know..."

"Yosec's dead, Petran."

"No... No... I saw... just th'other day... He was..." His eyes slipped shut again, but he was still breathing. Just.

He wasn't talking about Sotha Ponac, of course. It was the other one – Erane Reidl. The girl he'd nearly killed me over, before changing his mind.

Except... If I understood him, if he was telling the truth – and wasn't he too delirious not to be? – Erane was a Chrysomancer after all. A loyal one, as far as I remember.

Not that it meant anything. As far as anyone in the seminary, apart from Yosec, was concerned, I was loyal, too...

But if she'd known – or simply guessed – Erane would have done something about it. Something decisive. Something permanent.

Had I gotten it all wrong, years ago? Simply assumed it had been Petran, just because I'd preferred to believe it? The attempt had all of his trademarks, after all, but the reversal was drastic, even by Petran's standards. Had she tried to kill me, using methods they'd learned together, but Petran found out in time, and saved me.

Twelve years, and I'd consistently hated the man who'd saved my life.

This time, I did shake him awake. I wasn't in the mood for delicacy. "Petran! What happened to Erane? Where is she now?"

His eyes fluttered but didn't open. He smiled though – his best, most self-satisfied grin. "Hopeless with women ... Wil..." He raised a hand and wiggled his fingers. It fell back to the ground after barely five seconds, even that had been too much for him. "Dance..." he croaked.

A marionette! Dancing to a women's fingers on my strings! It wasn't an attractive comparison.

"What happened to Erane, Petran!"

"What ... you think...?"

"You killed her?" It made me felt sick and hollow just to think it, no matter that she may well have deserved it. She was a beautiful girl, and I'd loved her. I guess I still did. Don't they say you never stop loving your first?

"Watch her ... Wil... She's good... Very good... Don't know where she learned..." He flopped again. I kept holding up his head, ignoring the screaming ache in my hand and arm. Eventually I realised he wasn't going to come round again. Not this time.

I lowered his head gently to the ground and stood. Petran Steganesh was finally dead. A day ago, I would have been elated. Now, I didn't seem able to feel anything.

"A stiletto to the base of the skull," I heard Batrix saying from somewhere far away. "Hastily done. He should have died instantly."

"Would you have preferred that he had?"

She tilted her head on one side. "I expressed no preference, Scilli. But the method of execution would normally result in instant death. That Steganesh lived so long is testimony to a certain carelessness."

"Sotha Ponac didn't strike me as the kind to get careless. Maybe she was distracted."

"Indeed." The walls weren't around us anymore. Echosic and Romino were back exactly where we'd left them. Neither looked particularly surprised to see us.

I had an uneasy feeling neither Batrix nor I had been away at all. At least, not as far as the other two were concerned.

"How do you do that?" I muttered.

She shook her head. "I just do." If I hadn't known better, I'd have said she was overawed.

I needed something to occupy my mind. I reached Romino in three strides and caught him by the lapels. "The time has come, my friend, for a friendly chat."

He tried to wrench my hands free, but the discomfort of sprained arms didn't bother me anymore. I released one hand, fisted it, and drove it as hard as I could into his stomach. It hurt like hell, but I'm betting it hurt him a damned sight more.

"Let's try again, Romino! You didn't kill Ecozar or try to shoot me. Am I right?"

"Go to—"

I hit him again before he said anything that might annoy me.

"I'm suffering *chavet* withdrawal, Romino. Soon enough it's going to get very unpleasant for me." His eyes flickered. A vicious form of hope was about to kindle inside his greedy heart. I slapped his face. "Not soon enough for you, my friend. Right now, it's just making me very, very irritable. Now, try another answer."

"No. Of course I didn't. Why should I want to kill Rhys? I needed as many alive as I could. Although I'm beginning to wish whoever did shoot you had made a better show of it!"

"They were an even worse shot than you think." I was convinced by now it had been Petran, looking out for me yet again. It was Sotha he'd been aiming at, but his skills were Chrysomantic, not with guns. He'd been my guardian angel all along, and I'd just wanted to see him dead. Even his ridiculous pretence that he was responsible for the passage through the various levels of this dream-world... Even then he was trying to help me, put the real culprit off balance long enough for me to...

If only he'd said something...

I hit Romino again, just for the hell of it. "Then, what was the point of the chimeras and the worm?"

He dragged in a ragged breath. I don't think he liked me hitting him; I don't think he liked me at all, anymore.

"Nothing to do with me, Scilli... I just thought they were manifestations of the dream-world... Or something that Spook magicked up..."

Petran had admitted to that, sure enough, at the same time he'd admitted to doing exactly what Romino had been doing. "I don't know if I should believe you, Romino. The people on this trek seem to be having awful problems with the truth."

"It's the truth! I wanted everyone alive! To test out against the power!"

"Don't let anyone ever say you've no heart, Romino."

"All I did was bring us here!" He was beginning to babble, either with fear, or he thought he could see a way out. I let him think it. "The creatures, Rhys's death, the Grif Ditya imago – all of these were beyond my control. I had nothing to do with them!"

I'd had enough of his self-justifications. I punched him twice more: one to the gut, then to the jaw. It couldn't hurt my hands anymore.

He collapsed like a flag on a calm day.

Echosic was standing barely an arm's length away, watching me. He'd made no attempt to stop me beating his protégé. Not that he could have. The look on his face was defeat. He'd been betrayed too often over the last few days and was close to giving up.

"He used me," he croaked. "By heaven, sir! He used me!"

"I don't think heaven had much to do with it." I half-turned. Batrix was still standing motionless, her stance hadn't changed. "But that's it, isn't? We're stuck here. Unless you can shift us all out of here like you did a moment back."

There was a pause, and I honestly believe she was trying. "I cannot," she said eventually.

"So we're trapped, just as surely as those poor souls Romino destroyed with his tinkering?"

"Perhaps not."

I felt my pulse quicken. "Don't make jokes, Batrix. Not ones like that..."

"I was not joking. I believe there is a way we can return to our own world."

"Then what is it, madam?" Something like animation was seeping back into Echosic's face.

"That, I do not know."

I started to get angry once more. "Stop playing games, Batrix!"

"No game!" She raised her hands and looked at them again, as though they were something entirely new to her. "I feel – instinctively – that I can remove us from this place, but I do not know what to do. I cannot think."

I stepped forward, urgently. "Then go with the instincts! Please! Just do whatever they say."

She looked at me; plaintively, I thought. "I have never followed my instincts before, Scilli. I do not think I know how to."

I started waving my own hands about. "Don't think – react! Toss all that self-control to one side and do what your heart tells you!"

"Easy for you to say, Scilli."

"And for you to do! Forget you're Batrix the heteromorph, pretend you're human. Do something irrational."

"Madam, I implore you," Echosic joined in. "For all our sakes, if there's something you can do, then by heaven do it!"

Her face swung back and forth between us. Even behind the masking eyeglasses, I could see her uncertainty. The godlike radiance spilling out couldn't disguise the frightened mortal underneath. All her life, the heteromorph must have rigidly followed only what her reason told her was correct. Never had a hunch, never made a wild guess, never shut her eyes and jumped in with both feet. Now, the two of us were asking her to do something she didn't – couldn't – understand: act in blind, simple faith.

And worse, perform magic. The one thing in the world that Batrix hated above all else.

It was like someone asking me to jump off a cliff and fly.

"Please," I said, softly. I was suddenly aware that I was soaked in sweat. Was it an effect of withdrawal, or simple fear? "I'll beg, if you like. I wouldn't ask if it wasn't so damned important—"

"I am aware of the importance!"

"Then try. That's all I'm asking. I know how you feel, and what I'm asking of you—"

"I very much doubt you know how I feel, Scilli. How could you?"

She turned away. I stepped back, certain that was it. Fear and prejudice had won; we were stuck here.

And at the same moment, out of the corner of my eye, I saw Echosic raising something. I began to turn, and realised he'd picked up Romino's pistol. I stepped forward. It had occurred to me that he was going to shoot the younger man, and some random, generous impulse wanted me to stop him.

It took me much too long to realise that he wasn't aiming at Romino, that the muzzle was pointing straight at Batrix's back. He fired before I could stop him.

CHAPTER TWENTY-FIVE

I BEGAN TO SHOUT, to call a warning, alert Batrix, even though I knew it was too late. With more primitive pistols using flint and loose gunpowder, there'd be a hang fire – a moment before the lit priming powder fired the loaded barrel. No more, thanks to the late but ingenious Professor Alva. Primer caps are as near as dammit instantaneous. No one can duck a bullet.

Or so I thought. Looking back, I don't know whether it's my faulty memory, the way events seem to slow down at moments of stress, or if Batrix really did stretch time. In that place, I guess anything's possible; especially adding in the power that possessed the heteromorph.

I swear I saw the bullet as it left the barrel amid smoke and flame. It seemed to stretch as it pierced the air between the gun and Batrix. I thought I could have reached it, kicked it aside, but if the bullet was moving slowly, I couldn't move at all. I was nothing more than a spectator.

Curiously, my strongest memory is of Romino's face, clearly visible a few feet away; he was consumed with fear. Not for Batrix, obviously, but for the possible collapse of his plans now he was so close.

Then Batrix was no longer there. As I'd been watching Romino's selfish despair, she'd simple blinked out of existence. The bullet kept on going, through the space that wasn't Batrix any longer, and off into the darkness.

Echosic yelped in fright. Batrix was now standing behind him, as abruptly as her vanishing trick. Her brilliant aura flared even brighter, and the gun sagged and dripped as though it were melting fat. Echosic dropped the gun with a scream and fell to his knees, nursing his hand. It must have been as hot as it looked.

Then Batrix spread her arms around the crouching figure, her aura flaring out like wings of light. Time clicked back into its normal pace.

"No!" I leapt towards them. I didn't know what Batrix intended, but it didn't look good for Echosic. She simply saw him as a threat, one to be dealt with as quickly and easily as possible. The thing possessing her was just a bit too amoral for my taste. "Don't!"

She looked up at me, but she remained stooped over Echosic like a luminous raptor. Her expression challenged me to give one good reason why she should let Echosic live.

"Batrix! Leave him! He's an old man. He's frightened!"

Weren't we all? The light behind her eyeglasses was making them glow like blue lamps. Romino must have been as insane as he'd acted if he believed he could control this force, once released.

"He tried to kill me." As though she was commenting on the sky being blue.

"With a gun? Is that a serious threat to you?"

She backed away, lowering her arms. The wings of light vanished. Echosic scrabbled away as fast as his bulk and fitness allowed.

"Perhaps you are right."

"Come on, Batrix! I know you're in there somewhere. Speak to me. Don't let it submerge you!"

She straightened. The pose seemed less threatening, somehow. I allowed myself to believe it was more the rigid, stiff-backed stance I knew so well.

"Batrix ... please..."

"Scilli." That was her; I was sure of it. "I think we are all in great danger..."

"Still the master of understatement..."

She waved an impatient hand. "No time for your usual protective levity, Scilli! The moonstone – the entire dream-world – is inside me! I *am* this realm. It has the power each generation of humanity has given to it. Anything the human mind can conceive – has conceived – the potential rests in me..."

"Yes. You are a god, Batrix!" Romino was up and raving again. "Let me..."

She just looked at him, but it was sufficient. There was power and threat enough to tilt worlds in that glance. Romino shrank back; I think it was finally occurring to him what he'd unleashed.

Batrix's eyes returned to me, and she continued as though Romino didn't exit, hadn't interrupted. "...but it is more than a little insane, I think. Not only dreams of the strong and wholesome have taken root here: there is greed, murder, rapine – every form of monomania. I can feel the most repulsive thoughts, the earnest wishes of the world's most diseased minds, crawling like worms over my senses. Before long, Wil, I shall be as insane as it is..."

I saw the tears running slowly down her cheeks. I couldn't be sure if they sparkled in her cast light or glowed with their own.

"Batrix, you must get us out of here. If you have all that power, you can take us back…"

"…and release this on our world?"

I shut up instantly. I hadn't thought of that. I was too eager to get home. And the torment in her voice was enough to silence anyone. I renewed my vow to kill Romino, whether we got out of the bizarre realm or not. He was going to suffer.

Another arctic spasm knotted my guts, reminding me that I might not have the time after all.

"There must be a way!" I didn't sound too convincing, even to me. "If Romino's right, you're pretty much a god. Doesn't that give you some kind of omnipotence?"

For an instant, her eyes flashed disconcertingly. Her hands flexed, too much like talons for my peace of mind. Then she was in control again.

"I do not believe in gods."

I almost laughed. "And the Archimandrite doesn't believe in magic! Batrix, this isn't Ramini. Human laws don't count here. An entire House of senators couldn't legislate you out of existence. What you … what we all prefer to think, doesn't matter a damn. We're all out of our depth, here!"

"Perhaps you are, sir," Echosic rasped in my ear.

I glanced at him. His face wasn't pleasant – it looked too much like a week-old corpse's – and his eyes were sunken, but he was standing, and a sight more upright than I was.

"But I am at home here. In part at least, by heaven. Yes, by heaven, sir!"

I'd forgotten he was a shaman. Or had been, before a war that really wasn't his affair had stolen half his voice.

"Do you think you can help?"

He grunted a sort of laugh. "It's all continuous, sir. Thought and action, dream and reality. Where does one end and the next begin, eh? Can you tell me, eh? You were taught by wizards, weren't you?"

"Chrysomancers are peculiarly rational sorcerers, Echosic. They believed only in what they could achieve with their little bits of stone."

"Such a limited creed!"

"If you can do something, *gosigné*, I suggest you do it now." I took another look at Batrix, and it was obvious the power was in the ascendancy again. Her face was dominated by the cold light from her eyes, her stance becoming gradually more predatory.

Echosic steadied himself with a hand on my shoulder and called out. "Lieutenant-Commander Batrix!"

Her head swooped in his direction, shoulders hunching. He'd got her attention – I just hoped it was the right kind.

"Listen to me, Commander. You can fight it, you can win. But you will have to trust me." His voice had taken on a peculiar crooning. Somehow, it drifted past his ruined throat smoothly, easily. "You have to learn to accept what you are."

Batrix shuddered. "And what am I, *Gosigné* Echosic?"

"You are flesh and blood, just as I. Just as your friend, Scilli. But we do not belong here. This world must only be visited by the dreaming soul – a spirit shaped from the same dream-stuff that forms this realm. Our coming here has upset a delicate balance, it has allowed things that should never touch to make intimate contact..."

"Of that I am fully aware!" I saw the predatory thing slip back over her personality for a moment.

"You must separate again. This realm must never be allowed to enter the world of the flesh..."

"You begin to bore me, Chato Echosic. There will be no more talk of separation."

"Let me help you, Batrix. I know the secrets of dividing body and spirit to voyage the astral seas..."

"You failed in that many years ago, old man! You no longer have the skill." Batrix's personality seemed to be completely submerged. The white-haired goddess was becoming something much more threatening.

"We shall see, eh?" Echosic launched himself forward, using my shoulder as a spring-board. He hobbled closer to the demonic figure that had been Batrix just a short while ago. I thought he looked like a man with an egg-spoon approaching a landslide.

Tall as he was, when Echosic was within a few paces of Batrix, it was still as though she was stooping to look him in the eye. One of her hands drifted close to his face, almost caressing the old skin.

"You must believe, Batrix!" His crooning took on an insistent edge. "Your atheism is its best weapon – it has no barriers of faith to overcome. You simply refusing to acknowledge its existence is no defence. Better to refuse to believe in the reality of a cannonball aimed at your head."

"You talk well, old man. I will give you that. But I no longer have time for talk. I must take my leave of you." She began to draw back.

Echosic snatched one of her hands between his own. Light spilled between his fingers like radiant liquid. "Batrix! I am speaking to the heteromorph known as Batrix!" His voice was calm and powerful, no longer the coarse rasp, but something underlying it told me how much agony he was having to endure, clasping Batrix's bright hand.

"Batrix," asserted the bright creature, its voice massive.

Echosic shook his head. "Batrix! Here's my hand – take it!"

There was a pulse, and the light ceased dripping from Echosic's hands. I clearly heard his gasp of relief.

"*Gosigné* Echosic," Batrix said. She sounded lost, terrified. "It has almost overwhelmed me…"

"Courage, Commander." He was comfort personified: his voice soothing, caressing. "Consider it a bad dream, one that shall be soon over…"

"I do not dream…"

"All the better. There will be no danger of confusing your dreaming soul with the thing attempting possession. Come. Take my hands in both of yours…"

She clasped her other hand over his.

"Now, Batrix, we can only attempt this once. To escape this realm you must use the power, but at the same time you will have to eject it. Do you understand?"

There was a pause. "I understand, *Gosigné* Echosic. But I fail to see how we can accomplish it."

"Leave that to me. All I will say to you is this: the power cannot be simply cast off, like a cloak. It will have to go somewhere."

"Into another?"

"Quite so."

Slow I might be, but I worked out what they were saying only too quickly: Echosic was offering himself as the host. And in all likelihood, shaman or not, he stood no more chance of surviving than his wife, or any of the other damned remnants that haunted this world.

"Echosic! Don't! Not this way!"

I doubt either heard me, they were wrapped in their own struggle.

I saw Romino to my left, watching events as avidly as I. His expression torn somewhere between fury and relief. Furious, that he might be about to lose his life's work. Relieved, that it wasn't going to destroy him after all.

I moved closer. I didn't want him changing his mind at the last moment and trying to interfere.

The spasm chose that moment to hit hard. I clutched at my side, hugging the cramp, and stumbled. When I could stand upright again, Romino had disappeared.

Batrix was the only light in the world. Beyond her was total blackness. It didn't take much imagination to believe the entire realm had been absorbed inside her transmorphed frame.

Which begged the question: where exactly had Romino gotten to?

I cocked my repeater and began to search inside the sphere of light cast by Batrix. The cramps were getting worse, and I was finding it harder to concentrate. My vision seemed to be suffering, too; the light was flickering slightly, almost in time to my pulse.

I saw Romino suddenly, dodging in and out of the illuminated area. I guess he was trying to get around without being seen. But to what purpose, I couldn't guess. His hands were empty: no gun, no scrap of parchment. But why try to fathom the behaviour of a madman? And, he clearly was mad, although not in the way he'd tried to pretend earlier.

I ran at him. Or rather, I limped towards him as fast as I could. He froze, watching me. Maybe he couldn't believe what was coming at him.

I didn't try to grab him or fire a shot – my arms still ached too much to be trustworthy. I just swung my pistol as hard as I could. The barrel whipped across his face, and he fell back with a cry. Before he vanished into the absolute darkness beyond, I saw blood spray from a shattered nose.

I was going to dive after him, follow him into the blackness, but my eyesight seemed to deteriorate even further. Flashes of light danced across my vision: throbbing white, yellow and purple. A drumming began in my skull, matching each pulse. Somewhere, a huge horse was galloping across a plain. The pain in my guts flared to an agonising pit of acid. I know that I dropped to my knees.

Then everything came apart in jagged, needle-sharp shards of colour, and I fell down through a hole in the world.

CHAPTER TWENTY-SIX

I FELL FOR AN eternity, through corridors of light. Stars blossomed in the distance, rushed forward, spiralling off their contents into smaller and smaller patterns. Crystalline shafts flew past me like huge javelins. I wondered what it would be like to be impaled by one.

Then the swirling chaos resolved itself. I was on a featureless plain, in the middle of a battle that stretched to all four horizons. Men in every conceivable form of armour or uniform killed or defended themselves, endlessly. A colossal, three-faced figure appeared over one horizon, sweeping the ground with a sword the length of a Wael-Edra street. It strode over me, scything through the tight-packed mass of humanity. Within moments, it had vanished beyond the opposite horizon, leaving a wide swathe of harvested dead in its wake.

The Sun rose: a glowing, opalescent stone that looked like a spectre of the real star. Night's shadow fell back, and as each warrior was touched by the Sun's cold rays, they collapsed to dust. By the time the palely glowing orb was at its zenith, the plain was covered in nothing but fine, wind-borne powder.

And I realised what was really happening: I was still in Doctor Bezdichnij's surgery, having my new face moulded. Everything I'd experienced was nothing more than a dream, continuing on from the one that began as I'd sunk into his sorcerous trance. It was a comforting thought.

Then everything vanished in a painful jolt. I opened my eyes to find myself staring up at a luminously perfect blue sky. Nothing marred it. I found the Sun that hung in this wonderful sky: it was harsh, bright, and very hot. Familiar.

A withdrawal cramp twisted my guts in icy talons, forcing me into a disappointing change of heart. This was no dream.

I dragged myself into something like a sitting position. All around was desert and sculpted, blood-red buttes, contrasting sharply against the blue of the sky. And a lake, a vast lake that mirrored the sky and sprouted vertical-sided stone buttes of its own.

Qaijente. The real one. Or so I thought, anyway. And that was the lake, the holy lake of the Anesicci: Grémasicci Boya.

Which meant Batrix had gotten us back.

There was only one thing wrong: I was looking down towards the lake, and too many of the huge rock pillars around me rose to eye level, which meant I was actually on top of one of the buttes. A big one, yards across the top, and a hell of a long way to the bottom. I didn't feel like peering over the edge to check exactly how far.

I scrabbled to my feet, ignoring all the various pains that selfishly demanded my attention. I was back, but what about Batrix? And Romino and Echosic?

I saw something white flashing in the brilliant sunlight, just a few feet away. Breaking into a lop-sided run, I hobbled towards it as fast as the cramps allowed. It was Batrix, her hair, still silver-white, fanning across the red sand. She was sprawled in an uncomfortable-looking, worryingly twisted, pose.

I dropped down beside her, trying not to wince at my own discomfort or the rigid paleness of her face. I slid an arm under her head and raised it. Feeling her neck, I found a pulse: weak, erratic, but definitely there. She'd survived.

Her eyes flickered, then twitched open. Her irises were green, the luminous, unearthly green of a Full Moon. And it occurred to me she'd lost her ever-present, blue-tinted eyeglasses. I looked all around and spotted them only a few paces away. I'd almost crushed them underfoot on my way over.

"Scilli?" Her voice was harsh yet timid. She licked bloodless lips and tried again. "Did I succeed?"

"Seems like it. The two of us, anyway."

She struggled to sit upright. I tried to help, but it was an awkward and fumbling attempt, and she shrank away from my touch. I could take a hint. "Echosic? Is he not with you?"

"Last I saw, he was holding your hands…" I could hardly say he was offering himself as a sacrifice. Later, maybe.

"We came through together…" She got to her feet, staggering slightly. She brushed a hand across her eyes. "My spectacles?"

"Here." I placed them in her free hand. She slipped them on and instantly seemed to stand up straighter, taller; arms folded in the small of her back. Even in her ripped, dirtied, and ill-fitting tunic, she was, once more, every inch a Bureau officer.

"There." She pointed towards what looked worryingly like the edge of the drop down.

Shielding my eyes against the glare, I could just make out a dark hump. A human shape? Maybe. "You've got damn good eyesight," I muttered.

I started towards it tentatively. If it were Echosic, and he was perched on the rim of the butte's top, I wasn't eager to be squatting right next to him. Batrix overtook me, her longer legs eating up the distance. By the time I reached them, she was already checking the unconscious shape of Chato Echosic for life. She leaned back, apparently satisfied.

"He is not well, but he still lives."

I eased myself down next to her, concentrating on Echosic. Anything but look at the great load of nothing yawning right beside him. He was a deathly colour, with ugly dark patches under his sagging eyes, but he was certainly breathing.

"But I thought he—" I started before thinking what I was saying.

"You thought he was going to channel the power into his own body, thereby destroying himself," she finished for me.

"Something like that."

"I believe that was his intention. He saw no other way to solve the problem. But there was another solution."

"Romino?" I looked around, but my eyes obviously weren't as sharp as Batrix's. I couldn't see any hint of him.

"As you so accurately pointed out, Scilli, I was godlike." There was an unhealthy serving of self-loathing in her tone. "There were certain things I was able to do."

"You switched that power into Romino?"

"Echosic's own shamanic talents helped me separate myself from the power that possessed me. At the same time, I threw that power at the gate between the worlds, allowing it to reflect back and consume Gen Romino..."

He'd got what he'd wanted after all. I had to admit, it had a certain irony to it.

Batrix's perfect lips were twisting into ugly shapes. I couldn't imagine what was hurting most: the memory of what she'd almost become – the antithesis of her deepest beliefs – or what she'd done to Romino to escape that lousy fate.

"It's over now," I said quietly. "Romino started it. Now he's paid. Perfectly, I'd say. Just tell yourself everything that happened over there wasn't real."

She stood upright, rigid, shoulders squared. She looked down at me through opaque lenses, her face all calm, smooth planes. "I am sorry, Scilli, I do not understand."

I sighed and nodded to myself. I'd let it go.

"What is that?" she was saying.

I glanced up. Batrix was pointing back towards the centre of the butte. Thankful it wasn't anything beyond the edge or below us, I stood, turning to face what she was gesturing towards.

There was a stone ruin growing almost organically from the red rock. It was so weathered and smoothed by the scouring wind that I couldn't tell if it had been carved from one hunk of rock or assembled from brick and stone. Easy to overlook when you're panicking about how far up you are.

The ruin appeared to be only one storey, but anything above the first level could have fallen decades – centuries – ago. There were several tiny windows, all set high up. For no obvious reason, it reminded me of a gaol.

"Who'd put one up here, though?" I muttered.

"One of what?" Batrix asked.

"Prison," I answered, not looking back at her. I wouldn't do that again until we were many more paces closer to the ruin. "It reminds me of one. But why would anyone build one up here? So high? And how would anyone reach it in the first place?"

"Ordinary humans would never manage it, certainly," she said, voice thoughtful.

"But wizards could..."

She didn't reply. Instead, Batrix began walking towards the eroded ruin. Somehow – maybe it was the assurance with which she moved – I had the feeling that she wasn't surprised by the stone hut.

I forced myself to look back at Echosic. He didn't look good. Even if he didn't fade off into death soon, he looked as though he could topple over the edge into the lake far below. I didn't want that responsibility. But I didn't want to leave Batrix to wander blindly into some forgotten prison in the sky either, no matter how much she wasn't telling me.

I knelt at Echosic's side, pretending the void beckoning just beyond him wasn't there. He stirred faintly, his eyelids quivering.

"Echosic!" I muttered, putting an arm around his shoulders. A frigid cramp rattled my own body in sympathy. We'd both shake ourselves over the edge at this rate.

"Scilli?" His voice held a note of disbelief. I tried not to take it personally. "Are we free?"

"We're back, Echosic. Batrix did it. And she paid back Romino at the same time."

"By heaven," he rasped, his voice coarser than ever. "She is a wonder, sir. That she is..."

"I won't argue." I glanced over my shoulder – Batrix was halfway to the ruin.

"Lift me up, Bureau man." His eyes just about opened, and a feeble hand groped for my arm. "I want to see!"

I raised him into a slouched sitting position. Between his frailty, my touches of cramp and still sore arms, it wasn't too much like moving a mountain.

He sighed. I suppose his eyes were open enough to appreciate the view. I didn't feel like checking. "Magnificent, sir. A marvel; a true marvel."

"If you say so."

"Thank you, Bureau man. And thank your unique friend for me, too."

"For what?"

"I'm here. Now I can die. Anej is waiting for me in the next world, and she was never a patient woman."

I'm sure I could feel him shrinking, growing slacker, under my fingers. They were still too numb to be certain, though.

"I like you, Bureau man. You're a trump, sir, a trump."

"I like you too, Echosic," I said, wondering if it was true. A moment later I realised it didn't matter if it was or not, he hadn't heard me.

I got to my feet, stepping away. His body stayed sitting on the edge of the rock, gazing blindly across his precious Grémasicci Boya. At least someone had died happy.

I didn't waste any more time. Checking quickly, it was obvious Batrix had reached the ruin and gone inside. I thought I was supposed to be the impulsive one.

I began to run across the hard butte-top. It rapidly turned into some kind of grotesque fast limp. A sharp pain was starting to gnaw persistently at my left side. The nearest to relief I could get left me twisting like some misshapen carnival freak. By the time I reached the ruin, I was shivering, soaked in greasy sweat, and half-bent to my left.

Not much of a hero.

There was a doorway on the far side of the pile. I found it after a quick circuit. With all of my instincts bellowing in outrage, I walked straight through it.

Inside, it was virtually lightless. Even after my eyes had adjusted to the blackness, there was little I could make out. What little sunlight got though the small high windows fell onto the dusty wall facing them in small, pale squares that weren't reflected.

It was a corridor, or hallway. That's about all I could make out. A blacker rectangle in the shadows at the far end hinted at another door. I'd come too far now to get nervous of the dark, so, feeling giddily reckless, I forged ahead.

It was a tiny room, about ten feet square, with a collapsed apology for a bed against one wall. Rusty chains lay across it, all but useless now, too corroded to hold anything. Another small excuse for a window, high up on the left, threw a single ray of light across the room, smoky with raised dust. There were two figures in the room, sketchily outlined by the meagre scattered light: Batrix and Sotha Ponac.

"Made it at last, Wil," came Sotha's voice. "Don't be shy. No one's going to hurt you; and I doubt your heteromorph colleague can be of much hindrance."

I stepped closer. Sotha and Batrix became clearer as I drew nearer. Batrix was standing to attention against the wall to my right, watching the other woman carefully. Or maybe it was the gun in Sotha's hand she was watching. It was an old one, a single shot flintlock, probably almost a century old, but it gleamed with the care someone had lavished on it. Old or not, it would still make a very large hole in anyone standing in the way of its lead slug.

Just to make things awkward, Sotha was also pointing the pistol's identical twin straight at my face.

CHAPTER TWENTY-SEVEN

THE SHIVERS WERE COMING with monotonous regularity now. I stared at the pistol-muzzle like a fool, periodically hugging myself and trying not to double up.

"How did you manage to escape?" I asked. It was all I could think of saying. "You're not—"

Sotha Ponac laughed. "A Chrysomancer? Certainly not, my dear, something much purer than those Spooks of yours. They're nothing better than alchemists, with their ludicrous attachment to their bits of stone."

"Not a shaman?"

"I see I'll have to answer your curiosity, Wil. You..." she waved one of the pistols at Batrix "...on the bed, there's a bag. Fetch it for me, will you?"

Batrix stiffened even more. For a moment, it seemed like she was going to be proud and stubborn, then she stepped carefully around Sotha and moved towards the collapsed bed. Sotha watched her briefly, then glanced back at me. "I'm sorry I missed the transformation. She's quite the stunner, isn't she."

"Romino thought so."

She cocked her head to one side; I don't know if she was consciously imitating such a typical Batrix gesture. "You must tell me what happened at some later time."

"You could have waited around to watch."

Her eyes glittered. "No, Wil, my dear, my time was precious." She was keeping part of her attention on Batrix, now at the bed. I could just make out her shadowy form stooping to retrieve something. As she straightened, I wondered if she'd just throw it, and hope Sotha didn't manage to shoot both of us. But after a considered pause that seemed to last forever, she walked back towards us, tossing a small draw-string bag lightly in one hand.

"I'll take it." To my confusion, Sotha lowered the gun trained on me and tucked it into the waist of her skirt. Then she held out her free hand toward Batrix. The heteromorph placed the bag she was carrying into the upturned palm and stepped away. The second pistol hadn't wavered; it might have been tethered to a spot somewhere between Batrix's eyes.

"Tell me, Scilli," Batrix said. "What are your views on the monarchy."

She'd thrown me again. One day I was going to get irritated by that. "What monarchy?" was all I managed to say.

"The old one, of course." If Batrix had meant to annoy Sotha with her question, it didn't seem to have worked. "The rightful heirs to the throne of Ramini."

I still felt as though I was missing something. "Maybe the history I was taught back in the seminary was biased, but I don't recall anyone ever mentioning Ramini being ruled by one King."

"Don't be obtuse, my dear." Sotha was loosening the strings of her purse. She pulled something out. "You recognise this, I think." She handed it me.

I gave an ill-timed shudder and almost dropped the tiny object, but I clamped my fist around it and held on until the spasm passed. Uncoiling my fingers I saw there was a small, milky-white stone nestling in my palm – one shot through with traceries of fine gold veins. A fragment of abaston. One old enough for all its crystalline edges to have been worn smooth, its entire surface polished. It was almost certainly exhausted. But cut into it, so sharp it might have been done yesterday, was a cameo. The profile of a king who'd been dead for centuries.

I'd seen one just like it before, several months earlier, among the ashes of a group of suspected anarchists in Scan Leroth: people who'd rather destroy themselves than be caught by the Bureau.

Or, a thought struck me, maybe they'd just transported themselves elsewhere, leaving a pile of convenient ash behind.

I handed the cameo back. "So you're with the *Plytath a'Pyndr*?"

Sotha laughed and dropped the fragment back in her purse. "Despite all appearances, you're still a product of the Republic, aren't you, Wil? There are other countries across the oceans you know, other forms of magic. Chrysomancy might have enjoyed a brief fashionable ascendancy, but that's all over. Its day has gone. It's time to return to the older, purer forms."

"Very pretty speech. Doesn't answer my question, does it?"

She pursed her lips. "No. I'm not involved with any Pyndrian secret society. For one thing, I'm not Pyndrian; for another, they don't allow women to join."

"But that profile is still of an old Pyndrian ruler."

"The *Plytath a'Pyndr* is one of the prime movers!" She sounded angry; I almost got the feeling I was supposed to know all this already. "But the stone is merely a badge, something the far-flung membership use to identify each other. As I said, there is more to the world than Ramini. History didn't start with the discovery of abaston over here."

"So the whole world's ganging up on poor little Ramini? Doesn't sound fair."

"Not Ramini. Just this pathetic idea of a republic. Now the Chrysomancers have lost control, there's no reason why rulership shouldn't return to where it belongs..."

"In the hands of royalty," supplied Batrix.

Sotha merely smiled. "Of course. There are enough members of the old aristocracy left – either fled abroad or ex-Chrysomancers themselves. Most of the body is in place. All that is required is the head."

"The King." Batrix again.

Another thought hit me. "Or maybe even Queen?"

Sotha laughed out loud at that. "You credit me with too much ambition, Wil. True enough, I am directly descended from the kings of Steatl; but not the closest to the throne."

A few things were finally beginning to fall into place. "Of course. Varghas of Steatl, who led the last combined assault against the Chrysomancers when it finally sank through their dense aristocratic skulls that the Spooks really were in a position to overthrow the old order. He came the closest to becoming a genuine High King of all the kingdoms..."

"And as such, his descendants would have a strong emotional – if not historical – hold on the hearts and minds of the people." Batrix didn't sound surprised; it was like she was quoting verbatim from some report she'd read.

"So, you somehow persuaded Rhys Ecozar to include you on the trek to Qaijente. Presumably, Petran Steganesh recognised you. It was him who shot me, but it you he was trying to hit, so you took the first chance to remove and kill him, banking on our mutual antagonism to lessen the chances of him passing on what he knew. Shame the tutors at Madrasaté didn't teach marksmanship along with magical skills – it would have saved so many lives. You also killed Ecozar, probably something you passed to him was laced with *kraich,* and just before the worm struck."

"Very astutely reasoned."

"Taking a risk, though. If the worm hadn't attacked at just that moment, Ecozar's sudden death would have looked even more suspicious."

"I admit that was fortuitous timing. I was ready with a tale of Rhys's poor health – his ailing heart, you know – to explain it, but fate smiled upon me."

"Not quite enough..."

"Yes, I didn't anticipate you recognising the signs of *kraich* poisoning. Steganesh wouldn't have bothered to check."

She was probably right there. "But I don't see why. Why here? What's so special about a chunk of rock sticking out of a lake in the middle of old Anesetl?"

"Blame your tutors again, Wil. Another piece of history they conveniently ignore. King Varghas wasn't killed in the Battle of Axsté, nor was he executed afterwards. The Archimandrite thought it amusing to spare his life, and imprison him instead."

I looked around the dark, crumbling room. "It was here? No

wonder the place looks like it's about to crumble. It must be centuries since Varghas died."

"He never died, Wil. That's the point. Sendivogius sentenced him to life imprisonment – a life that would never end, not through natural causes, anyway."

I thought of the bizarre dream-play I'd seen back in the citadel, where the King was fooled by the Archimandrite and imprisoned, chained to a rock. It made sense now. It wasn't some analogy – not in the purest sense – but a fanciful retelling of history. Sotha's mind must have supplied the images...

No, that couldn't be right. Sotha Ponac was in some other part of that unreal citadel. I had no reason to believe I'd witnessed the thoughts of someone elsewhere in that dream-world. But Batrix was with me. And Batrix hadn't acted surprised through any of these revelations.

"You knew all this," I said. "Risnek briefed you, but didn't see fit to tell me. Both of you knew all along that this wasn't just some Anesicci pilgrimage!"

Batrix had the grace to look uncomfortable. "It was necessary for you to remain in ignorance," she said through facial muscles that were almost immobile.

Sotha laughed again. "It certainly was, my dear! They were hardly likely to tell you the truth!"

I thought Batrix was about to say something extra, but her mouth tightened around the words, biting them back. Surely, there wasn't even more she was keeping back? Something she'd almost spilled by accident?

"So where is he, then?" I asked, looking around the grim cell. "This undying king?"

For the first time, something like uncertainty tainted Sotha's face. "I've not been able to find him," she said quietly. Obviously, this was an admission that left a bad taste in her mouth. "The chains suggest he may have been confined here once. But I have yet to search everywhere," she added, almost defiantly.

I glanced up at the tiny window that was supplying light so reluctantly. "Night's drawing in," I commented. "If you want to search properly, I'd get on with it."

I didn't really know if it was growing darker, I was just guessing, comparing how dim it seemed to have gone since we'd come inside. Sotha acted convinced, though. She nodded rapidly and waved her pistol at Batrix.

"Come, all of us." She glanced at me – almost shyly, I thought – and bobbed her head again. "Will you lead?"

"Why not?" Arranging my stiff arms as casually as I could, I sauntered out through the cell door. Or as close to a saunter the constant aches and shivers would allow. I didn't exactly want to curl up and die – not just yet – but hugging myself and whimpering pitifully felt like such a good idea at the time. So did being violently sick. Sadly, neither of them was an option.

I turned right. It was as good a direction as any. I had no idea where I was going anyway, or what to look for. How would an undead king who'd been wasting his time on this rock for centuries appear? Pretty desiccated by now, I thought.

"What's he look like..." I called over my shoulder "...your king?"

"Very funny," replied Sotha. The enigmatic touch.

"I do my best. It's all in the timing."

I wasn't imagining it: the light was definitely going. From dim to inky. Pretty soon I'd be falling over my own feet.

"You wouldn't happen to have a torch, I suppose?" I asked.

"We won't need one." Her tone puzzled me. I was irritating her with all the questions, but for some reason she was holding her annoyance back, burying it under what sounded almost like deference. And I wasn't the one being covered by a gun. For the same reason? Was I supposed to be trustworthy?

I was going to ask another question, just for the hell of it, when the smell hit me. It was absolutely rank: the stench of a thousand unwashed bodies wallowing in their own excrement. By comparison, Scan Leroth's public dock-front water closets seemed like rosewater.

"Well, we've certainly found something," I mumbled around a hand vainly trying to screen my mouth and nose. The stench had one thing going for it: it took my mind off *chavet* withdrawal.

Sotha's face was a picture of disgust. "This isn't right," she muttered. I got the impression she was trying to talk without breathing.

"It isn't healthy, either," I added. "Are you sure this king of yours isn't dead? Maybe Sendivogius let him live but forgot to halt the natural process of aging." That was a pretty image, and just the sort of thing the Archimandrite would think of as funny. The moment the words were out, I was wishing I hadn't considered it.

"Are you both so certain this smell has any connection with your mythical ruler?" Batrix was being typically pedantic. I couldn't argue, but judging by the expression on Sotha's face, she dearly wanted to.

"Of course, you're right," she said, not sounding like she agreed at all. "Some dead animal, no doubt..."

I tried pinching my nose. "Then it's either a very big bird or a mastodon with remarkable climbing skills."

"Be quiet!" Sotha's respectful attitude towards me was showing signs of strain. But I didn't feel like easing up. It isn't in my nature.

"Perhaps we should look," suggested Batrix. "I think it will prove more fruitful than standing here arguing."

Sotha composed herself with an effort. I think she would have taken a deep, calming breath, if the air hadn't been so foul. "You're right again, heteromorph. Wil. If you'd be so kind…"

I was the guide again, and this time I had something to follow. Unfortunately, I was growing used to the stench, vile though it was, and the shivers were back. I decided I was feeling miserable.

I made my way down a corridor that wasn't quite as black as my original coat. There was a door at the end, thrown into outline by the fading light leaking around it. It was open, just a crack. And the smell was most definitely coming from behind it.

"Odd place for a sewer."

I stepped closer, only too aware of Batrix and Sotha immediately behind me. I heard a rustle: Sotha drawing her second pistol. She'd be safe then, with two guns, and me going in first.

Then I felt a wooden grip pushed into my palm. My fingers closed limply around it, just before a spasm tried to shake the pistol loose. I was growing more intrigued by the moment.

"Expecting trouble?"

"Always."

"Then you'll forgive me not being a gentleman…" Clutching the pistol as tightly as I could – which wasn't very – I shoved the door wide with my shoulder.

Inside was lit by the last rays of the setting Sun. By some freakish alignment, the cell was aflame with red sunlight. It was probably the only light it got all day, and although it gave everything the feel of an apocalyptic painting, it also pinpointed the figure cowering in the far corner.

It was filthy, its clothing nothing but soiled rags that covered nothing. It was huddled in a puddle of its own waste. It was male, and quite clearly insane.

And the face it tried to shield from me was identical to the one good Doctor Bezdichnij had given me back at his surgery in Wael Edra.

CHAPTER TWENTY-EIGHT

EVERYTHING FELL INTO PLACE. Maybe if I hadn't been feeling so sorry for myself, I would have worked it out earlier.

No wonder Petran had commented about my features: pale of face and with bright red hair. Features that weren't exactly designed to blend in and remain unremarked; ones that, once Sotha Ponac had seen them, helped her decide Rhys Ecozar wasn't needed any longer. Features that Risnek had no doubt planned for me, and ones Batrix knew all about.

I was a decoy. A set-up. A little extra something up the Under-Director's sleeve. My innocence would only add to the deception. If Sotha had been any kind of wizard, she'd have been able to smell lies out in a midden.

I looked down at the wretched thing in the corner. He was cowering away from me, dribbling a thick yellow phlegm. Those bright blue eyes didn't hold anything close to intelligence, just a bestial fear.

"Hello, cousin," I said.

I heard Sotha draw in a sharp breath, then laugh softly. "Are you trying to tell me you knew all along?"

"Not hard to guess, is it? We've so much in common."

Batrix chipped in. "Do you not think the resemblance is a little too close? What are the odds?"

A strange gambit, arguing against a ploy of which she was so obviously a part. Even stranger, Sotha seemed to take the warning seriously.

"What are you getting at, heteromorph?" The gun was unwaveringly aimed at Batrix's face again.

"I have heard that certain Chrysomancers were able to recreate heteromorphs in exact likenesses of living persons."

I'd never heard that before. I was almost certain that Batrix was bluffing – such a technique could have been used to devastating effect in the war – but I couldn't be sure. Who knows what secrets the Spooks kept to themselves, even now, just waiting for the right moment. Besides, I thought Bezdichnij's techniques, which were pretty much what Batrix was describing, was a Bureau secret. I'd hate to think we were still playing catch-up

Even an unimaginative clod like Risnek would find such a thought bad for his sleep.

"And you think Wil might be just such a creation?" Sotha laughed again. "He doesn't act much like a Shifter to me."

"Are you such an expert on heteromorph behaviour, then?"

"No. But I'm pretty good with men's."

"Is it all right if I join in this conversation?" I said. "Might I point out that, unlike Batrix, I didn't 'morph under the moonstone's influence."

"Perhaps it was possible to create a heteromorph with a stable body structure."

"What's your game, Batrix?" I sounded impatient, and it wasn't much of an act. She simply stared back blandly through her lenses. I was going to get no answers there, so I side-tracked. "If we can get back to that poor thing lying in the corner, I assume that it is the undying King Varghas. Left here to rot forever by Sendivogius?"

"Quite right, my dear," said Sotha. "I had thought to find him still sane, but it appears I was hoping against all likelihood, there."

"What happened?"

"Varghas was a devout man. A follower of the ancient Crosantic rites. He begged the Archimandrite to let him retire to a monastery after his defeat. To become a monk. He swore on the lives of all those lost at Axsté he would never interfere with Sendivogius' rule for as long as he lived."

"Some oath."

Her mouth twisted unpleasantly. "In that desperate moment he had no idea how long his life would be, but Sendivogius couldn't find it in himself to believe even such a devout soul as Varghas's. Something to do with his own treacherous nature, no doubt. As an added joke, he left a succubus to haunt Varghas every night. A temptress to test his devotion to the Crosantic vows of fidelity. It wouldn't have mattered to Varghas that his wife died centuries ago; he'd still be faithful to her memory."

There was something very familiar about her growing fervour, her blind faith in the filthy thing grovelling on the floor. It was Anej Echosic all over again, the same failure to grasp the bitter truth. She couldn't see what Batrix and I could, smell what we smelled. To her Varghas was still a noble king – all appearances notwithstanding.

She was like the extinct members of the Crosantic Order, with their naïve adherence to a code of chivalry that had precious little to do with the real world. Worshipping their one god, Crosatl and bound by a strict code of practise, they were anachronistic even before their Order was founded. Back in my happy schooldays at Madrasaté, the tutors had contemptuously referred to them as the Divine Suicides; later, to the Philosophic government, they were symbols of the stupidity of monarchy. The Crosantic Order didn't have a friend. The only wonder was that Varghas had managed to keep the Chrysomancers at bay for so long.

But now, in Sotha Ponac, it seemed those bizarre ideals were born again. It made me shudder – and not from withdrawal.

"Sadly, old King Varghas doesn't look as though he's ready for government again," I said lightly. "That succubus certainly took it out of him."

The zealot's light faded from Sotha's eyes. I think she was seeing the mess on the floor clearly for the first time. "The creature was more than just a temptress." There was disgust in her voice, but no pity. "If the victim allows himself to be seduced, he is dragged down further and further by increasingly degrading acts. Eventually, more than just the body is corrupted and vile."

"Looks like his soul went bad a long time ago, does it not?" I heard Batrix's hiss of disapproval, and I turned to her, smiling thinly

"Come on, Batrix, look at it! There's more than just moral or physical corruption here. As Echosic put it, just because you legislate against something, that doesn't mean it doesn't exist."

"The matter is academic." Sotha acted as though neither Batrix nor I had said a word. It took me a moment before I could figure out what matter she was referring to.

Batrix was ahead of me. "You mean the identical features on Scilli, here."

Sotha nodded. "Who will know the difference?"

"I will," Batrix replied, quite reasonably.

"Quite so. But you won't be leaving here, will you?"

"I expect not."

"Let me get this straight..." I butted in, simply for my own peace of mind "...Sotha takes me back, proclaims me the long-lost King, no doubt marries me, and Ramini becomes happily united under my benevolent rule. Am I close?"

"Perfectly correct, my dear. Don't you like the idea of being crowned ruler and marrying me?"

"Sounds heavenly, especially the marrying part. But I wonder just how long I'll be left breathing once you're Queen Sotha."

"You have a suspicious mind, my dear."

"Not just a pretty face..."

"How will you explain Scilli's natural ageing and eventual death, since Varghas is supposed to be under the Archimandrite's undying curse? This supposes he will live long enough to die from old age." Good old Batrix – always looking on the bright side.

"The glamour is obviously linked to Grémasicci Boya, specifically this butte. Once freed, he is able to live – and die – like any man."

"Obviously," I said. "I don't suppose you've overlooked anything? Like how we get off this aforementioned pile of rock?"

"The way it was originally planned to get onto it." Sotha opened her purse and took out a small, glittering ornament. She held it up for a few moments, letting us both take a good look before putting it back into the reticule.

It was a tiny model of an observation balloon – or something very like one – but with the hot-air bag rather more oblong than spherical.

My guess was that there was a full-sized one hanging around somewhere – literally – and that she'd just used whatever magic she practised to summon it. I had to hand it to her: it had all the markings of a well-planned operation. Which meant there was money behind it, a great deal of it, and plenty of people. I even began to wonder if the whole trek hadn't been a cover for this one thing. It had been done before.

"Neat," I admitted. "But in case you hadn't noticed, night's fallen. I don't want to take a long step into the lake in the dark."

"There will be light enough shortly," she replied, briskly confident again. "Until then, we wait."

"Does your succubus not appear in the dark?" asked Batrix quietly.

That I'd forgotten. "How will it react to visitors, d'you think?"

Even in the darkness, I could see Sotha's face was tense with indecision. "Perhaps we should go outside, after all," she murmured.

"So soon?"

The voice was repulsively slick. It oozed false sexuality. Outside the three of us, I could see nothing, but somewhere in the shadows was the succubus.

I tried to lick my lips, but my tongue was harsh as sandpaper. I didn't fool myself into thinking I was in the same amount of danger as either of the others: a succubus that had been left to torment poor mad Varghas would automatically target me first. My deliberate resemblance to the King put at the front of the queue.

But there was no guarantee Sotha wouldn't get the full treatment, either. It depended on how bored – or inventive – the thing was feeling.

Batrix was an unknown. Would the demon even recognise a heteromorph?

"Where is it?" hissed Sotha. She grabbed the second pistol from my unresisting hand and began waving them both in a worryingly panicky manner.

"Careful with those," I muttered. "You've only got two shots. I'd hate for you to waste one on me."

"Besides, I very much doubt it can be killed with mere bullets," reasoned Batrix.

"Such an unfriendly greeting, don't you think, lover?" The voice was behind me, in the same corner as Varghas. I turned, just in time to see the creature appearing out of the darkness, just as if it was turning up some internal lamp. The wretched figure of Varghas strained towards it, all fear gone from a face only too clear in the succubus' light.

For a moment it looked like Erane Reidl, then its features shifted to someone else. Something else. It had the ripe, voluptuous body of a woman married to a young girl's face. The archetypal girl-woman, with a few extra tricks beside. All for Varghas, his deepest fantasies and most shameful desires made real. It burned with rampant sexuality; I was sweating as though I stood only a few steps away from a furnace. It looked at me – coyly, seductively – and smiled. A smile shared just between the two of us. I knew it wanted me, above everyone else; only I could satisfy it.

I couldn't drag my gaze away from the gorgeous, lambent eyes. They were lamps in a window to welcome back the forlorn traveller...

...and it was all bullshit. If I'd had my repeater, I'd have taken great delight in putting a bullet through each one.

Something like a tiny frown marred the perfect brow. "You cannot resist, you know," the creature purred. The words stroked each one of my vertebrae in turn. I shivered, withdrawal forgotten. "My lover, here, thought he could... He was wrong."

It stepped in front of Varghas. He tried to move towards it, his hands reaching for its ample curves. It seemed unaware of his shaking, clumsy grasp.

"Don't try extending your part," I said, my voice sounding harsh. "You were placed here for his benefit, not ours."

"Oh, I was never told I couldn't play with strange men ... if they should ever show."

That sounded reasonable. The Archimandrite might have anticipated a rescue attempt. What better guard could Varghas have than his seducer?

"I think we may have a problem," I muttered to the two behind me.

"Indeed," sighed Sotha. "The things its look is causing me to think—" She broke off, pretending to either be coughing or clearing her throat, and I wondered whose face she'd seen, no matter how briefly. She'd admitted to thoughts no decent, well-brought up young woman should ever have. Despite her scheming and obvious ruthlessness, she still couldn't break years of social conditioning. She was actually embarrassed.

"How about you, Batrix?" I asked.

There was a pause, far longer than I'd imagined. I almost turned to see if the heteromorph was still with us, mentally, anyway. Then she answered, her tone as measured and neutral as ever.

"I see a creature, obviously tailored to appeal to the most basic lusts. I can even appreciate what the appeal might be, but the creature stirs no desires in me. Whatever seductive magic is at work here, it does not work on heteromorphs."

"That's what I wanted to hear."

The succubus pouted soft, red lips. "Your white-haired beauty doesn't like me. I think she could, if she tried. I could help her..."

"None of us like you," I muttered. "So I think we'll just leave."

"Without Varghas?" I'd expected slightly more outrage from Sotha. Her protest sounded little more than token.

"I don't see any way of getting him out, do you? Besides, I doubt he's in any condition to do much reigning."

"We've already agreed," said Sotha, her voice distracted. Her gaze was fixed on the demonic thing. "I have you."

"So much for the nobility of the Crosantic Order."

"I never actually joined. Women are not encouraged. But the idea's strong enough to get both of us crowned." She tore her eyes off the succubus and swung one of the guns in my direction. Suddenly, I wasn't so trustworthy. Strange the things power and lust make people do. I wondered what was uppermost in her mind at that moment. "Now back out, slowly. And watch that creature. Heaven alone knows what it might be able to do."

"I might do many things," the succubus crooned. It made no attempt to stop us as we backed out through the open cell door. "We might do so many more, together. I think you already know that; I can see it in your eyes."

I felt Sotha's anger. I didn't need to see the pistol to know she was levelling one of them.

"Don't!" I hissed. "You can't hurt it that way, and as long as you ignore it, you'll be safe enough. We might need the bullet later."

"It's foul!" she spat. "Foul!"

"On the contrary, it works through pleasure. You might like to think on that, once we're out of here."

"I'd beginning to wonder about you..."

"It's always good to be thought about."

We'd made it as far as the corridor. There wasn't even the doubtful help of a window out there. At best, we'd keep walking into each other, at worst, the demoness could pounce without warning. I reached out both hands, touching two separate people with each one. Neither felt what I imagined the succubus would be like – not that my sense of touch was all that trustworthy at that moment.

"Sotha!" I hissed. One of the handfuls twitched. "You take the lead. You've got the guns. We'll be behind you, so if anything gets in your way, shoot!"

"Very well." The handful jerked itself out of my gasp and rustled towards the building's exit. I turned to face where I imagine Batrix was standing, though she couldn't see me any more than I could see her.

"I'm going to have to ask you to take the rear—"

"—because I seem to be immune to the succubus' dubious charms," she finished for me. "Quite understandable, Scilli. Almost military in its thinking."

"I hope it's more original than that. Come on." I moved off in the direction of Sotha's rustling clothes. If it was Sotha, I had an image of the succubus' far from substantial cloak making a not dissimilar sound. Which made me think of the thing's body...

I had to admit, it was good at its job. Once seen and heard, it lingered on the mind worse than turned milk on the palate.

It felt like hours. I doubt it was even a full minute. Time wasn't playing fair, any more than it had back in the dream-world. Trapped in almost total darkness, taking my route from the feel of crumbling stone against my fingers and the noise of Sotha's skirts, trying to concentrate past the all-too regular pain and ague of withdrawal, my pulse fit to burst from throat and chest, the seconds wound down to the length of hours. I was on the point of believing we'd gotten trapped in an endless labyrinth, when the walls disappeared, and the black ceiling suddenly blossomed into an arch sprayed with a million stars.

I was never so happy to see the night sky.

Batrix emerged a moment behind me. I looked around. Sotha was already heading for the butte's rim. She seemed to be looking for something. The Moon might still have been full, but it didn't look bright enough for her to see much.

I was very wrong.

Because suddenly, the Sun – or its baby relative – rose up over the butte. The flat table of rock was flooded with harsh, cold light, throwing all relief into stark black or white.

CHAPTER TWENTY-NINE

I STOOD MOTIONLESS, IMPALED by the light like some stupid bug. The ball of light seemed to hang for a moment, and I got the strongest feeling it was looking for something. Or someone. Then I saw Sotha, waving both hands like a castaway just spotting a passing ship, still clutching both pistols. The flying light loomed forward.

"Our way off!" Sotha was shouting. She faced Batrix and I, while waving a hand at the approaching fiery beacon.

"On the back of a fireball?"

"By airship!"

The moment she said, it I realised what the light was: a huge searchlight cast from the cradle of a balloon. The model she'd kept in her purse was a charm, a sympathetic image of the real thing. When she was ready for it, she'd simply called it up – just like ringing for the maid.

"What is that thing?" Batrix's voice murmured in my ear.

"Strange lights in the sky over Wael Edra," I said.

"I imagine you will explain that to me one day."

"If we live long enough."

As the thing neared, I could just make out the black outline of an oblong gas bag, and the skeletal framework that must be the cradle underneath.

"That might be how we get down," I called to Sotha, "but it's a long walk back to Wael Edra. Or do you have horses waiting for us at the water's edge?"

She laughed and all but skipped back to me. Slipping an arm through mine she kissed me lightly on the cheek. We were friends again. "We don't need horses, Wil." She was trying to be mysterious.

I didn't feel like playing. "You mean the balloon's powered? Directable?"

She almost pouted. "I never seem able to surprise you!"

"I bet it's also been busy in the skies over Wael Edra these past months, ferrying co-conspirators and frightening the horses."

"Don't you admire it, Wil? You see, the late Professor Alva isn't the only genius this world has to offer."

"Alva may have been a genius, but he also made it his business to be answerable to no one. That little flaw got him murdered. I hope your pet engineer is more grounded in reality."

"You are cynical, my dear. Come! They're lowering ropes." She pulled away and walked towards a network of trailing lines that glittered in the light.

I thought of the climb, how high up the balloon was, and how thin those lines looked. "I can hardly wait."

The lines drifted closer, brought nearer by the drifting balloon, no doubt. I didn't get much comfort from seeing they were actually rope ladders; it wasn't the climb that bothered me, just the fall.

"Courage, Scilli," Batrix whispered from close by. She knew exactly what I thought of heights. "It is dark, you will not be able to see anything other than the top of the butte."

"That's why I have an imagination."

Sotha had already grabbed one ladder as it drifted past. Batrix and I moved in unison to seize a line each as they swept by. Shutting my eyes, I began to feel my way up the hempen rungs. They sagged way too much.

Then I heard the scream. I had to open my eyes and look about, but I couldn't see anything on the butte, already far too distant. I glanced at Batrix, she pointed to the ladder from which Sotha was hanging, at a distance above the woman's head. I looked. It was the succubus, inching down the ladder, face first. To me it looked like Erane Reidl again – an Erane who'd never existed outside my adolescent dreams. Distanced from the mad Varghas and his fantasies, I guessed it could look like anyone's desires, no matter how deeply buried.

"You can't leave me," the thing was crooning. "Stay a while. We can get to know each other—"

Sotha fired one of her pistols. It sounded like a cannon against the night's silence, but on the demon, it had about as much effect as a feather. The sensuous, too-young face split in a wide, tongue-licked grin.

"My sweet, sweet girl. Have you never heard that nothing can hurt true love? Come to me, or shall I come to you?"

"Keep back!" That wasn't terror in Sotha's voice, I'm sure, just a perfect imitation. She raised the second pistol.

"Don't waste it!" I yelled. I might just as well have kept my mouth shut. Sotha shot the succubus clean between the eyes. It didn't even leave a mark.

The thing laughed: a throaty sound that froze my spine. "My dear," it murmured, its voice a perfect imitation of Sotha's own, "come to me."

The woman began to climb the rope ladder, stiffly, like an automaton. I doubt she was even remotely aware of what she was doing.

"Sotha!" I yelled, but she was beyond me: whatever she saw drew her too strongly. The succubus' corrupted Erane Reidl features shot me a glance mixed from triumph and venom. It knew that I'd lost.

"Scilli!" Batrix called from slightly under where I dangled. I glanced down, trying not to see the ground sliding past a dozen feet below. The heteromorph was pointing again. This time, at the rapidly approaching ruin. The airship was about to fly straight over it, and anyone not high enough up the lines would be smashed against the ancient stone. Maybe not hard enough to kill, but they'd certainly be knocked clear. Which meant no ride home.

I began scrabbling up my rope ladder, aware Batrix was doing pretty much the same, but somehow with more dignity. Sotha was already higher than both of us, but in no less danger.

She'd reached the succubus, and the creature was stroking her face with one long-fingered hand. I was about to shout again, try and distract its attention, when my ladder was violently shaken. I clenched my eyes and hung on desperately. I guessed we were passing over the ruin.

The rope gradually stopped swinging. I managed to open my eyes again, instantly regretting it. The butte wasn't underneath us any longer, just a black void, and below that, Lake Grémasicci Boya. I could just make out ripples highlighted by the Full Moon. I wasn't grateful.

I looked up once more to where Sotha and the succubus were crouched. The creature was cuddled against the woman now, an arm thrown familiarly around her shoulders. Sotha was slowly and tenderly kissing each of the fingers.

Sotha Ponac may have ruthlessly manipulated me, poisoned Rhys Ecozar when she didn't need him any longer, killed Petran Steganesh, and left us all to die in the dream-world, but she didn't deserve this. No one did. I couldn't think of anyone I'd ever hated enough to sentence them to such a degrading fate.

I began scrabbling up my ladder. I think I had some half-formed scheme of reaching the airship, climbing back down Sotha's line and rescuing her. Maybe it would have worked, I never had time to find out.

Something snatched at one of my ankles. I lost my footing and nearly dropped off the ladder, barely hanging on with bruised hands and numb arms.

"Let her be!"

Heart beating hard enough to bruise my ribs, I looked down, wishing I hadn't. It was what remained of King Varghas, clinging to the ropes like a dried-out spider, his ravaged face glaring up at me. I still see that face on bad nights; it was like peering down into hell.

He must have seized the line as it dragged across his prison. Hard to imagine the desperation that had propelled him out of his semi-trance. The succubus had come to mean that much to him.

"Let her be!"

He lurched further up, his jerky fumbling making him look more like a spider than ever. He dug sharp nails into my legs. I don't know if he was trying to climb over me or drag me off the ladder. It didn't much matter; the result would be much the same.

I wasn't feeling generous. The drop no longer seemed that important, only this madman. I hooked my left arm around a rung and back-handed his face with my right hand, as hard as I could. Under the circumstances, that wasn't so much.

He jerked away, still managing to cling on. I hit him again. It was like punching a skeleton, and about as effective.

"Scilli!" That was Batrix, now level with me, but too far away on her own ladder to be of much help.

"If you've been keeping a gun back, now's the time to surprise me!" I tried freeing a leg enough to kick the disgusting immortal King away.

"Can you not fight him off?"

"Does it look like it?" I punched Varghas's ravaged face again. I was the only one who felt it. "Withdrawal and banged-up arms ... it's not exactly left me fighting-fit."

Batrix glanced up. At Sotha and her new friend, I guessed.

"See if you can help her!" Noble to the end. The King hooked a claw through my trouser-belt and hauled himself further up. I began to smell him. When I had a chance to look across, Batrix was already climbing.

Varghas's face was getting much too close to my own. He looked – and smelled – more demonic than the succubus. But at least he wasn't hanging off my legs anymore.

"*Let her be!*" he hissed.

I almost gagged on the stench of his breath. I didn't like to imagine what he'd been eating all these years. "I'm not the one doing anything!"

"*Let her be!*" He was beyond reason, beyond anything except his needs. For a moment I almost felt sorry for him; he was suffering the agonies of withdrawal as much as me, and neither of us had asked to be addicted. That had been the choice of others.

The moment passed.

Holding awkwardly onto the rungs with both hands, I managed to draw up both legs and lash out. The King's feet flew off the rungs, but his clawed fingers were still hooked around my trouser-belt. The jolt almost tore my own feeble grip free.

I pistoned a knee up into his chest. He snarled, but didn't move. I kneed him again. One of his hands was torn loose, taking a patch of worn fabric with it.

Before he could get his hold back, I looped a hemp rung around one of my wrists and seized at his grasping fingers with my free hand. Kicking at his dangling legs, keeping his equilibrium rattled, I slowly prised each finger loose. It was no harder that dragging three-inch nails free with my tongue.

And all the time, those haunted, haunting eyes glared at me.

Sweating, hurting, I finally unhooked his last finger. He didn't fall. Somehow, he lashed out and embedded his jagged nails into my palm, hanging off my own flesh.

I think I screamed. Anyone would. I snatched my hand back, kicking out blindly, and this time he fell. Taking a chunk of me with him.

I cradled my ruined hand, staring at a hole that had once been a palm. I'd lost a lot of blood to this venture. I hoped someone, somewhere, thought it was worth it.

Something moved above me. I looked up, thinking it was Batrix.

It was the succubus, still holding Sotha close. It had sprung across from its original perch to my own line – so lightly, I hadn't felt it. Sotha was lost, I could see that; her eyes were glazed, she was caressing the demoness' exaggerated curves with a perverse tenderness.

Erane Reidl's face drew close to mine. It leered in triumph and pursed its wonderful lips in a kiss. It waved a forefinger at me in an almost maternal chiding. I was a naughty boy, but it forgave me.

Then it began to laugh its deep, throaty laugh, and I fumbled Steganesh's last fragment of abaston from my pocket. I thrust it into the creature's mouth as hard and fast as I could. The laughter stopped. In a moment it became a scream; light and steam billowed out from between those inviting lips.

It tried to drop Sotha, but she clung on regardless. I don't think she was even aware of what was happening. A moment later the shrieking succubus fell from the ladder, Sotha still embracing it. They plunged down, trailing flame, looking like a small aerolite. I never saw either of them hit the water. Maybe the succubus could have made it back to the butte. I didn't care, but I doubted it.

I looked up towards the bulk of the airship. Behind the glare I could see the massive sausage of the gasbag, and the vast, spine-stiffened fins used to steer it. Whoever was up there, in the gondola, couldn't be any worse than what I'd just suffered.

I began to climb, pain and weariness seeming to grow worse with each rung. I made it to the top of the line, and hands I couldn't see helped me to the deck.

There, I finally surrendered to the darkness and jumped with pleasure into unconsciousness.

CHAPTER THIRTY

THE HOSPITAL WAS AS warm and welcoming as most, the nurses were more starched than their aprons, the bed was hard and the sheets, coarse. I was glad they were giving me top treatment, I would have hated being in the servants' ward.

I was in a small, semi-private room that held another nine empty beds. I had a window to myself – four storeys up, so I couldn't see much from my bed – and as much comfort as a private citizen of limited means could expect. I wasn't anyone special; I didn't deserve the best there was.

It had been almost two weeks since I'd been carried, delirious, half-dead, to bed. That much I knew from the ward-sister – an attractive brunette who seemed to think I was some kind of charity case, being paid for by a guilty and generous anonymous party. I couldn't remember much from the first few days, not until the worst ravages of the combined injuries and *chavet* withdrawal had left me. The withdrawal had been easy to fix, it always is – a few sips, and all symptoms vanish. I'd seen it many times. The blood loss, tissue morbidity and raging fever had been much harder to deal with.

Apparently, I had Batrix to thank for still existing. At first, my uncanny resemblance to the undead King Varghas had persuaded the airship's crew I was one of them; when they inevitably began to get suspicious – about halfway back to Wael Edra – Batrix had found a form of more direct persuasion, like a couple of pistols, or something. Details were scarce, and Batrix was being typically unforthcoming. I was left in this delightful hostel, more dead than alive, while the airship was secreted away in some Bureau bolt-hole for dissection and generally terminal examination. The crew, much the same.

But careful treatment and loving care brought me round eventually. That, and the careful application of some abaston magic by a kindly, aged relative who visited me often. An aunt I'd never met before and who I've not seen since.

It was good to know someone cared. Not Risnek, but someone much more interested in my continued health than the Under-Director.

The party in question visited me two days before Risnek finally showed his smug face. An anonymous figure in black, he slipped unnoticed into the ward, discussed several points with me, before drifting out again. The Archimandrite couldn't have done it more smoothly. Even if a nurse had actually seen him, they wouldn't have remembered for long.

Risnek was another matter. He burst through the ward doors, clutching a ridiculous bouquet that he hadn't chosen, dressed in white tie and tails, and a tall silk hat perched on his head. Maybe he thought he was off to the opera. I'd enjoy disappointing him.

The most convincing smile he could manage was on his face as he strode towards me, while his eyes caressed the shape of every nurse he passed.

He sat without invitation, tossed his hat onto the bed, and dropped the flowers to the floor. *Maybe they weren't for me after all.*

"Well, Scilli," he smiled. "And how are we?"

"I'm fine. I've no idea how you're doing."

The smile never faltered. It looked as though Doctor Bezdichnij had moulded it in place for him. "I see your humour hasn't been affected."

"You know how it is with us seminary scum."

He paused. The smile was fixed, but his eyes narrowed. Something like ice glittered behind them. "I've read your report. Is there anything you wish to add?"

"Such as?"

"We'll go over it." He made a great play of retrieving a brown paper folder from under his coat. *I wondered what my favourite ward sister would make of it.*

"First, you claim that *Ingosigna* Sotha Ponac was some distant claimant to the throne of one of the old kingdoms? And that it was her plan to reinstate this deathless King Varghas?"

"Pretty much. Marry him and be the power behind the throne. An old story – as old as Varghas, come to think of it."

"Yet she was prepared to abandon him."

"Thanks to the face you and Bezdichnij provided for me. At first, she thought I was another one with royal blood and, by some accident of heredity, born with Varghas's face. That's why she killed Ecozar—"

"The one who'd had her included on the Echosic's pilgrimage?"

"I think the whole deal was her idea. She presented it to Ecozar, and he persuaded Chato Echosic. Couldn't have been difficult, the man wasn't really thinking straight."

"And when she had no further use for Ecozar, she disposed of him. A ruthless woman. She could have been useful in the Bureau."

"No doubt. Towards the end, when it was clear Varghas was too corrupted to be of any use to her, I don't think she cared if I were royal or not. My face would be enough. She'd make me Varghas, and herself Queen."

He leaned forward. His breath smelled of peppermint and cigars. "Was she very persuasive?"

I took a moment before replying. "She had her moments."

He straightened. "But what of Petran Steganesh? You seem a little vague as to his motives."

"Before that, I want to know – why the face? How much did you already know? And why wasn't I told?"

He regarded me blandly. "We knew something like this was about to break. Our information was that any one of several such religious journeys would be used by the royalists. It was just your luck to be in on that one."

He was lying. But I wasn't going to tell him that just yet. "And the secrecy?"

"The heteromorph knew but was sworn to keep silent, and it always keeps its word. You know that. It was our belief that you'd play the part of an innocent caught up in events if you actually were ignorant. We didn't know what kinds of magic the royalists were capable of using. Truth-spells, mind-reading – either could be possible."

I began to wonder if he knew what truth was. Even an agent under deep cover for half a lifetime never loses all track with his reality. Sanej never did.

"You asked about Steganesh. He obviously knew as much about the royalist plot as you. And his actions seem to indicate he was there to prevent it. But as to who he was working for... He was a third *shakrat* Chrysomancer, after all, and the Spooks wouldn't want the royalty back any more than President Thinos..." I let the words trail off. Risnek could make what he wanted of the statement.

"Very well. Then we come to Gen Romino. You don't seem to have come to any definite conclusion, there."

"What more do you want? He was a remarkably powerful sorcerer of some kind, he could move himself and others into the Anesicci dream-world, and he died by the very power he was after."

"Do you actually believe he was responsible for the disappearances in Wael Edra?"

"Would these be the ones you dismissed so lightly?"

He drew back his thick lips in a snarl that was pretending to be a smile. It looked as though, more than anything, he wanted to light up a cigar and blow smoke all over me. "If it makes you feel better, yes. It seems you were right there."

"Hooray for me."

He glowered. He wanted more. If he knew how much there was, he'd be more eager to get off to whichever naïve opera starlet he was chasing.

"No, I don't think he took everyone. The properly witnessed disappearances into the ether, I'll grant him. There's no other suspects. But not all the incidents were actually witnessed; some people vanished when no one was looking. The senators on the steps of the Capitol, for instance..."

"That was witnessed by members of the President's private guard—"

"No. They watched the senators approach the steps, but like all good soldiers kept their eyes front."

"Are you suggesting members of the government were abducted under the noses of Sharpshooters?"

"Whatever happened, Risnek, it was behind their backs. And I don't recall saying they were abducted."

"They went willingly?" He didn't try to sound anything other than dismissive.

"There was something else reported during the mass disappearances, Risnek. Remember?"

For a moment he made it obvious he was thinking about it. "The lights?" he said finally.

"Right. The strange lights in the sky. And the brief scuffle between Sharpshooters and men described as foreign-looking. All that comes down to was the others were wearing unfamiliar uniforms. Ring any bells?"

"You seem to have the floor." I couldn't tell if he was looking uncomfortable. It was unlikely, just wishful thinking.

"What about the airship?"

His self-satisfied smile broadened; so it could move.

"Quite a find, Scilli. You are to be congratulated on that, too, I suppose. Our technicians have spent days crawling all over it."

"Good. Maybe they can put facts together faster than you. Call a few in here."

The smile evaporated. "I'm beginning to wonder if you're so keen to rejoin us after all, once you've recuperated..."

"I'll be back faster than you imagine."

The look he gave me was calculating. I wondered which set of figures he was adding up. "Very well, explain yourself."

"The airship was the source of the lights. I imagine it's been making quite a few trips between Wael Edra and ... wherever Sotha Ponac's people are basing themselves. Get the Sharpshooters who clashed with the so-called foreigners to look at the airship's crew, and I think you'll get a positive identification."

His eyes went misty, distant. He nodded slowly. "Yes. I can see that. But why the abductions?"

"Like I said, no one was abducted. Maybe Romino had already begun trawling the people of Wael Edra for his crazy scheme, but Sotha's people used it as a convenient cover."

"If I understand you correctly, Scilli, you're implying that more than a few people – senators included – left willingly!" He was properly horrified.

"You've seen that airship. D'you think you could research and build something like that on a handful of coppers? There's money behind it; money and influence. You know how it's powered?"

As though caught off balance by my question, he blinked at me stupidly for a moment. "Steam," he said eventually. "It's raised by hydrogen in the bag, like any balloon, then simple gas turbines turn four large propellers. It has several movable fins to guide its direction of flight."

It didn't sound so impressive, put like that. Just another step away from a basic observation balloon.

"Water has to be heated, to make steam," I said, enjoying myself. "Anyone who does that with dozens of cubic yards of hydrogen just above them is committing suicide."

"You obviously know better."

"Obvious is right. The water must be heated by abaston crystal, the same way as Alva's patent locomotive-engine was. Or is that information classified?"

His face grew dreamy again. "What's your point?"

"Only that hardly anyone knew about Alva's method for getting heat from abaston."

"Several I can think of, including yourself and the heteromorph..."

He meant the passengers on the maiden journey of Alva's locomotive train. Both Batrix and I had been on that trip, not many had walked away from it.

"Not one of whom hasn't either died since or left themselves open to blackmail. The Bureau knows how to keep secrets."

"There was that foreigner ... the Pyndrian writer, Boz. You were convinced he was part of an anarchist plot. If he is somehow involved, he'd be able to pass the secret on."

"Agreed, if Alva had been specific. He only admitted to abaston being involved, and that after several threats. It was Sanej who revealed how the process worked, and Alva's older partner, Thryme."

"He died shortly after returning to Scan Leroth," Risnek mused. The thought seemed to cheer him. "He wasn't well."

"The result of poisoning from prolonged exposure to the emissions from shattering abaston – Javier's Palsy. Which proves my point."

"How?"

"Even assuming that someone like Boz had learned that abaston can be used to heat water by exerting pressure across the crystal, he wouldn't know exactly how much. It took years for Alva to discover the precise degree of pressure to get the maximum heating without shattering the crystal. Experiments that caused Thryme's eventual death. It's only been a few months since that rail-train journey. Not enough time for anyone to have established the safest working procedures."

"Then I take it you are claiming someone within the government gave the details away."

"Not the government: the Bureau. We've got Alva's experimental notes locked away safer than the President's dirty linen. The only reason more locomotive-engines have yet to be built is because the Bureau won't tell anyone that one, simple detail."

"I never realised how deeply seated this morbid insecurity of yours was, Scilli. Originally you claimed Mawinnek was tipped off by someone in the Bureau, and now we're handing sensitive information to our enemies. Really," he smiled like a lazy alligator, "it's too much."

"Too much is expecting me to believe a fanatical royalist, a probably insane anarchist and an ex-seminary colleague of mine should all turn up together on the same trip."

"Coincidence, Scilli. And surely a fortunate one?"

"For whom, Risnek? Batrix and I are the only ones left alive."

"That you can be sure of; you didn't see Varghas die, or Sotha Ponac fall. I believe the ex-King was cursed with immortality."

"Only immunity from natural death. I doubt falling off a two hundred feet high butte counts as natural. And as for Sotha..." I kept my voice level, neutral. I wasn't about to give Risnek any satisfaction. "I hope she died. The alternative doesn't bear thinking on."

He raised an eyebrow. The bastard was going to make me spell it out.

"She had royal blood – thinned out a little, but it's there. That succubus wouldn't be too fussy who it visited each night, just so long as they had the blood of the kings." And he was right: I hadn't seen her fall. That creature would have done its best to save them both. I was tortured by the thought that it could have flown itself and Sotha safely back to the ruin.

Safely? I shook my head at the thought.

"So!" Risnek began to make leaving gestures again. "Although it appears the file will have to be kept open, my thinking is that the matter is pretty well wrapped up. Yes?"

"Well, with everyone either dead or unlikely to be seen again, I guess you might feel safe."

He looked at me, the self-satisfied smile still in place. I couldn't wait to see it finally and permanently crack.

"You had questions for me, Risnek. Now, I've got some for you."

"Are they necessary?" He made a great deal of fuss over taking out his watch and consulting it. No matter what he thought the hour was, his time was up.

"How long have you been a double agent, Risnek?"

I have to give him credit: his face didn't twitch by so much as a muscle. "I take it one of the injuries you received was to the head?"

"For months, someone has been passing out information, someone with access to the best, high-level stuff. People like Mawinnek have been laughing at the Bureau for months."

"You mentioned this theory before, Scilli. You've still to show me an item of proof..."

"Alongside which..." I pressed on as though I hadn't heard him "...the rather obvious fact that someone has been rather free with the details of Alva's steam-engine. You can't deny that."

He half-closed his eyes. "It does look that way," he admitted, his voice dreamy.

"You ordered Bezdichnij to give me King Varghas's face—"

"I've already explained that!"

"—in spite of standing orders that no operative will be given a disguise that is a copy of recognisable features or may – by its unusual nature – draw attention to that operative. You had me given Varghas's face – a face that any royalist would instantly recognise – and one with brilliant red hair that hardly slips into the background. I was a target, Risnek."

"It was a deliberate move, Scilli. We needed to attract the attention of certain people—"

"It certainly worked. One look at this face, and Sotha couldn't wait to bury Ecozar and bed me!" I didn't bother keeping the bitterness out of my voice.

"Thus proving how effective the plan was." Risnek was smugness incarnate.

"If that wasn't enough, you informed Mawinnek that both Batrix and I would be on the trek to Qaijente. He sent Steganesh to make sure we didn't survive."

Risnek's eyes slid open; they didn't look so dreamy anymore. "Where's your witness?"

"At a guess, you looked back through my files and found Petran's name. You saw the circumstances under which we parted, and, quite reasonably, thought he'd be the ideal executioner."

"An error of judgement, there." He'd given up his pretence of innocence. That probably meant he thought he could get away with it. Shoot me, or something. The room was empty, after all.

"You checked the wrong man. If you'd run through Petran's file fully, you would have seen just how much his own man he was. As long as I've known him, he's chosen his actions, and never offered explanations."

"An unfortunate trait, in an agent."

In anyone, I thought. If he'd told me that it hadn't been him trying to kill me years ago; if he'd told me why he was on the Echosic pilgrimage, what he knew...

I clamped down on those thoughts. Too many ifs. Regret wasn't the kind of luxury permitted by the Bureau.

"Did it also occur to you that Sotha Ponac..." I stumbled over the words. This was something I'd never be comfortable expressing. "You guessed I'd fall for her," I finally ground out. "Stick the inexperienced Scilli with a woman like Sotha Ponac, and he'll be worse than a crush-hit schoolboy. Was that only for laughs, or just in case I escaped your murder attempt? Did you think I wouldn't be able to kill a woman I'd fallen in love with?"

"I must admit, your ruthlessness did surprise me. It was generally believed that, if by some miracle you did survive Steganesh, *Ingosigna* Ponac would finish you. Either when she rescued the King, or realised you were a fake, or decided to use you as a substitute. Any would have resulted in your eventual demise."

"Glad to disappoint you."

"It doesn't matter." He pulled a pistol out from under his cape. It was a single-shot, highly decorated piece – identical to the ones Sotha had used.

"Just one last thing," I continued, as though the muzzle aimed right at my forehead wasn't intimidating. "Mawinnek is behind all this, right? His private security force has grown to the point where he can virtually challenge the government. Now he's playing all the minor interests off against each other: royalists against staunch republicans; the Spooks against foreign anarchists?"

"What of it?" He cocked the pistol's hammer.

"No such thing as coincidence, remember. So many on one journey, all with their own interests, all mutually exclusive. It was almost inevitable that the whole mess would collapse in on them.

Mawinnek's planning?"

"*Gosigné* Mawinnek has a flair for misdirection, but he also has several minor geniuses working for him. If President Thinos was assassinated tomorrow, you can be sure that the guilty party has already been chosen, tried and convicted."

"Like some disillusioned Ramini who's forged links with the Pyndrian *Plytath a'Pyndr*?"

"How well you understand us. Normally I'm loath to waste a valuable resource such as yourself, but I'm afraid you just can't be trusted."

"I knew my conscience would be my downfall."

"You were right." He pulled the trigger. The hammer stayed exactly where it was. Risnek jerked at the trigger several more times. Nothing happened.

I started breathing again. Not that I had anything other than full confidence in all of the Bureau wizards outside.

"The Spooks were working on a new glamour towards the end of the war," I said. "One that could twist reality just enough to stop any mechanism from working. Changing the rules, as it were." I reached out and snatched the useless pistol from Risnek's unprotesting fingers. "They could never make it work because they tried to cover too broad an area – such as a battlefield – and the spell just wasn't strong enough. No matter how many abaston stones they used. But the Bureau has been successful, to a limited extent. For a few minutes, an area the size of, say, a small hospital ward, can be rendered useless to anything mechanical. Like pistol mechanisms."

Risnek leapt up. "Very clever, I'm sure. That also means you can't shoot me as I escape."

"How far d'you think you'll get?" I asked his back. He froze and turned back to face me. "They're all around the building, Risnek. The moment you walked into the hospital, they cordoned it off with barrier spells."

He laughed: hollow, humourless. "I've been set up."

"Why did you think I was moved to your department, Risnek? Because all the other department heads had grown tired of me? Or because of the continual leaks? Leaks that had to come from one department and likely the Under-Director himself."

"You're a member of the Cadre!" he said, naming the Bureau's most private, internal security committee. Most people thought its existence was just a myth.

"Never heard of it. Now, I'd go outside and give yourself up, while the blanket spell is still working. Refined as it is from the Spook's original, it still doesn't last long, and I've got the gun."

It took him a moment, but eventually he got it. Once the spell collapsed, the gun would fire, even if no one was holding it. But I was holding it and aiming it straight at his heart. Or where it should be. I had no reason not to shoot.

He whirled around and leapt towards the door. He was framed neatly by the doorjambs when I felt the subtle shift: the spell had collapsed. The pistol fired.

Batrix & Scilli will return in

THE LOST VOYAGE